Also by

Sky

Data Mine

INHERITANCE

A NOVEL

LOU IOVINO

RARE EARTH
TRILOGY
VOLUME
ONE

For Ben & Charlie

"Her antiquity in preceding and surviving succeeding tellurian generations: her nocturnal predominance: her satellitic dependence: her luminary reflection: her constancy under all her phases, rising and setting by her appointed times, waxing and waning: the forced invariability of her aspect: her indeterminate response to inaffirmative interrogation: her potency over effluent and refluent waters: her power to enamour, to mortify, to invest with beauty, to render insane, to incite to and aid delinquency: the tranquil inscrutability of her visage: the terribility of her isolated dominant resplendent propinquity: her omens of tempest and of calm: the stimulation of her light, her motion and her presence: the admonition of her craters, her arid seas, her silence: her splendour, when visible: her attraction, when invisible."

—James Joyce, *Ulysses*

"There is no dark side of the moon, really. Matter of fact, it's all dark."

—Gerry O'Driscoll, Doorman, Abbey Road Studios, 1973

DARKSIDE STATION

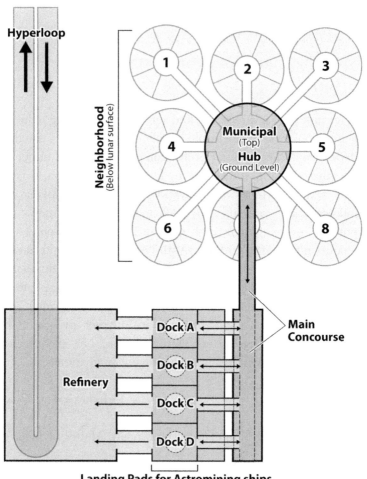

Landing Pads for Astromining ships
(Lifts lower ore containers to refinery access level
and crews to the Main Concourse)

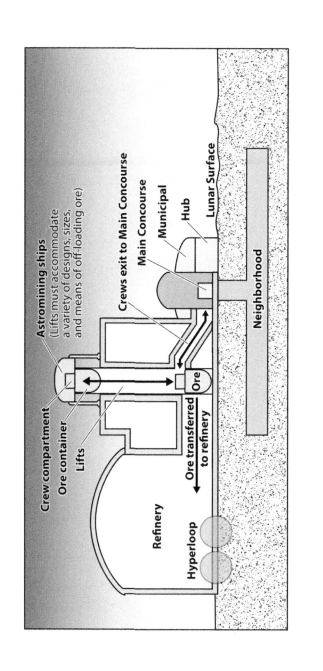

Astromining ships
(Lifts must accommodate a variety of designs, sizes, and means of off-loading ore)

Crews exit to Main Concourse

Main Concourse

Municipal

Hub

Lunar Surface

Crew compartment
Ore container
Lifts

Ore transferred to refinery

Ore

Refinery

Hyperloop

Neighborhood

PART I

Up and Away

After

"I REMEMBER THIS ONE TIME," the mourner begins, voice thick with emotion, walnut knuckles white from his grip on the lectern. "We had just wrapped up a haul and were heading home. It had been a pretty shitty trip—

"Darn. Sorry, Father."

Smile and a nod.

Forgiveness granted, the man goes on.

"Like I was saying, the grounds were pretty picked over, so we were only carrying maybe a few thousand pounds of cobalt and some gold. Junk, really. Probably just enough to pay the docking fees and put a few bucks in the crew's pockets.

"Well, about two days out from Darkside we came across an uncharted cluster. It looked like your typical rock pile at first glance. A bunch of small junk whipping around a few bigger boys in the center. The kind of thing you'd normally pass by without a second thought. But a couple of the smaller asteroids on the perimeter pinged the spectral sensors. Looked like maybe some traces of palladium and iridium. Our lucky day, right? Could save the whole trip."

Heads nod all around the packed house. A few chuckles. They know what he's talking about. They've been there.

"Now, we had an offload scheduled, and everyone wanted to get back for the holidays. But we ran the numbers and figured that we could adjust course, grab us up a few of the most promising rocks—you know, the ones we could just snag with the harpoon and haul straight aboard—and then get gone. Easy peasy. So we check the sensors, agree on this one little beauty, get in position, and I fire the harpoon.

"Well, it hits the goddamn thing square in the center and goes right through. Bastard was hollow.

"Darn. Sorry, Father."

Grimace this time.

Sign of the cross and the man goes on.

"As if that wasn't bad enough, the shot keeps on going and lodges deep into one of the bad boys toward the center of the cluster. A big, dense ball of iron and kiss-my-*youknowwhat*, spinning way beyond our orbital rate.

"Right away, we feel the tug. I thought it was gonna rip us in half. But no, sir. Scottie was on it. Man, I never seen anyone jump so fast. Don't think he even broke a sweat, neither. Like the freak he was—you all know, the man was a calculator—he figures the math in his head, adjusts speed and attitude, and lets out enough line to keep us from colliding with the stuff on the outer edges of the pile. All that in the time it took me to finish dropping a deuce right there on the bridge!"

Laughter erupts in the church.

Except from the dead man's daughter.

"And now I think, 'All right, let's cut bait and get outta here.' But no. Scottie's got other plans. Next thing I know, he's deploying the catch canopy. He wasn't gonna leave 'til he got what we came for. And sure enough, with some crazy unreal maneuvering, he managed to scoop up bits from the shattered

4

asteroid with just enough rare earths that we all had a pretty good Christmas that year."

His story is done; he's overcome. Adjusts the patinaed slide on his bolo tie and struggles to collect himself.

Then adds in a heavy voice before taking his seat, "That was just how Scottie was. He always took care of us out there. And back here, too."

She watches from the back of the room as he takes his seat and a few more of her dad's old colleagues stand up and regale the congregation with stories from the old days.

Dad fixing one of the Zephyr*'s air scrubbers with some coffee filters and zip ties.*

Dad and his crew getting drunk after topping the Leaderboard and ending up on the Hyperloop.

Dad's unlikely campaign for civilian operations liaison during his first year as a captain. Sonofagun almost won, too!

She's heard them all before.

As they share their stories, she focuses instead on the slide show running above the table with her father's urn. It was her job during his final weeks to go through old photo albums and shoeboxes and pick out memories to show during the service. Whenever she came across a picture that looked promising, she'd show it to him, hoping it'd spark some recognition. A little smile or an eyebrow raise. But none of them got a reaction. Nothing ever did those last days.

In the end she just grabbed a few handfuls at random and sent them to the funeral director.

"Would you like to say anything, dear?"

The priest, who she figures can't be any older than twenty-five and certainly not old enough to be calling her or anyone else *dear*, breaks her trance. Sincerity radiates from his bright smile and upturned palms, but they've never met, and she knows he's just going through the motions, doing what's expected of him. Just like everyone else here today.

Behind him, an image of her parents' wedding reception fades in. Mom in white, dad in dark gray with a white cummerbund and tie. Fresh off their vows, smashing cake into each other's faces.

Going through the motions too, it turned out.

"Ms. Watts?"

"Sorry, Father."

"Are you ready?"

"Sure," she says, shooting up from her seat and nearly colliding with him.

All eyes are on her as she moves behind the lectern and adjusts the mic, the burst of static an assault in the silent chapel.

"Hi. I'm Thea, Scottie's daughter."

She takes a folded sheet of paper from the back pocket of her jeans and spreads it out on the lectern. Stares down at the words. Words she threw together last night with the help of YouTube and a bottle of pinot.

Expected words.

Nothing words.

Meaningless words.

Words meant to check a box.

Just going through the motions, she thinks as people begin to exchange nervous glances.

"When someone dies," she begins, crumpling the paper into a ball, "people try to console you by saying the person isn't truly gone. That they'll 'live on forever' in all of our hearts and minds. Which is meant to make us feel good about the person we lost, I guess. And maybe even ourselves one day too.

"Listening to your stories today, I could certainly let myself believe in this very pretty idea. There's no doubt my dad meant something to some of you. And, for a time, the same could probably even be said about each of you to him. And you should feel good about that. Because my dad was picky about . . . well, everything. Especially people. So, mattering to him, mattered.

"But live on forever?"

She looks out over the church, then settles her gaze on her dad's silver urn.

"Over the last few years, I learned a secret," she continues after a lengthy pause. "And had any of you been around—any of you at all—you might have learned it too. But since you weren't, I'll share it with you now."

Ready?

Thea scans the congregants' puzzled expressions, watches them shift uncomfortably in their seats.

"In the end, none of you mattered to him."

She can see it in their faces. They weren't ready.

"I'm sorry if that hurts. The hard truth is that every one of you started getting erased a few years ago. Your names, who you were, what you did, where you and he met. Who you were married to, your kids. He forgot it all. Every bit of it. Before he died, you were all nobody to him. Not even ghosts, really. Just . . . nothing.

"But don't worry. It wasn't just you. At the very end, he didn't know me either. Whatever *we*," she says, pointing at herself and then around the room, "whatever we once were to him in his mind and in his heart slowly evaporated until everyone and everything was gone. Even himself."

She shoves her wadded eulogy back into her pocket and looks at the fading image of her parents flanking her at her high school graduation as it's being erased by a picture of her dad as a young man at the Houston launch facility, proudly holding his ticket to the newly established moon base.

"In the end, nothing lasts. No matter how much we wish it."

7

She pushes the microphone aside and steps out from behind the lectern amid stunned silence. She grabs her dad's urn, nods to the sincere young priest, and walks straight out of the church.

———

LATER. One hour. Two, maybe.

Thea scrapes the inside of the Jif jar, trying to rescue enough peanut butter to cover the other half of her sandwich. She gives up, smooths the little she's managed across the slice, then flips it atop the raspberry jam side.

A knock at the door interrupts her first bite.

She licks her thumb as she walks to the door. Glances through the sidelight at the visitor.

"Hey, Billy," she says, swinging the door open and letting in her dad's lawyer along with a blast of Texas summer heat.

"Hey, kid. Nice speech back there."

"Heard that, huh?"

"You know, your dad and I go back near fifty years. Two of us practically grew up together."

"That wasn't for you," Thea says, leading him into the kitchen and pointing at the seat across the table from her. "I'd offer you a PB and J, but I'm all outta PB."

"I'm good, thanks," he says, dropping into the chair with a heavy sigh. He sets his briefcase in front of him and clicks open the locks. "I was hoping to catch you at the luncheon. But this is probably better. This way we can talk."

He takes out a thick stack of paper held together by a binder clip and sets it on the table in front of her.

"That's your dad's will. I'm afraid there's a ton of legal stuff in there for you to read through, since other than this house, his truck, and a couple bank accounts, the rest of your dad's assets exist on the moon. Which is essentially like having them in international waters. Makes the paperwork a bitch, let me tell ya."

Thea shrugs and sets her jelly-skewed sandwich atop the stack.

"I'll cut to the chase. It's all yours. Your mom's not entitled to any of it, of course, per their divorce settlement. And I don't imagine she'll be coming for anything anyhow." The last part comes across as sort of a half question.

"Let her try," Thea says.

Billy seems not at all surprised by her response. "I was hoping she'd at least show up today of all days. How long's it been since you've seen her?"

Thea ignores the question. "What if I don't want any of it?" she asks, punching her index finger through the soggy bread.

"We can certainly talk about liquidating everything, if that's what you really want."

"It is."

Billy hesitates. "Look, Thea. I know your dad being gone all those years was hard on you. So dumping everything that took him away might feel like the right thing to do . . ."

She doesn't let him continue. "Hard? Billy, it's not like he was on business trips to Chicago or Miami while I was growing up. Do you have any idea what it's like to need your dad and know that he's two hundred thousand miles away? In fucking space. And when he's finally here, I mean *really* here to stay, all I get is the shadow of who he used to be."

"I just don't want you to make a rash decision, that's all. Take some time to think it through."

Thea flops back and swipes a tear from her cheek, angry that it's there in the first place.

"All I've had is time to think. Sitting here for the last three years, watching him disappear bit by bit. Toward the end, starting every day by introducing myself . . ."

Billy hands her a handkerchief. She dabs at her eyes, inhaling a trace of Old Spice from the soft cotton.

"I promised your pop that I'd never tell you this," he says, appearing to struggle with some weighty conundrum. "Should be okay, though. I mean, what can it matter now?"

Hell of a trial lawyer, her dad used to say about Billy, and Thea believes it in this moment, taking the bait despite the obvious twinkle in his eye.

"Out with it, old man."

"You know, he hated that you left school to come home and take care of him. But he knew there was no steering you away from it. You're just like your mom in that way. Once you decide on something, there's no stopping you."

The comparison stings, but she can tell he doesn't mean anything by it.

"Anyway, right after you got back, he made me get ahold of the astrophysics department and convince them to hold your spot."

"Are you serious?"

He raises three fingers indicating Scout's Honor. "He'd ask me about it nearly every time we spoke. Sometimes I'd get calls from your pop in the middle of the night, checking to make sure I'd talked to Cambridge. That your place was waiting for you."

"I'm sorry he made you do that. I told him I wasn't going back."

"I know. And it's not an option now anyway. The university held your spot for almost two years, but then they had to let it go. Broke my heart to tell him. But it was okay, actually, because by then he'd hatched a new plan."

Billy takes an envelope out of his briefcase.

"This came about eight months ago," he says, handing it over. "He said to give it to you after he was gone."

The handwriting on the envelope is shaky, but unmistakably his. Her name on the creamy paper, nothing else.

Billy snaps his briefcase closed and stands to go. Thea remains seated, unable to move.

"Take some time, then give me a call, okay?" He gives her a peck on the top of her head, picks up what remains of her sandwich, and heads out the door.

Thea stares at the envelope.

Sweat breaks out across her back.

She's afraid to open it. Because whatever the words, it'll mean the same thing. Something she hasn't let herself think about. *Couldn't* let herself think about.

In three years of doctors' visits, scans, pills, shots, infusions, specialists, and second, third, and fourth opinions.

Fights with him over the temperature in the house. The right brand of coffee. Old recipes. Scratchy slippers. The neighbor's evil cat. The grass, trash cans, TV shows . . .

All-out screaming matches over his asinine defense of his wife, her mother, who'd abandoned them both when things got hard.

The struggles day in and out over everything, anything.

Not once during those three years did she ever let herself think about what would come *after*.

And now . . .

She gathers herself, taps the short end of the envelope on the table, tears open the opposite side, and slides the letter out.

———

Sweetheart,

I have no right to ask. You've given me so much. Too much. But there's one last thing.

Please go see her. My Zephyr.
Sit in her chair and just listen. Feel. Give yourself that chance, honey.
I found myself up there. Maybe you will too.
Be happy.
Dad

———

And just like that, *after* arrives.

2

Fires

THE RAFT SKIPS across the tops of the waves, its dark black hull bouncing rhythmically on the low winter tide. Close to shore, a man jumps out into the shallow water and pulls the raft forward, beaching it as his companion kills the engine. After a thumbs-up to the one who will stay behind, the man quicksteps through the ankle-deep water, rubbing his upper arms in the chill air, moonlight reflecting off his bald head.

"Two hours late," the woman waiting for him grumbles as she stokes a small campfire. She tucks a few stray ringlets of hair into her beanie and stands to greet him.

"My God it's cold," he says as he rushes to the fire and holds out his hands.

"It's winter in this part of the world. What'd you expect?"

"It's July. My brain expects fireworks and hot dogs."

"Fresh outta dogs," she says, checking her watch. "But you'll get all the rockets' red glare you could hope for in a few minutes."

He tosses her a ziplocked bag containing a handheld device. She removes it, throws the empty bag onto the fire, then taps the glass.

A flight itinerary fills the screen.

"I don't understand. What's this?"

"We're pulling you."

Her brain crackles like the campfire as she tries to process what he's just said. She's worked so hard and has been so loyal. They can't do this to her. Not now.

"I've spent the last eighteen months getting in position," she says, her voice pleading. "I'm so close. I just need a little more time."

"This site has been deprioritized."

"By who?"

"That doesn't concern you."

"But this is *my* site!"

"Not anymore," he says.

A flash across the water draws their attention. Seconds later a thunderous roar drowns out all sound.

A sleek rocket appears in the night sky, a bloom of fire trailing behind it. It rises higher and higher until it disappears into the marine stratus hanging over the Mahia Peninsula.

"Leadership's making a huge mistake," she says as the basso thrum of the rocket's heavy engines fades away. She points to the smudge of light slowly fading from the luminescent clouds. "Taking this site offline will be a huge blow to astromining operations. They rely on it up there for a ton of supplies. It'll be a massive win for our cause."

"Things have changed. The system is too resilient for small setbacks."

"I'm not talking about a *small* setback. I'm gonna blow the whole fucking site to hell!"

"It won't *matter*. The Conglomerate and the national operations will just increase supply flights from the States or China or South America. Plus, Darkside Station grows less reliant on inbound supplies each day."

She lets out a long sigh, still struggling with the idea of

abandoning all her work but knowing she doesn't have much of a choice. *No* choice, really. They've decided, and they expect her to fall in line. Period.

"What's the plan?"

"We're gonna go straight to the source. More specifically, you are."

She looks down at the itinerary. Her flight out of Houston leaves in three days.

"How's this going to work?"

"We've arranged a position for you at Darkside that will give you broad access. Details and necessary clearances are all on there." He nods at the device in her hand, then reaches into his jacket and takes out a gun-shaped autoinjector.

"What's that for?"

He doesn't ask for permission before he grabs her wrist and pushes up her sleeve. "It'll let us track your movements," he says, placing the barrel on her forearm. "This is gonna sting."

Seconds later, her arm feels like it's on fire. She holds back a scream.

"Sorry about that," he says, sliding the injector back into his pocket and taking out a small handheld. As he taps the screen, a dull glow appears beneath her skin where the tracker is now nestled in her forearm. A few more taps, and the glow disappears.

"Anything else?" she says, cupping her throbbing arm.

"Settle in and wait for further instructions." He kicks sand onto the fire. "I'll be in touch in a few weeks."

"Understood."

"Good luck, Agent."

Then he turns and runs back to the raft, leaving her alone in the darkness.

3

Reunion

"WAIT A MINUTE," the customs agent says, double-checking her passport. "Are you Scottie's kid?"

"That's right," Thea says, switching her stuffed duffel bag to her other shoulder. She's probably overpacked. Billy said the buyer was motivated, so the deal should close quick.

"How's that old space pirate doing? Haven't seen him in years."

"He's dead."

Too matter of fact?

"Oh, shit," he says, cheeks flushing. "I'm sorry, honey."

"It's okay." She offers him a tiny smile to soften things.

"Wasn't on the job, was it? Think I would've heard about that."

"No. Alzheimer's."

There's a pause as the man looks for something more to say. But there never is.

He touches his computer screen, and the light atop the glass gates goes green as they swing open.

"Your dad was a good egg. I'm really sorry for your loss."

"I appreciate it. Thank you."

Man knew everybody, she thinks as she steps into the terminal.

———

THERE ARE three daily flights from Houston to the moon. Thea made sure to book the last flight of the day, hoping it'd be quiet in the terminal, but it isn't. The place is much too crowded for just last-flight passengers.

An announcement comes over the loudspeaker. "Attention, second-flight passengers. Once again, we're very sorry for the delay. We're happy to report that the issue has been corrected, and we are conducting final preflight checks. Stand by for further instructions."

She double-checks the time on her boarding pass, stashes her handheld in the side pocket of her duffel, and heads across the terminal to the large windows overlooking the launch pads. Pad one is empty, but pads two and three are occupied, steam cascading down the sides of the idling rockets. A truck with a scissor lift is parked next to the rocket on pad two. A maintenance worker on the top platform is winding up a thick cable as the lift slowly descends back toward the truck bed.

When Thea was in grade school, she and her mom would come here every time Dad left on a trip. They'd stand at this window, count down to blast off, then watch Dad's rocket vanish into the heavens. Thea would smash her cheek against the glass so that she could look up at the sky blushed with oranges, yellows, and reds, the fire igniting the clouds as the rocket soared.

By middle school, Dad's launches were more frequent, yet the sendoffs were more sporadic. Back when he was at the vanguard of astromining, money was good, but as competition grew, things got tight, and Mom had to take a job to help pay the bills. There was no time for jaunts to the spaceport to see Dad off for the hundredth time.

By high school, the tradition was gone altogether.

And then, not too many years later, when Dad got sick, so was Mom.

Thea drops her bag next to the window and leans forward, resting her cheek on the warm glass like she used to do as a girl. She looks up into the vast Texas sky, the last rays of the day streaking through wispy pink and purple clouds, lending a transcendent weight to her memories.

Nice try, old man, she thinks.

"Thea?"

She turns and sees someone pulling a small roller board toward her. Her eyes are struggling to adjust to the change from the bright sky to the dim, dingy terminal, so she can't make out the woman's face right away.

But her voice is clear as a bell.

"Darcey, wow," Thea says, stepping away from the window and holding out her hand, which Darcey ignores in lieu of one of those awkward hugs where your arms are pinned to your sides.

"Thea Watts, oh my God. How long has it been?"

"Been a while."

"Years!" Darcey says, finally releasing her.

Thea's old classmate looks fit and vital, her tight red jumper accentuating her thin runner's thighs and muscular arms. Wavy curls lustrous. Face aglow. She looks like she stepped out of the pages of a fitness magazine.

And she's about the *last* person Thea wants to see today.

"I heard about your International Astromining Alliance grant," Thea says. "Congrats on that. How'd it go?"

"My postdoc advisor was a real dick. But working with the IAA was great. In fact, the publication of my research just came out last month. Wait, I've got a copy."

There aren't a lot of women in astrophysics, so they stuck together in college and even collaborated on a few projects in the early years. Two outsiders bound by a common purpose. But that all ended the day Thea left Cambridge. And now, as she watches Darcey dig through her suitcase, jealousy crashes over her like a rogue wave.

"Here we go," Darcey says, thrusting a copy of the *Journal of Astrodynamics* into Thea's hand.

"Can't wait to read it," Thea says, sliding it into the front pocket of her duffel without a glance.

"So what are you doing here?"

"My dad passed away."

"Shit, Thea. That's awful. I'm sorry."

"Thanks," Thea says, desperate not to let this person see any weakness in her. "I've got a potential buyer for the *Zephyr*. I'm meeting him at Darkside in a few days for a tour of the ship and to discuss terms."

"I'm sure that's gonna be hard on you. Your dad's ship and all. But honestly, it's probably a good call. Civilian operations are mostly gone. Actually, I don't know of any flying these days. They just can't compete anymore against national crews. And certainly not against us."

"Who's us?"

"The Conglomerate," Darcey says, a sly smile spreading across her face.

"Really? You took a job with *them*."

"I know, I know. I'm a sellout. But after the grant and the paper . . . they offered me a role as a payload specialist on one of their scouts, with a chance to move up to a trawler within a year. I mean, how could I turn that down?"

Among Thea's fondest memories from her Cambridge days are the protests in London *against* the formation of the Conglomerate, the group of wealthy nations united around a singular purpose: control of the global market for rare earth elements. Darcey was always there right alongside her, the two of them waving signs and clenched fists at Parliament, then going to the pubs for mushy peas and pints.

And now, Darcey is one of them.

"I get it," Thea says, grinning at her old friend's weak convictions, jealousy quickly evaporating in the face of rising righteousness. "Sounds like a *great* opportunity."

An awkward silence stretches between them until another announcement comes over the loudspeaker.

"Second-flight passengers, please report to your gate for immediate launch prep and departure."

Darcey gestures toward the overhead speakers as if they are to blame for cutting their reunion short.

"Listen," Darcey says. "I don't know what your plans are after you offload your dad's ship, but . . . maybe I could put in a word for you? We always need good astral spectroscopy analysts. I bet you'd kill it at prospecting."

"Gee, thanks, Darc. I appreciate the vote of confidence."

"Come on. I didn't mean it that way."

"No, of course not." Thea waves off the comment, though she's tempted to remind her friend of her perennial position one spot *behind* Thea in their class rankings. Remind her of all the times she helped Darcey work out the "impossible" math. All the times she sharpened Darcey's obtuse or aimless hypotheses.

But she catches herself.

Why bother? Let it go.

Darcey won.

"Seriously, thanks. But I've got other plans."

Darcey does a bad job of faking her disappointment, then with a quick hug and promises to keep in touch, she jogs off.

As soon as she's out of sight, Thea pulls the journal with Darcey's article from her duffel and tosses it into the nearest recycling bin.

_____

NINETY MINUTES, two gin-and-tonics, and an ill-advised bean burrito later, Thea's flight is called.

She braces herself as she shows her boarding pass and ID to the gate attendant, not sure she can stomach yet another conversation about her dad—or anything else for that matter. Luckily, the man barely glances her way as he scans her pass and waves her to the queue forming at the top of the jetway.

Midweek shuttles only carry eighteen people, so the crowd is small. In fact, it appears that her fellow passengers are all part of the same group, all of them wearing dark blue body suits and speaking what she thinks might be a Scandinavian language. They seem relaxed and happy, which suggests they must all be heading back up after shore leave.

Once everyone is checked in, the group is ushered down the jetway to the pad three preflight area, which is just a large room with steel benches flanking a rack of space suits. Plastic rings indicating height ranges are interspersed along the crossbar between the hangars, like a system for organizing discount clothes at a department store. Thea finds her size, grabs a flight suit off the rack, and picks a spot on one of the benches away from the others.

The suit is sealed in a thick plastic garment bag. Even with the added weight of the bag, it's far lighter than the old, retired suits hanging in her dad's bedroom closet.

Laughter erupts as one of the other passengers struggles to zip up his suit. A woman rushes to his aid, pulling the zipper over the man's belly as his face turns red. "Too much brisket," the woman says, poking her friend's middle and sending the group into an apoplectic fit of laughter.

Thea kicks off her sneakers and stows them and her sweat-shirt in her duffel. Air immediately swells the garment bag when she breaks the seal. She runs her hand over the blindingly white spectra fiber, surprised at its smoothness, then takes the flight suit out of the bag.

She begins by thrusting her feet through the suit's crumpled legs into the attached adjustable footies. Once her feet are situated, she slides the suit up her legs, then stands and shimmies it over her hips. She works her arms inside, and just as she's zipping up the front, someone bellows for everyone's attention. She grabs her duffel and heads to where the other passengers have encircled two women in matching orange flight suits.

"Be sure *all* your belongings are safely stowed in your baggage," says one of the orange-clad women. "We do not have a lost and found, so anything you leave behind *will* be discarded. Then leave your bags in this bin and follow me." She points at a gray bin on wheels to her right.

The group follows directions, and Thea takes up the rear as they follow the two women down a long corridor to the staging area.

All along the walls are images of the Houston launch site's construction. Thea pauses before a picture of the ribbon-cutting ceremony and looks for her dad's face in the crowd. She knows he was there. She remembers how excited he was when he came home, scooped her up in his arms, and flew her around the living room.

She finds him a few rows back from the Texas governor. Toothy smile. Cheesy mustache. Dad.

She kisses the fingertips of her glove and touches them to the picture. Then races to catch up to the group.

The two crew members stop before a set of escalators going down. To the right of the escalators is a rack of helmets.

"These are one size fits all; it doesn't matter which one you take. Just like your flight suits, all helmets are sanitized between uses, so any bad breath you smell once you put them on is your own."

The others chuckle as they grab helmets, which are surprisingly lightweight. As soon as Thea seats the rim of hers into the collar clips, its interior illuminates. There is a quick flash of light right in front of her face, then the visor goes from opaque to clear.

"Welcome, Althea Octavia Watts."

The voice tries to pull off a regional accent, but the twang is over the top and mangles her name. She can only imagine how badly it's botched the Scandinavian names, but by the wide smiles behind most of the visors, it appears this one last bit of Texas flair, no matter how inaccurate and cliché, is welcome.

Green lights glow atop all the helmets but one, and the two crew members give that helmet a quick inspection and adjustment. The light changes from red to green, and they're ready to proceed.

"Okay, let's go. Clock's ticking."

They all shuffle onto the escalators, which empty onto a platform, where their ride is already waiting. It's a long vehicle, nine rows of two, and looks to Thea much like a roller coaster car.

"Everyone, please take your seats and follow your helmet's instructions. We'll be coming around to make sure you're secure for takeoff."

Thea's seat number appears in her visor, and she soon finds herself sitting down next to a young man who greets her with a quick thumbs-up and head nod. As she settles in, a video begins to roll on her visor, explaining how to secure her shoulder harness and seat belt. When she clicks the last of the anchors into the buckle at her belly button, her visor returns to normal.

A crew member is at her side moments later. "Nice job, Ms. Watts," the woman says, giving Thea's left shoulder strap a sharp tug. "Love your middle name, by the way."

"Dad was a science fiction buff."

"Really? Then you blasting off for the moon is probably blowing his mind, huh?"

"You betcha."

It doesn't take long for the crew to finish their rounds and take their own seats at the front. The cart jolts forward down a brightly lit tunnel with smooth, white, curved walls. It feels like traveling through a drinking straw.

Thea's suddenly very aware of her own breathing. The helmet's stuffy and suffocating, her suit smothering. She sucks in hard and closes her eyes, trying to calm herself. Her helmet responds with a cool puff of air radiating from behind her ears and wrapping around her cheeks. It smells like lavender, and a dim yellow light fills the interior of her helmet.

She breathes deep and steady, and after ten or twenty seconds, it starts to work. A tenuous calm settles over her.

She can't remember the last time she had a panic attack. She's always wanted to do this. She used to beg her dad to take her. And now, as she's finally about to go, she freaks out.

Why?

That's when it hits her.

Her dad is really gone. The truth lands on her heart like a stone.

I thought you'd be here with me, she thinks, glancing at the smiling young man next to her in the place where her dad should be.

Her eyes well with tears. *I can't do this.*

The rows in front of her suddenly turn upward at a ninety-degree angle. Gravity pushes her into the seatback as the cart climbs up along the side of the rocket. She looks to one side and manages to catch a glimpse of the night sky through the launch tower, the glow of Houston off on the horizon. But then the cart slides sideways into the fuselage, the rocket's bay doors close, and Texas is gone.

Her panic returns.

All she wants to do is get out of this damn seat and go back home. She's about to say something, hoping someone's monitoring her helmet audio, when to her surprise, the young man next to her grabs her hand.

She really takes him in for the first time. He looks like he just got out of high school. White-blond hair swoops across his forehead above a big bright smile and glittering crystal-blue eyes.

"First trip up?"

All she can do is nod.

"It's scary for everybody the first time. But you're going to be fine, I promise. I've done this dozens of times. It's a piece of cake."

Somehow this simplistic assurance . . . helps. Thea feels tension leach out of her as she stares, awestruck, at the angel seated next to her.

"My name's Jakob," he says.

"Thea," she replies, and squeezes his hand. "Thank you."

There's a loud clang as the cart locks to the interior frame of the rocket, followed by a mechanical whir from somewhere below that sets her teeth on edge.

"Welcome aboard. We'll be on our way to the moon momentarily. Our flight time will be approximately sixty-four hours. Once we escape the exosphere, you'll be free to move about the cabin. Your crew is here to assist with all your needs. Thanks for traveling with us. Enjoy your flight."

The video of a waving flight attendant, space helmet resting against her hip, is replaced by a sixty-second countdown.

Thea feels a low vibration at her back. As it grows, Jakob lets out a loud *woot-woot*, which is taken up by the other passengers.

Woot-woot! Woot-woot!

And something remarkable happens.

Something absent from Thea's life, something absent for far too long . . . returns.

She relaxes, closes her eyes, and remembers all the times her dad gave her a big wave as he left the terminal and went off on one of his many expeditions. That was when he was at his happiest, she thinks. His most *alive*. Like the young man to her right, holding his arms up over his head like you do as the roller coaster clicks its way to the top of a big drop.

The vibration becomes more violent, but she's no longer afraid. Her heart pounds as the vibration grows. Tears stream down her face. Happy tears. Sad tears. All the tears that she's held back for years and years, washing away her sadness and pain and anger and frustration. She lets them come. Welcomes them.

For the first time in a very long time, she simply *lets go*. Unclenches something deep inside and lets herself *feel* again.

"Woot-woot!" she cries, watching the numbers on her visor flash.

Five . . .
Four . . .
Three . . .
Two . . .
One . . .

4

Horizons

THE JINGLE IS UNMISTAKABLE.

Thea tosses the tattered paperback aside, scoots off the bed, and rushes to the window. Sunlight streams into the room as she throws aside the sheer curtains. The window frame is warped from the Texas heat, and she has to strain against it, rocking it side to side, in order to shimmy it up inch by inch. She sticks her head out as soon as it's high enough.

There it is!

She vaults across the covers like a bandit across the hood of a getaway car, kicking *A Wrinkle in Time* to the purple carpet in the process, and grabs a fistful of change from the top of her dresser.

"Whoa, where you off to in such a hurry?" her mom asks as Thea pounds down the steps and rips around the corner toward the front door, her bare feet slapping against the foyer hardwoods.

"Ice cream!" she calls over her shoulder, then smacks down on the door handle and flings the screen door wide.

She leaps from the porch and races to the mailbox, nearly

ripping off the upturned red flag as she uses it to change direction. Up ahead, Mister Softee is just turning the corner.

"Hold up!" she shouts, waving her arms and running, all while making sure not to step on the sidewalk cracks and break her mother's back.

The truck stops and waits for her.

Mission accomplished, Thea slows down, sucking hard at the soupy air, thick with the scent of honeysuckle from Old Lady Morris's bushes. The sun roasts her shoulders, the straps of her tank top offering little protection to her pink and peeling summer skin. Heat from the concrete sautés the soles of her feet, so she hops onto the cool grass next to the curb as she jogs the rest of the way to the truck.

The driver slides open the service window and waves at her, his red-and-white paper hat slightly askew. She wipes sweat from her forehead and enthusiastically waves back, deciding in that moment to go for lemon water ice instead of her usual choco-vanilla swirl with rainbow sprinkles.

A breeze kicks up. She raises her arms over her head, reveling as the gentle air cools her sticky armpits and sweaty cheeks.

The breeze stiffens, accompanied by a low whistle. The whistle grows louder, then shifts to a deep growl as the wind intensifies even more.

She scampers to a tall Texas ash and looks up through its bending limbs. Leaves strain to hold on to their branches. A robin's nest breaks free, light blue eggs caught in the torrent. Two smash on the sidewalk next to her, oozing yellow streaked with bright red. She positions herself so that the trunk bears the brunt of the wind.

The sky blackens with clouds racing in from the west. The ice cream truck driver's hat is whipped off his head as he scrambles to shut the service door. Thea can't help but watch it fly, caught on the wind like a sail. It gets snagged in a holly bush, but only for a few seconds before it's ripped away by the gale.

The screech of rubber draws her attention back to the truck. Its wheels are skidding and skipping across the asphalt as it skitters down the street.

Thea feels a tug at the center of her chest. It gets stronger with each second, her tank top ballooning out and braids lifting from her shoulders. The truck leaves a streak of black rubber in its wake.

And that's when she realizes . . . the truck's not being pushed by the wind.

It's being pulled.

And so is she.

A swirling vortex of garden gnomes, potted plants, porch rockers, mailboxes, trash, dirt, Harriet Jane's tricycle, and other bits and pieces of her neighborhood are being sucked into a dark void, a black nothingness poked into the fabric of her world like a finger through tissue paper.

She pushes her back up against the knobby wood of the tree, slides her butt down to the ground, and anchors her bare heels in the grass. The canopy overhead is being shredded, branches and limbs cracking and splintering under the weight of the suck.

The rear tires of the ice cream truck smoke and tear apart as the driver desperately tries to reverse away from the vacuum. But the tug-of-war lasts only a few seconds before the back end of the truck rises off the ground.

It rises, drops, then rises again.

And flips end over end, tumbling toward the black hole.

Thea watches it bounce away like a ball toward a storm drain, the crunch of metal a bottom note to the truck's shrill death cries.

A hand touches her shoulder.

She startles awake, the event horizon of the dream receding.

"I'm sorry, Ms. Watts," says one of the crew members. A rhythmic, gentle chime sounds from the cabin speakers. "We'll be landing soon."

Thea tries to sit up, but her sleep sack holds her in place. She twists away from the brightening overhead glow and shields her eyes. She's utterly exhausted. She spent most of the first day floating between the cabin windows, looking down on Earth or out into the depths of space, which amused the rest of the passengers and crew who were old hats at space flight. Since then, unrelenting, merciless heartburn has prevented any solid rest. Her stomach and zero-g aren't on speaking terms. She managed the last few hours of shuteye only after eating an entire tube of antacids that one of the crew members found in the back of a storage bin.

"How are you doing, Thea?"

"Pretty rough," she says, hitting the button to retract the divider between her seat and Jakob's. She finds him sucking on the end of a food pouch. "Explain to me again why no one has figured out how to get artificial gravity onto these shuttles."

"They just can't handle the weight. I hear they're working on lighter superconductors, though. So maybe a few years from now?" He squeezes the last bits of his breakfast into his mouth.

Thea suppresses a belch, afraid of what might pop out.

"You'll feel better once we get on the ground."

She unzips the fabric cocoon down to her waist and adjusts her seatback so that it's upright again. The moon fills the window next to her. Lunar highlands drift past, crags and craters speckled across the vast grayness. Spires of ancient rock give way to valleys of rubble and dust.

Growing up, she had a lunar mobile hanging above her

bed. She used to lie there at night, staring up at it, imagining what it'd be like to be inside one of the little plastic ships spinning around the glow-in-the-dark sphere. And now she's here, about to land on the *actual* goddamn moon.

A flash of light outside the window draws her attention. Sunlight bouncing off something reflective. Something cutting across surface.

Something straight.

God doesn't build in straight lines.

She fumbles with the zipper, shimmies her legs out of her sleep sack, swings out of her seat, and pushes off. A little too hard, she realizes, when she smacks against the window. She stares down in awe at the Hyperloop, a glass and steel aberration amid the ancient lunar flatlands. She follows the luminescent line and finds the edge of the shipyard glowing at the base of a massive ridge.

The shipyard began as a hotel and playground for the famous and ultra-wealthy at the height of the space tourism movement, a time when the ferocious pace of innovation the world had enjoyed during the preceding century seemed like it would go on forever. But then we began to run out of rare earth elements, the critical ingredient in all of our technology.

We scoured the globe for untapped sources of these essential metals. Dredged deeper in the oceans than we'd ever dared. Some discoveries were made, but it was never enough. Earth's supply eventually ran dry, and technological progress stalled. To move forward again, we needed to find new sources of rare earths. And we did. But not by looking down as we always had, but instead by looking up.

There are thousands and thousands of rare-earth-rich asteroids that orbit just beyond the reaches of the moon. All we needed to do was figure out how to catch them.

The original plan was to create an Earthside astromining

hub. But the new space-based industry was unpredictable, and safety concerns for Earth's satellite network—not to mention the planet itself—ultimately led to the conclusion that this approach was simply not feasible. Instead we pursued the creation of a base on the far side of the moon, the dark side, which is why the astromining base completed a decade later was called Darkside Station.

It was then that the old moon hotel and landing pads were expanded to become not just a shipyard, but the world's most important shipping and receiving hub ever built. The two lunar outposts, old and new, were connected by the Hyperloop, and the era of astromining officially began.

Soon after, a fleet of commercial and international ships began to replenish the world's supply of rare earth elements.

Ships like Thea's father's.

Now, *her* ship.

"I'm sorry, Ms. Watts. You're going to have to take your seat. We'll be landing shortly."

Thea nods to the woman, takes a final glance out the window, then floats back to her seat.

Jakob is smiling at her, head bobbing along to something in his headset. "Cool, right?" he says way too loudly, pointing toward the window.

Thea fastens her waistbelt, then reaches over and pulls the nearest earphone off his ear. "So much cooler than I imagined. How many times have you ridden it?"

"Oh, I ride the Hyperloop all the time," he says, taking off his headset. "I'm low man on the crew, so I have to travel with our catch and supervise the offload."

"By yourself?" Thea pulls her shoulder straps into place and buckles them.

"It's not so bad. I usually leave right after breakfast and can get back to Darkside Station before last call at the bar."

Thea tries to do the math, and it doesn't add up. "Wait, how fast does the train go?"

"I don't know. It's only about a five-hour trip each way. No big deal."

One of the crew members addresses the cabin. "Attention, everyone. We'll be coming around to make sure you're all secure for landing. Please stow everything in your seat compartments. We'll be on the surface in about fifteen minutes."

"Do you guys have plans tonight?" Thea asks Jakob.

"Unfortunately, we're heading over to Darkside right away. Our ship, the *Lillehammer*, leaves at dawn tomorrow."

"I didn't think there were any trains today."

"No passenger trains. We're hitching back in a boxcar."

Thea nods, trying to hide her disappointment.

"Do you want to come with us?" He brightens. "It's not very comfortable, but that's what the aquavit is for, right?"

Thea takes a second to enjoy the look on Jakob's face, eyes twinkling with youth and adventure, and a smile that can melt your heart and weaken your knees. If only she were ten years younger.

"Thank you, but I reserved a room, and sleeping in an actual bed sounds really good right about now."

"Maybe we'll see you over at the docks?"

"Probably not. I won't be here very long. But the next time you're in Texas, you look me up." She puts her hand out, so thankful that he was here with her.

He takes her hand in his, kisses the back of it, and makes his promise just as they start their descent to the surface of the moon.

———

SIXTY MINUTES LATER, after a landing process the exact opposite of their takeoff, Thea's in her room at the shipyard.

The chilly air smells of metal, and the harsh furnishings and hard surfaces belie the fact that she's standing in what was once one of the most expensive hotel rooms in the known universe. But with lunar tourism now dead, the room's aspect aligns more closely to its purpose: a stop-over. A place to kill time on the way to somewhere else. Like a Route 66 motor lodge, but in space.

Yet the comforts of space travel, or lack thereof, are the furthest thing from her mind as she stands there, forehead pressed against the glass of her hotel room window. Below, a crane lowers a pill-shaped shipping container onto a platform. As the arm of the crane swings away, the platform slides forward and feeds the container into the end of a glass and metal tube that stretches away into the distance.

"How does it work?" she asks as a thick, circular door swings closed over the tube opening, sealing the container inside.

"It's basically a big railgun," the porter says. He drops her bag on the bed and proceeds to peck away at a handheld device. "Something to do with electromagnets, I think. Your entertainment system has a video about it."

As Thea watches, a steel arch above the tube comes to life. Five red circles appear across the span of the arch, one at a time, until all five are lit. The lights glow for a few seconds, then suddenly go dark like at the start of a Formula One race.

"There it goes!" she says, watching the tube shudder as the container flies down its length and shoots toward Earth.

"Cool," the young man says without looking up from his tablet.

The container streaks like a bullet on what looks like a collision course with Japan, which is slowly coming over the horizon. Like most people, she's seen footage of the collection crews retrieving containers from various landing sites all over the world, but seeing the process from this vantage point increases her admiration for the math and science and mechanics involved in transporting the bounty of space back home.

"Sorry, this is my first time," she says when she finally loses sight of the container amid Earth's swirling atmosphere.

"No kidding."

"That obvious, huh?"

"Eh, you're good," he says, a subtle smile appearing on his face as he finally tears his eyes away from his tablet. "Make sure you check out the flag too. You'll kick yourself if you don't."

She raises an imaginary camera and clicks a picture.

"It says here you're on the first train to Darkside tomorrow, is that correct?"

She nods. "Anything I need to do? Do I need to check in or something?"

"Nah, place is empty, so you'll be fine showing up just a few minutes before your departure time. Welcome to the shipyard. Let us know if you need anything else."

The porter departs, and Thea flops backward onto the bed, reveling in the simple fact that she can. Loving the slight bounce her body makes as it hits the firm mattress.

"My God . . . artificial or not, I love you, gravity," she says to her empty room, exhaustion flowing over her. She closes her eyes, trying to let it take her, but her mind is racing. She can't believe she's here.

She rolls off the bed and goes back to the window. Down below, another container races down the railgun barrel and is hurled toward the planet, which is big and blue and beautiful and everything she ever hoped it would be. You can look at all the images and watch all the videos and enjoy all the augmented reality and read all the descriptions of being on the moon and looking down on your planet. How insignificant it makes you feel. How tiny in the grand scope of things. The perspective it grants and the illusions it shatters.

But nothing comes close to the actual thing.

Never a poet was born who could do justice to this experience, she thinks, but then realizes she can't remember the last time she's read any poetry.

She glances back at the bed, realizes the futility of trying to sleep right now, and instead heads out the door to explore.

5

Shipping and Receiving

"It got knocked down. That's the only thing that saved it."

Thea stares at the tattered and torn flag hanging from its crossbar like a cheap curtain on a rod. The tarnished aluminum flagpole is slightly bent at the tip, which is fixed in a clear block secured to the moon's surface with metal straps. A spotlight from somewhere above casts the flag in harsh white.

"What do you mean?" she asks.

The man is cleaning his squeegee blade with a dingy rag. He holsters his spray bottle and then does a wide sweep across the glass separating the visitors' area from the Apollo 11 flag.

"Aldrin and Armstrong couldn't drive the pole into the surface very deep. So when they took off, the exhaust from their ship knocked the whole thing over. That's why the pole's bent at the bottom. It all got buried until engineers found it during the original excavation of this site."

"But how'd that help it?"

"There's a plaque over there with the whole story if you're interested," he says, nodding toward a tall brass fixture on the far wall.

"I know. But you've got such a *nice voice*," she says.

This gets a booming laugh from the worker, whose facial topography seems to match the place he calls home. "All righty, then. Polished the damn thing enough over the last twenty-odd years, I know it by heart."

"Wow, twenty years. Amazing."

He points at the plaque. "After Eleven, NASA made damn sure the other Apollo flags stuck. But over the decades that followed, radiation, micrometeorites, regolith showers, regular old moon dust . . . all of it beat the shit out of the flags, pardon my French. That's why they're all gone now. Only that one right there's still around. Getting covered in dirt and dust saved it in the end. Guess you could take that as a kind of life lesson or something, if you're so inclined."

Thea gazes at the flag through the sparkling clean glass. Red, white, and blue now a sort of pinkish and gray. Dimmed stars blending into a bleached background. Motes of space dust orbiting faded glory, once more giving proof through the night.

"Thanks for the history lesson," she says.

"My pleasure."

The worker twirls his squeegee and uses his shirt sleeve to wipe a smudge only he can see off the glass. He tips his cap, grabs his bucket, swipes his badge, and disappears through a service door, leaving Thea to wonder if he was real or if she made him up. Some Dickensian ghost unbound by time and space.

Thea pauses to look at the tall brass fixture as she passes, but she's certain after reading just a few of the words etched into its burnished face that she got the better version of the tale.

She follows the signs to the observation deck. The causeway opens onto a tall space with a twenty-foot glass wall.

Couches and tables are scattered around. She runs her fingers through the plastic fronds of a decorative plant at the center, then heads for the glass, wondering why they'd dedicate such a big space to viewing what amounts to shipping and receiving.

But then she looks down onto the shipyard floor.

At a giant pile of gold.

The gleaming yellow rock fills one of the wide storage bays that line the walls of the processing center. Adjacent bays hold what look to be smaller but still massive piles of silver and a ruddier copper-colored stone. All these once-precious metals, now made ubiquitous and therefore worthless by asteroid mining. Still, they're impressive to behold in such vast quantities. She imagines that was even more true when astromining was just getting going and things like gold and silver still held some value.

She remembers her very first bucket of golden brick Legos. She'd build rockets and houses and cars out of them, then set them on her bedroom windowsill so that they'd glow in the sun. Her dad gave her enough of them that eventually she had an entire golden city in a corner of her room. She thinks it might all be in the attic now, along with a bunch of her other crap. But maybe not. A lot of stuff got trashed once her mother left.

Down below, a red light in the processing center begins to whirl above an exterior door with the word *INTAKE* painted across its middle. Seconds later, steam bursts around the edges of the door as the chamber on the other side pressurizes. When the burst stops, the door irises open, and a tubular boxcar slowly enters, pulled forward by what look like sleds evenly spaced along a track that arches in a big U from the intake door to its twin on the same exterior wall, simply marked *OUT*.

The boxcar slows and comes to a stop, and the intake door irises closed again. After a few seconds, the boxcar rotates clockwise, the magnetic sled beneath it working to slowly spin it along its length, like a football in a tight spiral. After a few degrees, the top edge of the tube hinges open, and as the rotation grows, so too does the opening, until the boxcar eventually spills its glittering contents onto the processing room floor.

A small crew dressed in bright orange jumpers emerges from somewhere beneath the observation deck. Three men are carrying push brooms with what look like heavy metal bristles, while a fourth heads to a front-end loader parked near the furthest storage bay. After a minute, the tumble of rock eventually stops, and one of the men jumps into the boxcar and starts sweeping out the remaining rocks. When he's finished, he twirls his index finger over his head a few times, signaling to someone to begin rotating the boxcar back to its original position, then he joins his coworkers clearing the track.

The guy on the front-end loader maneuvers the vehicle into position and scoops up a bucket full of gold as the empty boxcar heads for the *OUT* door. The door swallows the boxcar and closes, a burst of air escaping around its edges to complete the cycle.

Thea's still watching the broom crew when she hears a bright beep. She turns to see a "crew members only" door swinging open near her, and a woman steps onto the observation deck. She's dressed in orange like the men below and looks completely exhausted, her muddy brown hair a rat's nest as she whips off her hard hat.

"Hi there," Thea says, too loudly for the empty space. "I was wondering . . . how many shipments a day come here from Darkside Station?"

"I don't know. Ten or twelve, maybe," the woman mutters. "Listen, I don't wanna be rude, but I'm coming off a fourteen-hour stint and ain't got the energy to chat. Sorry."

She spares Thea only the tiniest of glances before beelining for the exit. As she leaves, Thea notices the door the woman came through is still in the process of swinging closed.

Thea doesn't let it.

She slips through. The air is stunningly cold. She creeps down the spiraling metal stairs to a control booth that looks out over the work floor. The lights in the booth are off, the only illumination coming from the control panel, which is why she doesn't notice the man enter behind her. Until he flicks on the lights.

"You lost, honey?"

The man is rail thin, his greasy hair falling over his hollow cheeks as he leans on his broom handle two-fisted, like he's holding a butter churn.

"Sorry. Curiosity got the best of me, I guess. This place is pretty amazing."

"Got that right," he says, eyeing her up and down. Two of his coworkers join him at the entrance to the control booth, looks of surprise on their faces at finding a stranger on the floor.

"Sorry, I know I'm not supposed to be in here. I'll leave."

"That's all right, sweetness. No bother at all," the man says with a mischievous smirk to his buddies. "Hey, I could give you a tour. Show you how things are done, shipyard style."

His coworkers cackle with him as he hops around, riding his broom like it's a bucking bronco.

Thea tries to push past to the stairs, but he cuts her off.

"Whoa, now. Hold on. You don't know what you're missing."

"Let me by," she says, staring him down.

"I usually don't go in for colored chicks, but for you I'd make an exception."

Thea's palm thrust knocks the sneer off his face. He drops his broom as he stumbles backward. Thea grabs it and points the bristle end at his head.

"If I wanted to stomp dumb rednecks I could have just stayed in Texas."

"Stupid bitch!" he growls, a bloody bubble blossoming on his swelling lower lip. He pushes free of his friends' grip, ready to go after Thea, but then a voice booms out from across the work floor.

"Oy, arseholes! Get the fuck out of there!"

The loader driver is standing next to his vehicle, waving his coworkers over. He's nearly as wide as he is tall, and his square jaw is thrust toward them, his bushy gray goatee a feral threat all by itself. Thea imagines he could probably haul as much weight in his tree-trunk arms as in his loader's bucket.

Her would-be attacker is still furious, looking like he's ready to re-engage, but after some coaxing, his two coworkers guide him away. The three of them head down the stairs to the work floor.

When they arrive, the driver catches her eye through the window of the control booth and points up at the door leading back into the observation deck. "You can't be down here. So fuck off."

Thea flips the bird to her skinny combatant, who spits out a glob of bloody phlegm in response, then heads back up the stairs. She slams the door behind her, the last vestiges of adrenaline fleeing her body.

On the floor below, the skinny douche and his cronies are getting their asses chewed by the loader driver. She watches him thrust his pointer finger in their direction a few times, enjoying the sight of them cowering under the barrage. But then she feels the beginnings of a migraine blooming in her skull and decides to call it a day.

One *hell* of a day, at that.

———

Too few hours later, and despite oversleeping, Thea makes it to the Hyperloop terminal with a few minutes to spare.

She scans her boarding pass once, twice, then a third time, which turns out to be the charm. The gate swings open just as the departure announcement comes over the loudspeaker. She races to the platform, then stops short. Her train is seven cars long, but she realizes only one of them is a passenger car, and it's the very last one. Her bag digs into her shoulder as she jogs to the end of the line and jumps through the closing doors of the passenger car with seconds to spare.

The car could hold twenty passengers, but since it's a midweek transport to Darkside Station, it's mostly empty. To her surprise, Thea finds herself seated across the aisle from the hulking man from last night.

He glances at her as she sits down, then lets out a groan.

"Good to see you again, too," she says, catching her breath as she buckles her shoulder straps.

He pulls his beanie down over his eyes and crosses his arms across the acreage of his chest. She doesn't imagine he'd have any trouble at all holding this position for the next five hours, and decides not to let him.

"Look, I didn't mean to cause a problem yesterday. I'm sorry."

No response.

"It was an impulsive mistake. I don't know what I was thinking. It's my first time here, and I was super interested in the process."

Still nothing.

"You can only learn so much by watching the infovids, right? So I figured I'd check it out firsthand."

Dead silence.

"I'm sorry about your friend, too. But he had it coming."

"Not my friend."

Got him.

"I mean, that buddy of yours has got some nerve. Total jackass. As if I'd ever—"

"Look, luv," he says, pushing up his beanie and staring her down. "I get that you're all excited about *being on the moon*. But all's I wanna do is catch some blessed shuteye before I start my next twelve-hour, ball-breaking shift pushing around space rocks. At my *second* job at the refinery. So if you'll kindly leave me the fuck alone, that'd be greatly appreciated."

"Okay, okay. Jeez! I was just trying to find out what it's like up here."

"The moon's great. Shipyard's great. Did ya see the fucking railgun? Holy shit, right? It's great! It's all super great! That what you're after?"

"Why do you stay if you hate it so much?" Thea asks. "There's plenty of jobs for heavy equipment drivers back home."

"You don't know what you're talking about." He turns away from Thea and stares straight ahead. "That ain't why I'm up here."

"Why, then?"

He doesn't say anything at first, choosing instead to try and bore a hole in the seatback in front of him. But as the silence stretches out, he chances a few peeks over at Thea, who is patiently waiting for an answer, projecting that there's no way she going to let him sleep until he gives one.

He relents. "I'm a pilot," he says. "Used to be, anyway."

"What happened?"

"The fucking Conglomerate happened. That's what."

Darcey's smiling, smug face comes to Thea's mind as she watches the veins pulse in the man's thick neck.

"They came up here and squeezed all the little guys out. Made it impossible to compete. Sucked up all the good fishing spots and undercut everyone. Some guys tried to survive by mining scraps like gold and cobalt. But most just gave up."

"Is that what happened to you?"

"I flew with a civilian crew for almost seven years. We had it good for a while there. But then our ship took some damage from a rogue meteorite and my boss couldn't afford to fix her. So he packed it in."

"Good pilots don't grow on trees. Weren't there other crews you could fly with?"

"No one's hiring, except the Conglomerate. And I'd sooner shovel shit than work for those bastards. So that's exactly what I'm doing. Shoveling. It ain't the glamourous story tourists like to hear," he says, meeting her gaze once again. "But it's the truth."

Thea knows it is. She's heard versions of the same story from her dad and his circle for years.

"I'm not a tourist," she says.

"Don't tell me you're one of them."

"My dad was an independent operator like you. He died recently, so I'm up here meeting a buyer for his ship."

"What outfit?"

"Watts Astromining."

The man brightens instantly, slapping his knee as a broad smile breaks out across his face.

"I knew your dad!"

Of course you did.

"Even flew for him every once in a while, when he was back home on shore leave. *Zephyr*, right?"

"I'm Thea," she says, holding out her hand.

His hand swallows hers, but his grip is gentle. "Rory Abernathy. Your dad was a good man. I'm sorry to hear he's gone."

The train lurches forward, sliding slowly into the lunar darkness and picking up speed steadily as it leaves the shipyard behind.

"I know you need to catch some sleep, so I'll leave you be," Thea says. "Sorry again about last night."

"Gotta tell ya," he says, pulling his beanie down again and settling back into his seat. "I got a real kick outta watching you put that twat in his place."

Thea smiles, settles back into her seat, and follows Rory's lead.

6

Tender

SHE'S HEARD about the Leaderboard her whole life. Her dad used to chronicle the *Zephyr*'s movement up and down the rankings, gleeful after each big score of platinums when he and his crew climbed toward the top, despondent with each backslide when fishing was bad. She and her mom used to keep track of his progress on a whiteboard in the kitchen, using magnets to represent the various ships.

Now she's staring up at the real thing.

Mining crews and station workers flit around her with tremendous purpose as she stands in the tumult of the Hub, but she's hardly aware of them. Her gaze is fixed on the board above, its glowing green characters listing the crews and their tallies above a live shot of the refinery floor, where the fleet's catch is being processed.

The Conglomerate holds a commanding lead over Luxembourg, with crews from China, Japan, and Russia close behind. Thea scans the list looking for a single civilian operation, but doesn't see any. Just the eight-hundred-pound gorilla and a bunch of national crews. Things have changed since the days of those kitchen magnets.

A young girl appears behind the information counter below the board. She's pecking away at a handheld tablet, buds in her ears.

"Excuse me. Can you tell me how to get to Dock D?"

The girl doesn't answer—or even register Thea's presence —so Thea taps on the window a few times. When that doesn't work, she pounds the glass.

"Yeah?" the girl finally says, tossing her tablet onto the countertop and unscrewing a single earbud.

"Dock D. How do I get there?"

"Umm, you follow the signs," she says, pointing a nibbled fingernail toward a digital display on a far wall. "Or the smell. Either will get you where you're going."

Thea considers reaching through the window and grabbing the smug girl by her collar, but she's already running late for her meeting.

"Thanks . . . Molly," Thea says, glancing at the girl's nametag. "Especially for the tip."

The girl rolls her eyes and sucks in a popped gum bubble. "Umm, what are you talking about?" She picks at the string of pink caught in her lip ring.

"The smell. That's really helpful advice. I'll let everyone at the docks know that *you're* on the job, making sure none of their visitors get lost." Thea gives the girl a wink. "That way they'll know exactly who to thank next time they come by."

"Geez, I was only joking," the girl calls after Thea, who's already heading toward the docks without looking back.

———

It's impossible not to notice what's different about this part of Darkside Station: the place is empty. The general buzz of the Hub and the main concourse quickly gives way to an eerie quiet. Locked metal gates seal off most of the lifts to empty pads above. Dim and flickering lights create shadows that criss-cross the metal grated floor and peeling walls. The air is stag-nant and, as Molly foretold, fetid and funky. It feels like walking through the center of a rotting log with poisoned mushrooms growing off the top.

The *Zephyr*'s lift is at the very end of Dock D, which is about as far from the Hub as you can get. Thea runs her finger across the top edge of the placard for Watts Astromining, knocking a thick layer of dust to the floor. A spiderweb is laced across the control panel next to the lift doors. She's never considered that there are spiders in space, and she feels bad about ruining this one's web as she enters the code, which is her parent's anniversary. Not exactly secure, but that was her dad.

The lift sputters to life, lights glowing for the first time in years. A five-second countdown appears on the control panel while the lift repressurizes. When the countdown hits zero, the doors open with a hiss of stale air.

A silver food wrapper flutters out at Thea's feet. She picks it up and sees that it's a wrapper for a PB&J Bar, Dad's favorite. She puts the wrapper to her nose, hoping to find some trace of him, but all she smells is plastic and absence. With a sigh, she tucks the wrapper in her pocket and gets on the lift.

The ship's cargo bay is dark when the lift doors open. She can tell that life support is operating because there's air and gravity, but the air is unbelievably cold and hurts to breathe. The only light comes from the lift, and she doesn't know where the control panel is. But finding it will have to wait because she's shivering so hard her teeth are chattering.

Using her handheld device as a flashlight, she finds lockers along the far side of the cargo bay. She hurries over and searches a few until she finds a cache of jumpers, grabs one that looks like it'll fit her, and pulls it on. She can tell it's one of the original ones by the logo of a puffy cloud blowing out a stream of air. Her dad had it designed based on a drawing Thea made in first grade. She zips it up to her neck, her hands shaking to the point that it's hard to hold on to her device, which chimes with an incoming message.

I'm here.

She sends the potential buyer the code for the lift, grabs him a jumper from the lockers, then goes in search of the control panel. She has *got* to get the lights and heat going or this is going to be the quickest blown sale in history.

"Holy Christ," the man says as he steps off the lift, silvery briefcase in hand.

"Sorry! Just now found the controls." Overhead floods pop on, blinding Thea as she makes her way back to the man and hands him the spare jumper.

"How long has she been sitting?" he says as he struggles to pull the legs on.

"A couple of years. I'm Thea, by the way."

He zips up the front of the jumper, picks up his briefcase, then offers his hand.

"Peter Mazur with Conglomerate Acquisitions. Why don't we head to the bridge. It will warm up a lot faster than back here."

"Sounds good," she says, rocking back and forth, hands deep in her jumper's pockets.

For a moment Mazur looks confused that they aren't hurrying out of the tundra that is the *Zephyr's* cargo bay, but then with a broad smile on his face reminiscent of a jackal, he realizes why and leads the way.

"This is a first-gen trawler, correct?"

"Yeah, but my dad made constant modifications, especially to the engines. You got the spec sheet from my lawyer, right?"

"I've got to be honest with you, Ms. Watts. Even with the upgrades, this ship is ancient by current standards." Mazur pauses to try and turn a valve, using the fact that he can't as a case in point. "Newer vessels are far more fuel-efficient, which gives them greater access to untapped parts of the asteroid grid. Holds are bigger, they've got better towing capacity, more accurate spectral sensor arrays, more powerful harpoon rigs. I mean, have you seen the Orion-class ships? They're a work of art."

"If that's the case, Mr. Mazur, why are you here?" Thea asks, following him up a steep set of stairs.

"The Conglomerate's operation has grown to the point that it needs a small fleet of tender ships. Mostly for refueling and shuttling cargo back and forth to Darkside Station." Mazur pushes open a door marked *Bridge*. "With a little work, we think this ship . . . what's it called again?"

Thea walks onto the bridge and into her father's heart. "She's called the *Zephyr*," she says, looking around in a daze.

"Yes, right. We think she'll make a fine tender."

Thea looks out the large front window at the tapestry of light and darkness spread out before her. The starfield is infinite, its immensity impossible to conceive. But it barely registers on her as she returns her gaze to the bridge itself.

Leather and steel and glass and determination knit together harmoniously to create a sense of order, a sense of confidence in the ship and in the people brave enough to command her. Comforting and trustworthy. Weathered but sturdy, like a baseball mitt. Like her dad.

The would-be buyer prattles on about navigation systems and signal degradation along the *Zephyr*'s spine. Flaws and *obvious* inadequacies, obvious to all but her. But none of it matters as she stands where he stood all those years and sees what he saw. And finally, she thinks, understands *everything*.

She bumps her thigh against the console, which causes her to look down.

At herself.

It's third grade and she's dressed as a turkey. Red, yellow, and orange paper feathers poke out the back of a construction-paper headband. Big round eyes and an orange beak are glued to the front of the large brown paper bag she's wearing, a hole cut in it big enough for her head. Her dad is kneeling next to her, holding up an oversized fork and wearing a black paper pilgrim's hat with a pasted-on yellow buckle.

She's overcome. Needs to sit down.

She swivels the captain's chair toward her and drops into it. Runs her hand over the armrest, feeling the cracks and lines etched into the padded leather, worn down by years of use.

By him.

She closes her eyes and fights back tears. Thinks of the letter he left for her.

I found myself up there. Maybe you will too.

She should have made time. Should have come up here with him while he was alive. But she always had an excuse, was always too busy to come home from school or give up a ski trip during spring break. And when she finally made time for him, she came home to a shadow. Too little of him and far too late.

"Ms. Watts, are you okay?"

Thea opens her eyes and finds Mazur with his briefcase open on the console next to her.

"Sorry, it's just a lot to process."

"I understand," he says, taking out a stack of papers and handing them to her. "This is our offer. We think these represent very fair terms, especially for a ship in this state."

Thea takes the papers but doesn't look at them.

"Our offer expires in three days. Please let me know if you have any questions." Mazur snaps his briefcase closed.

"The jumper," she says, suddenly unable to tolerate the sight of this stranger wearing the *Zephyr*'s gear.

"Excuse me?"

She points at the jumper.

"I'll leave it by the lift," he says.

"No. I'd like it now, please."

He looks at her with a quizzical, somewhat amused expression. But when it becomes clear she isn't joking, he takes off the jumper, hands it to her, and leaves with a huff.

———

THE REFINERY IS A MAZE.

Thea has no idea where she's going but decides to head in the direction of the most noise. She figures that's her best chance of finding the spot where raw materials from the fleet are sifted and sorted for the processors.

She walks along a perimeter catwalk that encircles an open floor plan below. The main floor looks like a cross between a nuclear power plant and an oil rig. Four- and five-story-tall ultrasound processing units are intermixed with open, swirling vats of solvent. Helium processors the size of corn silos line the exterior walls. Thick cables snake everywhere as attendants in white coats troll the space, tablets in hand.

She's about to ask someone for guidance when she sees signage for the *Payload* area.

She takes a set of switchback stairs down to ground level and finds herself in a huge room filled with massive piles of grayish-brown rock. A few loaders weave around the piles, adding to or taking from them. Thea stays to the perimeter and watches, looking for him. But he finds her instead.

"Oy, what are you doing here?"

She turns and sees Rory walking toward her, a toolbox tucked under one arm.

"I'm looking for you."

"What for?"

"Wondering if you want a job."

7

New Parts

RORY INSISTS on an exhaustive structural integrity scan. Afterwards, despite the all-clear from the shipwright drones, he conducts his own visual examination, meticulously working his way from bow to stern. He crawls over bulkheads, airlocks, and pylons, checks thruster ports, communication arrays, and canopies, tests portal seals, bay doors, and docking clamps. He's like a two-hundred-fifty-pound spider in a spacesuit, working his way around a web. Then he goes inside the ship and starts again, from tip to tail. Electrical systems, conduits, cooling vents, air scrubbers, hydrogen tanks, reactor coils, waste systems. Nothing escapes his scrutiny. Meanwhile, Thea's job is to listen, learn, and keep the list.

It takes a full six weeks before he declares his inspection complete, proclaiming the *Zephyr* to be *not too fucked*.

"Let's have it, then."

Thea hands him the tablet. He examines the list of supplies they'll need to get the *Zephyr* airborne.

"I've got a buddy at the shipyard who can get most of this for us. A couple of these things are in high demand, though, so it'll cost a premium."

"How much?"

"I covered a bunch of this guy's shifts when he was Earth-side last year on a heater in Vegas, so he owes me." Rory transfers the list to his handheld and hands the tablet back. "But he's still gonna need some cheddar to bump us to the front of the line."

When Thea decided to get the ship flying again, Billy transferred her dad's life insurance to a Darkside Station account. An outstanding balance on docking fees took a big bite out of it, but there's still enough money to get them going.

"Appreciate you calling in any favors," she says. "The more you save, the bigger our cushion."

"There's one problem."

Rory grabs a reddish sphere from a nearby workbench and gives it to Thea.

"There's no way in hell we're gonna find a replacement for this up here, and it'll take months to get one from back home. You're going to have to find someone who can repair it."

"What am I looking at?"

"It controls our main hydrogen electrolyzer. Without that, we won't be able to convert ice into fuel."

The device looks like a mechanical heart. It's made from some sort of translucent alloy and has several thick blue cables dangling from a central connection point.

Thea tosses it casually into the air and catches it in her other hand like a juggler's ball. "No fuel. That'd be a problem, right?"

"Bloody hell, woman!" Rory snaps, looking ready to throw himself on the ground to save the critical part from hitting the deck.

Thea laughs. "I'll head over to the ship builders' office this afternoon."

"No, they'll screw you over there. One look and they'll know you're fucked without it. I'd sniff around the Conglomerate docks. There's usually a bunch of engineers hanging around, hoping to get on their roster. You can probably strike a deal with one of them. Just make sure they're good."

"And how will I know that?"

"I don't know. Trust your gut."

"Last time I did that I ended up here. I think my gut's got shit for brains."

Rory lets out a deep bellow. "We'll talk about crew when I get back."

"Hey, Rory," she says, just as he's about to get on the lift. "Thanks. For everything."

"See you in a few days."

————

THE HUB IS PACKED with people, most of them staring up at the blank Leaderboard.

"What's going on?" Thea asks an anxious-looking man, sweat beading on his slick forehead, a finger poised above his tablet's screen.

"New tally's about to be posted," he says without peeling his eyes off the board.

"Ooh, do you think there's gonna be a new number one?"

That gets his attention.

"What? No." He looks at her like she's just farted. "But I've got a grand riding on Luxembourg falling to third. I'd love to explain it all to you, but—"

The board suddenly lights up, cutting off the sweaty man's sentence as effectively as a razor to the throat. Groans go up around the Hub. The man throws his tablet to the ground and stomps on the screen.

The Conglomerate's lead has widened. Their tally is now more than five times Luxembourg, who are still fixed in second place, much to her companion's chagrin.

"Is it ever close?" she asks the man, who's bending over to retrieve his ruined tablet.

"No," he says over his shoulder, then slams his device into a trash bin and storms away.

The crowd thins, and Thea sees her old pal Molly manning the information desk. She hasn't seen the teen since their run-in on her first day at Darkside. Thea gives her a sarcastically cheerful wave, which is met by a mighty eye roll and middle finger, then follows everyone to the main concourse.

There are a lot of crews in town, so the concourse is packed. Thea anxiously scans the crowd. Luckily, Darcey is nowhere in sight. Thea's managed to avoid her former classmate since deciding to reignite the family business; she's not interested in a repeat of their last awkward reunion. She adjusts her backpack so that the shoulder strap hides the *Zephyr* logo stitched on her jumper, then heads to the Conglomerate docks.

She passes a bunch of redshirted crew members high-fiving their latest tally. It stands to reason, with this being a space operation, that the Conglomerate would have chosen something other than red as their official color. But no one seems to mind the association with the ancient television show.

"Pitches this way!" someone yells, directing people toward a small crowd near Lift Three.

A line has formed across from a man and woman in matching red jumpers sitting on folding chairs behind a table. The man waves forward the first person in line.

"You have sixty seconds," he says.

The woman at the front of the queue steps forward and scrambles to unbox what looks like a shiny metal crab. She sets it on the table and quickly taps a command into a handheld device. The crab comes to life, its antennae waggling and pincer-like claws snapping.

"This looks like a standard Tesla miner," she says, "but I've improved its sensors and upgraded the AI so it can autonomously identify rare earths in any asteroid." She gives an awkward wave of her hands as she speaks, like a birthday party magician. "It can also withstand ten percent higher g-forces than the latest models, so you won't have to worry about it spinning off into space."

"We aren't interested in miner tech at this time," the man behind the table says, waving the crestfallen engineer away. "Next!"

The woman barely manages to tuck her invention under her arm before she's shouldered aside by a man with a Gandalf beard and wild puffs of gray at his temples.

"Hello, Dr. Klaus. What do you have for us today?" asks the woman behind the table.

With a flourish, the doctor pulls a marker out of his breast pocket. "I have devised a new approach to calculating the optimal laser boring rate," he says, then begins to scribble an elaborate equation on the tabletop in front of the two Conglomerate representatives.

They lean forward with smirks on their faces, clearly enjoying the show.

"You see, by solving for drilling overshear, we can accurately predict the resultant debris field and employ the appropriate orbital adjustments to minimize risk to craft and crew."

"Won't work," says a thin Asian woman looking over Klaus's shoulder.

Klaus looks back at her, incredulous. "This is of no concern to you, missy."

"You're right about that," she says, crossing her bare arms over her all-black jumper and looking directly at the two Conglomerate members. "But sure as shit, it'll be a concern to these two when they shatter their payload."

Klaus huffs dismissively and tries to get back to his performance, but the Conglomerate woman is curious.

"Explain," she says.

The Asian woman slides in front of Klaus, but not before snatching the marker from his hand. "You're assuming gravity is a constant, which it is not. Every cluster out there is unique, and gravity can be different even within the same rubble pile." She circles a portion of the equation and then hands the marker back to Klaus. "All you've created is the equivalent of holding up your thumb and squinting before smashing a wall with a hammer to find a stud."

Klaus goes a deep shade of red, clenching and unclenching his fists. "How dare you! Of *course* I have considered the impact of gravity, and I have determined it to be negligible within this predictive construct."

"Then instead of just being wrong, you're a moron," the woman says, running a hand through her dark mane, shot through with various shades of purple.

"Listen to *me*, little girl—"

"Go ahead. Call me *little girl* one more time, you old fuck, and see what happens."

The two Conglomerate representatives have had enough. They signal to one of their security goons.

"All right, both of you. Move along."

"That's not fair," says the Asian woman. "I didn't get to go."

"Doesn't matter." The Conglomerate woman eyes her up and down. "You might be good at math, honey, but you're not exactly Conglomerate material."

The woman storms away, leaving the security guard to deal with Dr. Klaus, who is furiously trying to defend his honor.

Thea follows the thin Asian woman and catches her just as she pushes her way through the crowd and onto the main concourse.

"Hey, hold up!"

The woman spins around. "What do *you* want?"

"I saw what happened back there."

"You're going to tell me I should respect my elders and all that shit? Forget it. That guy was dead wrong."

"Yeah, plus he was a dick," Thea says. "And you're right about the gravity."

The woman's attitude softens, and an unmistakable look of curiosity appears on her young face, highlighting the constellation of freckles scattered across the bridge of her nose.

"I study astrophysics," Thea explains. "Well, I used to." She holds out her hand. "I'm Thea."

"Lola." The woman gives Thea's hand a quick shake.

Thea slides her backpack off her shoulder and kneels next to it. She unzips the main compartment and takes out the *Zephyr*'s busted electrolyzer.

"I'm assuming you showed up for that demeaning bullshit back there because you're an engineer," she says, handing the device to Lola. "Ever seen one of these?"

Lola turns it over in her hands, examining the surface. She braces it against her thigh and uses a purple fingernail to slide open a thin slot that Thea hadn't noticed.

"Not since high school," she says, then blows into the open slot and peers inside. "Don't tell me you're still flying with this thing."

"I'm not flying *anywhere* right now. But I hope to be soon. Can you fix it?"

"Yeah, but I won't."

"Why not?"

"If I do, you'll just be back in a month or two complaining that I did a shitty job." Lola hands the device back. "These things suck. You need an upgrade."

"Yeah, and how much is that gonna cost me?"

Thea senses a shakedown. Heeding Rory's warning, she already checked on the price of having a replacement sent up from a factory in Florida, so she has some frame of reference.

"It'll probably take three days to design and fabricate. Let's say fifteen hundred."

Thea needs only a split second to decide. "Deal," she says, tucking the obsolete device back into her pack and then shaking on it with Lola.

"Half up front."

As they're transferring the money between devices, Thea catches Lola looking at the logo on her jumper.

"What's with the happy, puffy cloud there?" Lola asks, a smirk on her face.

"Bring the new electrolyzer by Dock D when you're done, and I'll show you."

8

Takeoffs and Landings

A YEAR into his Alzheimer's—when it was clear he'd never fly again—Thea arranged for her dad's stuff from the *Zephyr* to be shipped back to Texas. She never told him she'd done it, for fear that it would break the little spirit he had left. She just slowly integrated those clothes into his regular rotation and spread the pictures and knickknacks from the ship throughout the house, thinking he'd never notice. But occasionally she'd find him holding a sweatshirt or turning a trinket over in his hands, puzzling out something just beyond his reach.

Consequently, there's only the barest minimum left in his quarters—now *her* quarters. A couple shitty pillows, a prison-thin mattress, a threadbare blanket, and a single LED in the ceiling illuminating the gunmetal-gray everything. Thea's managed to tolerate the barrenness thus far, but with her goal of getting the *Zephyr* flying again now in sight, she decides it's time to do something about her new home away from home—and the excruciating kink in her neck.

The Hub is anchored by a massive general store where crews can obtain all sorts of home goods, clothes, international delicacies, liquor, books, magazines, and other recreational items. It does its best to provide all the comforts of a home hundreds of thousands of miles away, and in Thea's case, it succeeds. She's giddy as she roams the aisles, and she spends more than she probably should. But when she leaves the store, she knows that tonight she'll not only be sipping a nightcap, she'll hopefully be getting a good night's sleep for the first time in almost seven weeks.

The rest of the Hub is a bazaar of vendor tables and tents where machinists, engineers, and systems technicians offer services to the fleet. The refinery ship builders handle most flight support and large-scale fabrication. For everything else, you come here. Custom EVA suits, specialty miners, ion coils, power cells, propulsion tubes, sonic ordnance, and plasma welders are just a few of the items for sale. Thea shows the *Zephyr*'s electrolyzer around and is pleased when all the engineers she talks to echo Lola's assessment. She ends up selling the busted device for a few hundred credits, which makes her feel better about her earlier extravagances.

Grabbing a hot tin of some sort of saucy noodle dish from one of the vendors, she takes a seat directly beside the massive, curved window overlooking the docks. As she delights in the tingly chili aroma, a Conglomerate scout untethers and slowly maneuvers away from the station. From here, right at the very edge of the Hub, she has a perfect view. She wonders if it's Darcey's ship. Imagines her on the bridge, elegant and thin and brilliant, her crewmates hanging on her every word of scientific magnificence. As the sleek ship's engines engage and it jets away in a burst of blue flame, she sucks in a noodle so hard that it whips against her cheek, leaving a red-orange streak in its wake.

The napkin holder on the table is overstuffed. She tugs and tears at them, and when she finally wiggles a few napkins out, they fly from her grip and flutter to the ground. She bends down, collects the napkins, and wipes the sauce from her cheek.

When she sits back up, she finds herself staring at the nose of a huge trawler, impossibly close and heading straight at her.

Thea falls backward in her chair as she tries to get away. Her head smacks on the metal grated floor. She bites her lip. Tastes blood. Stars swim in her vision as she scrambles backward across the floor, trying hopelessly to get away from the hulk that's about to smash right into the Hub.

Someone grabs her under her arms and hauls her to her feet. She joins a crowd of panicked people fighting, like her, to get away from the inevitable impact.

But the bow of the trawler suddenly, miraculously, pulls up, mere meters from the station window.

The ship bucks backward and continues its slow skyward arch, giving everyone in the Hub a view of its underside and the damage around its open cargo bay.

"It's the *Victor Hugo!*" someone screams.

Parts of a launch pad tethering mechanism hang from the torn hull of Luxembourg's ship like seaweed. Cargo streams from the ship's opening, striking the Hub window, walls, roof. The station shudders under the concussive blows.

When the stern rises past the window, everyone finally sees what saved them. A harpoon line extends from the ship's rear. Its far end is attached to a bolt stuck in the lunar surface.

With the collision averted, everyone reverses course and rushes back to the window to get a better view of the calamity continuing to unfold outside. The ship's momentum makes it swing like a bob on the end of a pendulum, its path taking it back toward the docks. A blast of blue fire from a starboard side stabilizer slows the ship's progress but doesn't stop it entirely.

"Why the hell aren't they releasing the harpoon line?" someone yells.

"They're gonna take out the docks!"

"Wait! Look!"

A figure comes gliding down the harpoon line using a carabiner connected to an EVA suit. They have what looks like a bright yellow jackhammer or some other type of heavy tool strapped across their back. A second figure follows a few meters behind, holding an oval-shaped tank with a blue hose extending from the top.

They unlatch themselves before reaching the surface, letting the moon's gravity carry them down next to the harpoon bolt. They quickly connect the tank to the yellow tool.

A bright arc of energy rips from the tip of the device.

"What are they doing?"

"Cutting the line," Thea says.

A few seconds later, the harpoon line snaps.

The trawler's engines fire. The blast sends the two crewmen tumbling backward amid a cloud of regolith. The ship climbs high enough to clear the dock.

A cheer ripples through the crowd gathered at the window. But their delight quickly turns to gasps of horror as the ship's engines sputter and then cut out. The show isn't quite over.

The ship starts to list. It turns over.

Tumbles toward the surface.

Its stabilizers fire again just before Thea and the rest of the people gathered by the window lose sight of it. But they all know it crashed when a cloud of lunar dust rises up from behind the docks and envelops everything.

———

THREE HOURS LATER, the all-clear comes.

Security doors had sealed off Dock B from the main concourse. Luckily the dock never completely depressurized, and a Japanese crew was able to get to one of the dock's decompression closets, don the emergency EVA suits inside, and quickly contain the breach caused when part of Luxembourg's damaged lift punctured the south wall.

The *Victor Hugo* wasn't so lucky.

Information is scant, but it appears the ship failed to completely detach from its launch pad during takeoff, which resulted in a blowout in their cargo bay. No one can understand why the pilot proceeded with takeoff while still partially tethered, or how the launch mechanism malfunctioned in the first place, or why the ship's environmental fail-safes didn't adapt to the blowout, or why they couldn't release the harpoon bolt from the line. And unfortunately, no one can ask the pilot or captain, the two people who might be able to provide some clarity, because their frozen corpses were found near the impact zone.

Asteroid mining is a dangerous profession. Everyone expects things to go wrong from time to time. But an accident this bad hasn't happened in more than a decade. Everyone hopes the ship's logs will clear up the mystery. But only time will tell.

Thea looks down from the bridge of the *Zephyr* at the crash site, which is only a few football fields away. A station security detail is combing through the wreckage. Lights from their helmets dart and dance across the crumpled hull as they canvass the scene. Most of the investigation seems concentrated near the cargo bay.

A vehicle with a high cab sitting above a solid, rectangular bed and heavily treaded tires stops near the starboard side of the crashed ship. Three people get out of the cab and climb down to the surface. The driver is dressed like the investigators already on-site, but the two passengers are wearing Luxembourg colors. They unspool a thick cable from the back of the vehicle and plug it into a port in the ship's midsection. Red and white navigation lights illuminate along the starboard side, and a faint glow leaks out through one of the ship's crumpled airlocks, indicating power is at least partially restored. They're joined by a few of the investigators, and they all enter the ship through the airlock.

A chime from the comms system startles Thea. A call from the shipyard.

"What in bloody hell happened?" Rory says before Thea can even say hello.

"The *Victor Hugo* went down, and her pilot and captain died."

Rory is gobsmacked, and Thea has to repeat parts of the story several times. He's clearly trying to puzzle out what could have led to this disaster. But the one thing he's sure of, he says, is that this couldn't have been human error.

"This had to have been a *major* malfunction."

"Why do you say that? Couldn't it have just been pilot error?"

"No. I know Roxy, she wouldn't do that. Besides, even if she did, safety systems would have prevented this. No, whatever went wrong here, it had to have affected multiple systems in ways that... well, really shouldn't be possible."

"What does that mean?"

"I don't know," he says. "But we're gonna run a system-wide diagnostic as soon as I get back."

Down below, the two Luxembourg crewmen leave the *Victor Hugo*, each carrying a duffel bag. But instead of getting back in the vehicle, they start walking toward the external airlock adjacent to the *Zephyr*'s dock.

"Listen, I gotta go," Thea says. "I'll see you tomorrow."

She ends the transmission and darts off the bridge. She can't help but feel weirded out by her conversation with Rory. What could have brought down that ship?

When the lift reaches the bottom, she hurries to the external airlock. Gets there just as the two men enter the dock, helmets and duffel bags in hand. The taller of the two is maybe the handsomest man Thea's ever seen. His woolly blond hair and matching blond goatee perfectly accent his toffee-colored skin and deep brown eyes. He looks like a steamy caramel macchiato. Next to him, at least eighteen inches closer to the ground, is a young man with a dark, swept-back mane and handlebar mustache.

Thea steps in front of them. "Hi, sorry. I don't mean to bother you."

"Can I help you?" the tall man asks.

"Was that you guys?" she says. "The ones who cut the harpoon line."

A reluctant nod. "We really don't want to talk about it. Sorry." He turns to go.

The shorter man smiles apologetically. "It's been a long day, *ma chère*." He speaks with a thick French accent. "Please excuse us."

They start to walk away.

"I just wanted to say thank you," she says, feeling compelled to call after them. "What you did was awesome."

The tall man stops in his tracks and turns, a weary look on his face. He rubs his chin as if considering something, then takes a step back toward her.

"If it was so *awesome*, then why is my ship lying in a crater out there? Why are my pilot and captain dead?"

Thea swallows hard, immediately realizing her mistake.

"We didn't do anything special. We did what we were supposed to do. We tried to save our ship. It was our job, and we failed." He takes a deep breath, stepping back again. Seemingly drained. "Trust me, there's nothing awesome about any of this."

Thea's cheeks burn with embarrassment. "I didn't mean," she starts, but then stops trying to find a defense of her words, realizing there isn't one. "This whole thing is a terrible, terrible tragedy. I can't imagine . . ."

Then words abandon her, and she just stands there.

"Forget it," the man says in a way that she's sure is meant to let her off the hook.

"No, I'm an asshole," she says. "I was in the Hub when your ship . . . when everything happened. What I meant to say, what I should have said, is that we all owe you a debt of gratitude. The whole station. Your actions saved a lot of people today. And I'm really sorry for your loss."

The tall man softens. He pulls off his right glove and offers his hand. "I'm Elliott. This is Bastien."

"Everyone calls me Beetle," the Frenchman says with a quick wave.

Thea introduces herself, but then pauses, wanting to ask but afraid to upset them again. But Elliott spares her by preempting her question—everyone's question.

"We don't know what happened," he says. "It's inexplicable. None of it makes any sense."

"Give it some time," she says. "They'll figure it out."

"Maybe," Elliott says. "I hope so."

"What will you do now?"

"Try to get work with another crew, I guess."

"There *is* no work," Beetle interjects. "And I won't go work for those bastards. I'd rather break my back at the shipyard or go back to France than put in with the fucking Conglomerate."

Sounds like someone else I know, Thea thinks.

Instantly the notion in her head grows from seed to bud to sapling to oak.

"I have an idea," she says, a broad smile breaking out across her face. "Can I buy you guys a drink?"

9

Checks and Balances

"How CAN you stand there and tell us that your agent's first assignment was a success? People died!"

The man being interrogated swipes across his tablet, changing the image on the conference room screen from the wreckage of the *Victor Hugo* to a shipping manifest. "Yes, that was unfortunate. But it's being handled," he says. "We've created a false paper trail that will reveal the pilot was smuggling in large quantities of MDMA and psilocybin. Combined with a fake disorderly conduct arrest during her last shore leave, we'll be able to paint the portrait of yet another drug-abusing operator struggling to cope with the stresses of space. The Luxembourg government and its space agency will have to defend their astromining program, which is already under tremendous scrutiny because of the state of their national economy. In fact, I think this might take them off the board entirely."

"That still doesn't explain the launch malfunction," says one of the man's bosses.

"It won't need to be explained. In response to the accident, a station-wide systems update will be pushed out in the next few days. This new 'fix,' along with the emerging story about the pilot, should be enough to keep Municipal from digging deeper."

The people in the room don't seem satisfied.

"I still think we should replace her," one of them says. "Put someone more prudent in place. Someone less aggressive, less reckless."

The man waves off the notion before it can take root. He sent his person up to the moon, and he's going to make sure she stays there.

"I've been handling agents since this organization was founded, and I promise you, pulling her now would be a mistake. She is too well placed. We'd never get another agent in as deep."

"I disagree," says another of the leadership, eliciting a few nods from his counterparts. "It'll just take time."

He knows he has to end this now, so he changes tack. He slaps the table.

"We're out of time!" he snaps.

Shock ripples around the room, the leadership clearly unaccustomed to this tone from a subordinate.

"The days of international rationing are over. Astromining has flooded the system with rare earth elements. If we don't curtail it soon, decades of work will be wasted."

A woman at the head of the table speaks up, unfazed. "We've had this debate *numerous* times. Most of the inbound elements are still going to renewable energy efforts, carbon capture, and the medical industry. Our window is still open."

"Maybe. But for how much longer? A year? Two at most?"

He pushes back from the table and makes his way to the front of the room. Rubs a palm back and forth over his bald dome, collecting himself.

"I still believe in our cause. But I think we are at a tipping point. If we allow rare earths to become ubiquitous, society is doomed. The creative spark that drove humanity for thousands of years will die, and we'll become slaves to artificial intelligence, social media, augmented reality, pharmaceutical exploitation, all of it. And when the singularity comes . . . that's the ball game.

"*But* . . . we can stop it. It's up to us to end humanity's technological march to our own doom. We need to return to the *human* condition. Remind ourselves who we are. Reset the world."

He makes sure to make eye contact with each person in the room before continuing.

"It's up to us and us alone. That's why we have to keep going," he says, palms facing heavenward as if in prayer. "This is our best chance. I beg you. Please don't let it slip away."

The men and women in the room exchange glances.

Some silent agreement is reached.

"Okay. We'll let you proceed. But you need to let things cool off for a little while."

"Understood," the man says, relief flooding through him.

His bosses get up from the table to leave, but not before giving him a parting directive.

"Get her in check. Or we will."

Warm Welcomes

"Oy! Who are you?"

Elliott hands Beetle his spanner and stands up.

"I'm Elliott. This here's Beetle. And you?"

"I'm the one asking the questions. What do you think you're doing?"

"The drive nut is misaligned," Beetle says, shining his flashlight into the open gearbox. "We need to recalibrate it, or the actuator will eventually seize."

"What do you care?"

"We can't do our jobs without the crane, man."

"Your jobs, eh?" Rory says, dropping the two large duffels he's carrying onto the cargo bay deck. "Where is she?"

"The captain?"

"Yeah, the *captain*."

"She's on the bridge."

"Don't touch anything," Rory says, waggling his finger at the two of them before storming off.

———

A RIBBON of digital asteroids is displayed on the opaque glass of the bridge's forward viewscreen. Thea is standing on the console in front of the screen, circling a tight cluster of objects with a grease pen, when Rory stomps up behind her.

"You're back!" she says. "Take a look at this."

"What are you doing?"

"I was digging around in my dad's old files and came across this beauty. Assuming some elliptical decay, which of course there will be, this bad boy should be in range in the next month or so. Pop had it tagged as a high-yield cluster, so I think we should go after it."

"I'm not talking about the fucking rocks. I mean what are you doing with those two blokes messing with the crane?"

"Oh good, you met Ell and Beetle. I hired them."

"You hired them?"

"Yeah."

"You?"

"Yeah, why?"

"All by yourself?"

"Now hold on a second," Thea says, hopping down from the console. "What's the problem?"

Rory goes red and tugs at his beard. He looks like he's about to say something, then just puffs out his cheeks and grunts.

This puffing and grunting happens a few more times.

"You having a seizure, buddy?"

"What in the hell do *you* know about this job?" he spits.

"Really?"

"Yeah, really!"

"My dad helped start this whole thing!"

"Yeah, *he* did. This is *your* first time up here. And you've never been out *there*!" he practically shouts, pointing at the projection of the asteroid band. "How in Holy God's name do you think *you* know who to hire?"

It's her turn to puff and grunt.

She takes a step back to collect her thoughts. Rory does the same.

She wants to scream about being the boss. Her ship, her rules, and all that. But she knows she could never get Rory to buy it, because she doesn't buy it herself. And she needs Rory. Without him, she might as well pack up and go home.

After a beat, she decides on a different approach. The honest one.

"When my dad got sick, everything fell to me. No one told me how I should take care of him. No one could. My mom was gone, and no one else was there to help. I was completely on my own. It was overwhelming. I had *no idea* what the fuck I was doing. Considered giving up at least once a day. It would have been so easy to just stick him in a home and be done with it. But over time, it got easier. I figured things out day by day, little by little, and it slowly got better. And in the course of doing it, *having* to do it, being self-reliant became a weird source of pride for me. I'm good at it.

"But then my dad died, and I came up here. To this place. This ship. With no idea what to do all over again. So I got back to work the only way I know how."

Rory strokes his beard, going red again, but Thea assumes —hopes—that this time it's for a different reason.

"I should have talked to you about Elliott and Beetle before bringing them on board," she says. "I'm out of practice. And for this to work, I know I'm gonna need to get better. I will. I promise."

He gives a grunt. "Sorry I flew off the handle," he says. "I'm just really picky about my team. *Our* team, I mean."

He fishes a handkerchief out of his pocket.

"We good?" she asks, unsure why he's handing it to her, pretty sure she let no tears fall during her diatribe.

"Aye, we're good. Now wipe that shit off the screen."

75

She turns back to the viewscreen with a smile.

"So tell me about these two characters," he says as she begins wiping her circles and arrows off the glass.

"I already did. Those are the two guys that stopped the *Victor Hugo* from crashing into the station."

"Why didn't you start with that?" He helps her down after pointing out a spot that she missed, then shakes his head. "The tall one looks far too *pretty* to have done anything that daring."

She makes a point of tucking his handkerchief into her back pocket. "You should go talk to them. They're quite a pair."

"Count on it. But we do the next one together, agreed?"

A chime comes over the comms system.

Thea steps back to the console and hits a button. The image of her dad's old chart is replaced by a video of Lola at the base of their lift, waiting to be buzzed up. She has a brown box under one arm and a green drink in her other hand.

"Agreed," she says with a mischievous smile. "In fact, let's start right now."

She hits the mic. "Come on up, Lola."

Rory goes red again.

———

Rory, Elliott, and Beetle shoulder in to get a look as soon as Lola steps back from the panel where she's installed the *Zephyr*'s new electrolyzer. It's glowing a soft purple, matching the accents in the woman's wild mane.

"That can't be right," Beetle says. "I don't see any bubbles."

Rory nods. "He's right. Where are the bubbles?"

"Sorry, no bubbles, boys," Lola says, pecking away at her handheld device.

Elliott looks over her shoulder. "But I *like* the bubbles.

They're reassuring. When you see bubbles, you know the reactor is doing what it's supposed to do. We feed it ice, it breaks down the H2O, makes us the power we need to fly. And we know we're good because . . ."

"Because you don't drift powerless into the void of space and die?" Lola says, turning to face him.

"No. Because we *see the bubbles*."

"Look, man, I already told you. My system uses a capillary design, so the hydrogen and oxygen gases don't have to travel through the electrolyte fluid. Near perfect efficiency and no gas crossover. You know what that means? It means your ship is less likely to blow the fuck up."

She makes the exploding brain motion.

"You want bubbles, drink a soda," she adds as she brushes past Elliott on her way out of engineering.

"I like that one," Rory says to Thea, who's doing a bad job of hiding her smirk.

"Me too," Beetle says.

"I still don't like it," Elliott says, rubbing his chin as he stares at Lola's fancy new electrolyzer.

Thea looks up at Rory. "So, what do you think? We got ourselves an engineer?"

"Oy, that we do." He calls after Lola. "Girlie, wait up!"

Her voice comes back down the corridor. "Call me girlie again, old man, and you'll be doing it a few octaves higher."

11

Make Believe

THEA'S ARMS ARE RUBBER. Her thighs spasm and her feet ache. She rotates her shoulder, cringing at the pops and crackles coming from her rotator cuff. Winces at the kink in her neck.

Thankfully, load-in day is almost over.

She's surrounded by crates, boxes, and barrels filled with a vast assortment of food, clothes, dry goods, paper products, toiletries, medical supplies, raw material for the 3D printers, brackets and fittings, hoses, clamps, screws, bolts, torches and welders, and a hardware store's worth of other stuff. If something breaks, she's confident they'll have whatever is needed to fix it.

Then there's the special things the crew can't live without.

Beetle nearly got arrested when he was caught breaking into the wreckage of his old ship to retrieve his high-end bread machine from Paris. Luckily, Municipal let it slide with a warning. Beetle had helped save the station from disaster, after all.

Rory and Elliott bonded while cleaning out the general store's supply of whiskey and rye. The carton of spirits is nearly as heavy as the one with Lola's collection of hot sauces, which she claims not only enhance shitty space food but can also double as handy solvents in a pinch. Thea believes it, too, after a nose-hair-curling sniff of a deep red tincture in a bottle with a flaming skull on the label.

This is really happening, she thinks to herself in wonder as she admires the stores filling the cargo bay.

The console chimes and the lift starts to rise. The crew is back.

Thea tweaked her lower back pretty badly early in the day, and it's only been getting worse since then, so she takes this brief respite as an opportunity to lie down. The metal floor grating isn't comfortable in the least, but it's cool on her sweaty back. She closes her eyes against the bright lights shining down from above and brings one knee up to her chest, trying to stretch whatever needs stretching.

The lift clangs to a stop and the doors hiss open.

"This better be the last load," Thea says. "I'm not cut out for this shit."

"Wait until you get out there."

That voice is unexpected. Pain knifes through Thea's back as she twists to see the person getting off the lift.

Darcey.

"What are you doing here?" she says as she struggles to her feet.

"Didn't mean to startle you. The lift was unlocked," Darcey says. "So it's true. You're actually doing this."

Thea simply nods as Darcey strolls around the cargo bay, admiring the stacks of provisions. She stops next to Rory and Ell's crate and lifts out a bottle of amber liquor.

"I was stunned when I heard you turned down our offer on the *Zephyr*," Darcey says. "What changed?"

"I don't know, exactly. Just . . . once I got up here and saw the ship, I decided to give it a go. Figured, why the hell not?"

Darcey slaps the bottle back into its cardboard slot and turns to face her.

"This isn't a game, Thea. You don't do this job because you've got nothing better to do."

"I know that. Better than you, in fact," Thea snaps back. "I've been around it my whole life. Remind me, how long's it been for you? Seven, eight weeks?"

"What about your crew?" Darcey says, ignoring the jab.

"They're solid. Got a few fleet vets on board and a rockstar engineer."

"You mean the kid with the purple hair that's been sniffing around our dock. Lola, right?"

Thea feels her anger rising. "That *kid*'s smarter than either of us. She's gonna be great."

"Being smart down here isn't the same thing. You'll see after you've been out there a while."

"Darcey . . ." Thea pauses. "What are you doing here?"

"Looking out for you. That's what friends do."

"I'm fine."

"Are you sure about that?"

"Yes."

"Your pilot bounced around from crew to crew—"

"Wait—you're looking into my crew?"

"Your pilot moved from crew to crew for years until he ended up doing grunt work at the shipyard. And some people are whispering that your other two guys might have contributed to the *Victor Hugo* crash."

"That's bullshit Neighborhood gossip."

"Maybe. Who knows?"

"We'll be fine," Thea says dismissively.

Darcey's tone changes. "Look, Thea . . . I know we lost touch, and I'm sorry about that. I still care about you, though. And I think you're making a mistake. You shouldn't be up here."

"*You're* here. How's that any different?"

"The difference is, I'm on the best team with the best

people. Not a ship that's been sitting at dock for years. And I'm not entrusting my life to some cobbled-together crew of misfits."

Thea clenches her fists, but a chime from the console stops her from saying something she might regret—or might not. The lift starts to rise, and Darcey glances over at it with annoyance. It appears that she's about to launch a final salvo, but Thea cuts her off.

"You should go."

Darcey shakes her head in surrender.

The lift arrives and the doors open. "You won't believe what we found, *ma chère*," Beetle says, setting a steel-gray steamer trunk at his feet.

"It's a second-gen pick-harpoon," Elliott says. "It cost a pretty penny, but it's worth it."

Then he notices Darcey. His eyes linger on the Conglomerate logo on her jacket. "Sorry, didn't know you had company."

Rory's less subtle. "Who the fuck are you?"

"Old friend of Thea's. But don't worry, Mr. Abernathy, I was just leaving," Darcey says.

She and Rory stare each other down for a beat, then she turns back to Thea.

Leans in so only she can hear.

"It's dangerous up here," she says. "Trust me on this. You should be careful."

Quick hug. Pure make-believe.

Then Darcey gets on the lift and is gone.

After an awkward silence, Lola asks the question that's on all their minds. "What was *that* all about?"

"Old rivalries," Thea says. "Nothing more."

Shrugs all around. No further explanation needed. Not among this group of people, who've all been there.

Thea opens the trunk and takes a look at the pick.

"Looks pretty banged up," she says to Elliott. "You sure it's worth it?"

"No doubt. Trust me."

"I do."

And with that, the crew gets back to the business of getting flight-ready.

Thea watches them with a broadening smile.

Two months ago, she was burying her father. Now she's on the dark side of the moon, captaining a mining vessel manned by a crew of wild cards she just met.

Her life savings are on the line—not to mention her actual life.

And yet she's never felt more alive. More free.

After years in dry dock, she's ready to spread her wings.

And fly.

PART II

Prospects

12

Firsts

EVERY BIG LEAGUE rookie wants to hit a home run their first at-bat. Anglers everywhere dream of that majestic first cast of the day and the mantle-worthy monster they'll haul in. And every novelist of every sort, everywhere, has fantasized about their best-selling, prize-winning debut novel.

Holes in one, love at first sight, one-try perfect SAT scores. None of us really expect these things, but we all secretly hope for them, whether we want to admit it or not.

Thea and her crew were no exception.

They had high hopes for a magical maiden voyage. A big score that would put the big boys at the top of the Leader-board on notice that there was a new contender for the crown.

That's not what happened.

On only their third day out from Darkside Station, their gravitomagnetic field collapsed. They spent the next thirty-six hours working in zero-g to repair one of their rotating super-conductors. Beetle kept them all entertained as they worked, spinning and flipping and twirling around the ship, showing off his own brand of wild acrobatics. He explained to the others that his skills were forged during his teenage years as a performer with Cirque du Soleil, but only now did he feel those skills had been perfected. Space was the ultimate acrobatic big tent.

Two days after the repair was completed, their sipper crapped out. They'd captured a berg and drilled to its icy core without a hitch, but the sipper's heating element never reached peak temperature, so instead of super-heated water, the system sucked slush up the straw, which naturally turned back into ice in the deep freeze of space before it could reach the *Zephyr*'s reactor. The whole line had to be abandoned, and they spent another several days floating amid the ice patch, fabricating a new sipper and running diagnostics.

A fried circuit here, a navigation system glitch there. Nothing they couldn't fix, but all adding more repairs, more headache, more delay.

Eventually, however, they made it out to the grounds, many days late but only a little worse for the wear. And the upshot, Thea thought, was that the crew forged faster bonds than they might have otherwise.

Which would prove to be a good thing. For she had no doubt those bonds would be put to the test in the days, weeks, and months ahead.

———

A FOAMY WAVE gently kisses the shore. Carnival clatter and kids' happy shrieks drift toward her from the pier glowing in the distance, mixing with the caws of gulls floating on the ocean breeze. Light glints off the Ferris wheel as it spins in the setting sun.

"Thea, we're almost in position."

She slows the treadmill to walking speed and wipes a sheen of sweat off her face.

"Roger. Be right there."

When her heart rate normalizes—or as close to normal as it's going to get given her current fitness level—she ends the program, notes her distance and time, and steps off with a final glance at the California coastline on the display.

Maybe I'll do it for real one day, she thinks, then makes her way to the bridge.

When she arrives, she finds Rory and Beetle huddled around Lola's terminal. Elliott is standing off to the side, staring out into space.

"We ready?"

No one speaks or looks at her.

"Guys? What's going on?"

After a big sigh, Rory waves dismissively at the forward display. "Go ahead. Show her."

Lola pulls up a visual of their first-ever target—the cluster Thea identified in her father's old charts. Ahead of the cluster, a series of red dots appears.

"I know I promised around an eighty-percent capture rate with this probe pattern," Lola says, still not meeting Thea's gaze.

She reaches out and strikes a key. Fireworks bloom on the display—along with a cat waggling its hips and shaking maracas.

Beetle and Rory burst out laughing and start to mimic the cat's dance.

"Girlie got us near ninety-two percent!" Rory says before kissing the top of Lola's head.

"Holy shit!" Thea says, pulling Lola out of her chair and swallowing her in a hug. Lola beams, then takes up the cat dance. Thea's about to do the same until she notices Elliott still off to the side, pensively staring at the display.

"You okay?" she asks, bumping up against him to break him out of his reverie.

He gives her a weak smile. "Yeah, I'm good." But Thea can tell he's not. He has a terrible poker face.

"No, something's wrong. Talk to me," she presses.

He hesitates. "It's just . . . after everything that's happened, I really want this to work. I *need* all of this to work. That's all."

"I do too," she says, squeezing his hand and pulling him toward the rest of the group. "We all do. And that's why it's gonna."

After receiving a genuine smile and nod from Elliott, Thea faces the others.

"One more time. We ready?"

"Roger!" they all shout in response.

Lola leans over her console, and her fingers fly over the keyboard. The computer-generated image of the approaching asteroid cluster disappears, and they are once again able to see the bow of the ship and the stars beyond.

Lola looks to Thea, awaiting her orders. They all do. They're ready to start this adventure.

And after a beat to savor the moment, Thea issues her first real command as their captain.

"Do it."

Lola punches a key.

Dozens of small projectiles stream away from the *Zephyr* in rapid succession. The probes start off on the same trajectory, then break off on individual flight patterns, disappearing into the darkness.

"They should be in position in a few hours," Lola says.

Rory and Beetle high-five. Elliott squeezes Lola's shoulders.

"Let's celebrate," Thea says. "Who's with me?"

To her surprise, her crew look at her uncertainly, then exchange glances. It's then that Thea sees Lola discreetly sending her a signal by pinching her nose between two fingers.

Ah.

Thea makes a show of sniffing her armpits, then amends her earlier offer.

"Who's with me in twenty minutes, after I've showered?"

It's cheers all around.

13

Away Game

"Damn it, you gotta goosestep! Goosestep!"

"How?"

"Like this!" Rory says, demonstrating on his own controller.

Thea rapidly triggers the button combination. Leans to the side so hard she nearly rolls off the couch.

"Fuh, I bit my tongue."

"To hell with your bloody tongue! Pass the ball!"

"I'm trying," she says, tasting copper as she lurches the opposite way, nearly landing in Elliott's lap.

Pushing Thea back into her spot, Elliott asks, "How long did you play rugby for Leicester?"

"Six seasons," Rory says, still smashing the buttons on his controller. "Blew my knee out in Year Seven training camp and that was that."

"You miss it?"

"Nah. By that point I'd been under the knife so many times I was contemplating hanging my boots up anyway. Shoulder, both ankles, left wrist. It was time."

"*Fils de pute!*" Beetle yells, then pumps his fists in triumph as the game whistle blows.

"Fucking hell!" Rory says, jumping up from his seat and pointing at the screen. "That's not a foul."

"Into the sin-bin with ya, mate," Beetle says, then high-fives Elliott. But his celebration is cut short when Rory drops on top of him instead of next to him, crushing Beetle deep into the couch cushions.

"Aren't you going to help him?" Thea asks Elliott.

"Little man can hold his own." He grabs a napkin off the table in front of them and hands it to Thea, who dabs some blood off her lower lip and tongue. "Trust me. He's picked fights with bigger men than Rory and lived to tell the tale."

Lola bursts into the room. The sight of Rory smushing Beetle into the couch gives her pause, but then she walks over to the game console and shuts it off.

"Oy, girlie. What gives?"

"Data's in from the probes. We got a hit."

"Too bad, boys," Thea says. She pops off the couch, pulling Elliott after her. "Guess we'll have to call it a draw."

Rory uses Beetle as leverage to get up, leaving him crumpled between two cushions. "Let's go, *mate*," he says, tromping after the others.

"Draw, my ass!" Beetle yells after them as he extricates himself. "Hey, wait for me!"

———

THE ASTEROIDS PASS through the *Zephyr*'s string of probes like small fish through a net. As they drift by, the probes' onboard spectrograms scan each object for telltale signs of rare earth elements. This is critical, because while the cluster can be thought of as a singular unit given its orbital dynamics, the composition of every cluster is unique. Spin rates, mass, shape, density, and gravitational fields differ for each asteroid in the cluster. A probe string's layout needs to be designed to capture the largest breadth of objects in its scan field to ensure it achieves the greatest analytical depth.

Lola's design pays dividends in this regard. Yet despite her eighty-nine percent capture rate, she's disappointed in the results. She expected ninety-two percent, and she keeps replaying the simulation of the scan field, pointing out idiosyncrasies in the cluster's behavioral pattern that contributed to her miscalculation.

"We could recall the probes and reset them before scanning the cluster again," she says to the rest of the crew, all of whom have gathered around her screen. "Gimme a week, tops. With some modifications, I can get the next scan well into the nineties."

"It wouldn't matter," Elliott says, nodding at the visualization. "The dead zones in the scan field are way inside the cluster. Even if we found something good in there, we wouldn't risk taking the ship in that deep."

"But I can do *better*."

"You did great," Thea says, squeezing her shoulder. "Where's the signal?"

Lola lets out a long sigh, then punches a few keys. The visualization zooms in on an asteroid near the outer edge of the cluster, a blue glow near its center indicating the location of the target elements.

"She's a big one," Beetle says. "And not much debris around her, either. Good catch."

Rory points at a spot on the screen. "We can slide in through this point," he says, "and match her spin rate with no problem."

"Yeah, but look at the density," says Elliott. "Crust is thick and mostly iron. Our harpoon won't be able to get through that."

Rory strokes his goatee. "Can you render it in 3D?"

Lola starts typing. "I'll put it up on the plotter."

Seconds later, an image of the asteroid appears above the holographic projection table in the middle of the bridge. Beetle immediately begins circling the table, examining the glowing, three-dimensional visual.

"I know what you're thinking," Elliott says, matching his steps.

"No, no, look. We can anchor here," Beetle says, tapping a spot on the image. The area turns bright orange where his fingertip contacts the projection.

"Yeah, I see what you're getting after, mate," Rory says with a nod. "Lola, increase the magnification and highlight areas where the iron is thinnest."

The image grows in size above the table, and reddish-orange blotches appear dotted throughout. Rory and Beetle identify a few spots around Beetle's potential anchor point where the iron density is less than a few feet, or where no iron is present at all.

"We're not ready for this yet," Elliott says.

"Come on, Ell. We've done this many times before," Beetle says. "And on harder and faster rocks than this."

Thea, confused, looks over at Lola, who looks equally bewildered. "Done what?" Thea asks Elliott. "Can someone please tell me what's going on?"

"I'll show you," says Beetle. He takes Thea by the arm and centers her near the image. "If we set low-yield explosives at these points where there are breaks in the iron, or where it's very thin, we can rip off a section of the crust big enough so we can get inside."

"Then it's business as usual," Rory adds. "We deploy the miners, get to the juicy parts, and start extraction."

"So what's the trouble, then?" Thea looks to Elliott, who's standing with his arms crossed.

"You have to set the explosives by hand," he says.

Now Thea gets it. Elliott's concern is well-founded. This is *not* how she envisioned their first trip. But with a payday, and possibly a substantial one, within arm's reach, she's not willing to give up.

"Walk me through it," she says.

Rory begins. "I match the asteroid's spin. It's nominal, so it'll be a snap. Then we use the harpoon to anchor to the asteroid at the thin spot Beetle found."

Beetle, apparently unwilling to cede the floor, given that this idea started as his brainchild, quickly jumps in. "Once the *Zephyr* is orbiting in sync with the asteroid, we trolley down the harpoon line to the surface and set the charges."

"Like you did at Darkside."

"Precisely."

Thea's following. She does her own circuit around the image of the asteroid, calculating in her head. "The problem with the low spin rate is there won't be a lot of gravity on the surface. Guessing maybe a quarter g at most."

"Point one five, give or take," Rory says.

Lola chimes in. "The crust is metal though, which is optimal for our EVA suits' magnetic boots, so that shouldn't be too big a deal. I mean, *I* ain't gonna do it. No friggin' way. But still."

"That's the spirit," Rory says, motioning for Lola to zoom out on the image. "Once the crew is back on board, I'll release the harpoon, move us to a safe distance, and trigger the explosives. If we've done our job, enough of the crust will get peeled back or blown away that we can then re-anchor and send in the miners."

The crew is silent as Thea considers the plan. After one full rotation of the glowing image above the table, she's made up her mind.

She doesn't need to ask Rory, Beetle, or Lola. She knows what their vote will be.

She turns to face Elliott. "What do you think?"

He shrugs. "Like Beet said, we've done this before. As far as manned missions go, this is a relatively easy one."

"And yet . . .?"

He lets out a deep sigh. "I guess I'm just a little skittish after what happened the last time Beetle and I had to do something like this."

"I can understand that." She knows the loss of his old ship and friends is still a raw nerve. "We should let this one go. For our first mission together, I want us all on the same page."

She watches him soften as soon as she says it, suspecting that the offer is all he's in search of, not an actual rejection of the mission.

"No, it's a good plan," he says. "Let's do this."

Lola's fingers begin to drum out a mesmerizing rhythm on the console, accompanied by *hell yeah*s from Beetle and Rory.

"One condition, though," Thea says, her gaze still fixed on Elliott, but her voice loud enough for the rest of them to hear. "I'm coming with you."

14

Descent

THEY SLOWLY MANEUVER through the debris field to the ancient, fifteen-thousand-ton leviathan. Their gentle approach conceals the violence they intend to inflict upon the beast, their plans to stab at the very heart of it and claim that which makes it special in the universe.

They draw to within two hundred meters and match the asteroid's rotational pattern and spin rate. They become momentary partners, cosmic companions pirouetting through the darkness. Graceful, harmonious.

Until the *Zephyr*'s harpoon shatters the illusion, piercing the asteroid's iron skin and lodging deep in its flesh.

Rory reels in the slack until the line draws taut, then adjusts their yaw and pitch. Once their orbit above the anchor point is stable, he calls down to the harpoon bay airlock.

"Let me say it one more time—"

"Rory, we've been through this," Thea says over the comms.

"This rock is barely spinning, and its axis is true. No fucking wobbles at all. She's a dream. The autopilot can handle it."

"Rory!"

"And the kid's here too as backup in case shit does happen to go sideways. With all her super nerd powers, I'm sure she could figure us a way out of a jam if she needed to."

"Thanks for the vote of confidence, gramps," Lola calls out from somewhere on the bridge.

"Let me go down there with the boys," Rory pleads.

"I'm going. End of discussion," says Thea. She gnaws the last bits of her antacid, twists her helmet into place, then throws the lever that seals the door leading back into the cargo bay. Next to her, Elliott and Beetle are loading the last of the charges into shoulder bags.

"Fine. But you stick to your assigned zones and let those two take care of the rest. Got it?"

"Yes, sir," Thea replies. "Oh wait, I thought I was the boss." She smiles at Elliott and Beetle, who seem to be enjoying the exchange with Rory a little too much.

Elliott initiates the process to depressurize the harpoon bay airlock. "Ninety seconds to exit, Bridge."

As she stands in the airlock—a liminal space between the safety of her ship and the hard vacuum of space—Thea's brain screams at her.

Stay on the ship.

Are you insane?

What makes you think you can do something like this?

And the truth is, she might *not* be cut out for this. But she's certain that she'll never feel confident in her dad's old chair if she doesn't try.

The light above the door leading to the harpoon bay turns from red to green to indicate the depressurization cycle is complete and the airlock atmosphere now matches that of the harpoon bay. By contrast, the entire perimeter of the *cargo* bay door now glows a bright red.

"You ready to go for a walk?" Elliott asks. Next to him, Beetle gives Thea a wink and a crooked smile.

Absolutely not, she thinks, swallowing hard. Then with a deep breath, she gives them a thumbs-up.

"Let's do this."

Elliott opens the door. Straight ahead of them is the harpoon cannon. The barrel is a mottled gunmetal gray shot through with red and orange hot zones that cast the mechanism in a bloody glow. Steam rises off the entire length of the barrel as it continues to cool in the deep freeze of space. Heavy, multicolored hoses feed into the side panels of the cannon and snake away to somewhere deep inside the bowels of the ship. Right next to the gun is a massive spool of thick tungsten rope line. A secondary bolt hangs above everything, ready to be loaded into the barrel, which is pointed down toward the asteroid through the open hatch in the ship's hull.

Thea's about to step forward when Beetle taps her on the arm. He holds up his carabiner and points to the one clipped at her waist. She unlatches hers from her belt and reels out some of the attached lifeline from the chest compartment of her suit to match his. Then the two of them fall in line behind Elliott.

As she approaches the spool, she notices the harpoon line quiver under the tremendous tension exerted by the asteroid. "That normal?" she asks, pointing at the line.

"That's perfect, actually," Elliott says. "Rory's got us nice and snug."

He opens a compartment next to the spool and takes out three cable trolleys. He snaps the trolleys to the harpoon line, then attaches his carabiner to the lead trolley. Beetle attaches to the second trolley and makes space for Thea. She snaps her carabiner onto the last trolley and then takes up the rear of their trio.

"Okay, let's go down slow and steady," Elliott says, twisting the speed knob on the side of his trolley.

Glowing numbers appear on his unit's display, descending from twelve to four meters per second, at which point he releases the knob. Beetle and Thea follow Elliott's lead once again, setting their trolley speeds to match.

Beetle holds out his hand, palm down, and looks to them both. They take the hint and place their hands atop his. With a nod, the mission is underway.

Elliott moves to the edge of the exterior hatch.

"Here we go," he says, then casually steps out and starts gliding down toward the asteroid.

A twenty-count later, Beetle's descent begins, leaving Thea alone in the bay.

Lola's voice crackles through the speakers in Thea's helmet. "You got this, boss."

Her mind reels. She steps to the edge of the open hatch, takes a deep breath as if she's about to cannonball into a swimming pool, and leaps into space.

It would be easy to focus, she thinks, on how insignificant we all are amid the vastness of the universe. The brief irrelevance of our lives compared to the timelessness of space. It would be easy to feel lost in all this darkness, crushed under the weight of the void. Struggle to comprehend the wonder and mystery and grandeur of the tapestry spread out forever and everywhere, beyond any person's fears or hopes or beliefs.

It would be so easy to let herself think all those thoughts. But as she descends toward the ancient celestial traveler below, one inelegant, unshakable thought takes hold.

This is so friggin' cool!

Her trolley slows as she approaches the bottom of the harpoon line. She looks up at the *Zephyr*. The glow from the harpoon bay and running lights along the underside of the hull is blurred by tears, and instinctively, she tries to wipe them away—only for her hand to knock into her face shield. She lets out a giggle, which grows into a fit of laughter. She can't help it. It's like a release valve for the hope and joy filling her chest.

You were right, old man, she thinks, remembering Dad's letter. She feels like she's found something that has been lost for a long time.

Herself.

Elliott and Beetle grab her as she reaches the bottom. The soles of her boots snap down and adhere to the asteroid's metallic surface. She tries to take a step and manages to do so only after much effort.

"Don't worry, they'll calibrate to your stride after you walk a bit," Elliott says.

She takes another step and feels a twinge in her left knee where she tore her ACL in high school doing hurdles on the varsity track team. But a few steps later, she's able to walk normally.

She reaches down to where the harpoon bolt pierced the surface of the asteroid. "How far in did it go?"

"About fifty meters," Beetle says. "Don't worry, she's in there good."

"Okay Lola, we're all set down here," Elliott says. "Let's get the grid up."

"Roger, Ell. Here we go."

A glowing green grid appears on Thea's heads-up display. As she pans left and right, the grid maps to the surface, with coordinates appearing at regular intervals.

"Just a walk in the park, Captain," Beetle says, then unclips from his trolley and heads off.

Elliott spins Thea around to face the immediate area. "Coordinates are in the dialog box on the right, but the system will guide you at every step," he says, pointing in the direction of her first target. "All three of your targets are within one hundred fifty meters, which is the span of your lifeline." He taps the lifeline reel at the center of her chest plate. "If you run into any issues with the charges, call one of us and we'll come. You can twist the locking mechanism like this to disengage the autoreel. That'll let you have some slack in the line so you can move around without it tugging at you."

He reels out some line to show her how the device works. "Twist it the opposite way to re-engage the mechanism, which will suck in the slack." He grabs her carabiner. "But stay attached to the harpoon line. No matter what."

"Roger that."

With a nod, Elliott does what he just warned her against— he unclips himself from his cable trolley and heads off in the opposite direction of Beetle.

Thea takes another glance up at her ship, then sets off toward her first target.

———

A GOLDEN-YELLOW LINE appears ahead of Thea on the grid, representing the path she should take, and the distance to her first destination counts down on her visor as she walks. She expected the metal skin of the asteroid to be craggy and rough, but with nothing to oxidize it, the blue-gray iron is smooth and mostly flat, with only a few gentle swales in her vicinity. She's able to track Elliott until he disappears over a low rise. She turns to find Beetle, but he too is out of view.

She's alone on the alien landscape.

After approximately forty meters, a pulsing red dot appears up ahead.

She quickens her pace, getting increasingly confident in her boots' ability to keep her grounded, and reaches a two-meter tear in the surface of the asteroid. Her first target. It looks like something burst out from beneath the iron, and she can't help but picture the xenomorph from that classic movie Lola forced her to watch right before they left Darkside Station. She kneels next to the upturned edge of the tear, turns on her helmet's headlamps, and peeks under the asteroid's skin at the substrate below. She estimates that the ragged edge of the metal is only about three feet thick.

"I've reached my first target," she says.

"How does it look?"

"The metal's peeled back pretty good. Plenty of room to fasten a charge to the underside of the tear."

"Just make sure it's not tucked in there too far or I won't pick up the signal," Lola says.

Thea slides off her backpack and takes out one of the charges. The device looks like a steel brick with a single toggle switch on one side. She flips the switch, and the opposite side of the brick glows red. Then she reaches into the breach in the asteroid's skin and attaches the red side to the underside of the tear. As soon as it clicks into place, the whole brick glows a soft green.

"Got it, Thea. Good work," Lola says.

Thea stands up and checks the coordinates for the next target. But before she can move, there's a quick flash of light from behind the rise where Elliott is working.

And a scream.

15

Time and Space

BITS OF ROCK and shards of metal stream out from behind the rise like confetti shot out of a cannon.

"Elliott!" Thea shouts. "Come in!"

No response.

"Come on, Ell. Talk to me."

Still nothing.

She starts jogging toward the rise, fighting her boots as they attempt to calibrate to her new stride and pace. Frantic voices fill the comms—Rory, Lola, Beetle calling for his friend—but there's nothing from Elliott.

Thea stumbles and lands hard on her bad knee. Pain fires through her thigh muscle and hips. She's struggling back to her feet when she sees him. Elliott comes over the peak, his right hand and forearm encased in a bulbous, pink substance.

Sealant foam.

He trips, then slides down the slope on his belly like a kid on a slip-and-slide.

"Elliott!" She starts toward him.

"No," he says, voice weak.

"Hold on. I'm coming," she says.

"Go," he croaks.

"Say again," Beetle says, his voice breaking through the comms chatter. He's breathing hard.

"Go!" Elliott shrieks.

Then the rise explodes behind him in a blinding flash.

———

THEA'S ULTRAVIOLET visor snaps into place over her face shield just a moment too late to protect her from the intense burst of light. While she tries to blink away the whiteness filling her vision, she can feel shrapnel impacts all over her body. She drops to her knees and instinctively shields her head, but something large catches her shoulder, spinning her around and dropping her onto her stomach.

A system alarm blares, interspersed with a modulated female voice. *"A breach has been detected."*

Thea rolls onto her back and stabs her finger at her wrist control pad. Adrenaline is coursing through her body, so it takes several tries before she can calm her shaking hand enough to key the right sequence and silence the alarm. But even with the alarm muted, the computer voice persists.

"Oxygen level, eighty-nine percent."

Thea's mind goes blank. Her heart pounds in her chest.

"Thea, do you read?"

"Yeah, Roger!"

"You're bleeding oxygen," Lola says, clearly trying to sound calm and collected despite her new octave. "Can you seal the breach?"

Breach?

Thea realizes gas is escaping in a steady stream from a tear near her shoulder. She looks around, but her pack is nowhere to be found.

"My pack's gone," she says.

"Then you need to get on board. Right now!"

"Where's Elliott?" She twists around, frantic to find him.

Lola blurts out something in response, but Thea can't process it. She's too stunned by the sight of what appears to be a frozen metal wave where the rise stood just moments ago. The iron skin of the asteroid is peeled away from the surface, the top edge jagged and torn, curling toward her like the top of a tin can.

There's no sign of Elliott.

"Oxygen level, seventy-seven percent."

Thea screams Elliott's name while Lola and Rory scream at her to get up to the ship. She scrambles to her feet, only to be instantly blindsided and knocked to the ground again. She thinks it's more debris from the explosion, until she's flipped onto her back.

"Stay still!"

"Beetle, what the hell?"

"No time!" he says, kneeling above her and frantically pulling out his lifeline.

He twists the locking mechanism, preventing his autoreel from engaging, then grabs his carabiner, the part that normally attaches to the trolley, and clips it to Thea's waist belt.

"What are you doing?"

"Saving him!"

Beetle punches something into his wrist pad and squats in a three-point stance. Pivots left. Then right. Hits the control pad. Then thrusts forward and launches himself into space.

"Beetle!" Thea screams, reaching after him.

But he's gone.

Thea scrambles to her feet again, terrified, desperately trying to make sense of what Beetle said before he jumped, tracking his flight from the surface of the asteroid.

And then she sees where he's heading.

Elliott is floating amid a sea of detritus from the explosion. Tumbling end over end.

Not trying to right himself. Not calling for help.

"Oxygen level, sixty-four percent."

"Thea, come in! What's happening?"

"What are his vitals?"

"Whose?"

"Elliott's, damn it! What are his vitals?"

"We lost his signal," Lola says. "Do you see him?"

"Yeah," Thea whispers, chest tight, on the verge of hyperventilating as she watches Beetle shoot through space toward their friend.

He's closing on him . . . fast.

Too fast.

Beetle covers his head as he flies through the debris field. Luckily nothing enters his path. Thea watches in disbelief, eyes flitting back and forth between Beetle and the coils of his rapidly disappearing lifeline at her feet.

My feet!

She enters a command to shut off her boots' magnetic soles, just as Beetle did. Checks his carabiner to make sure it's locked around her belt, knowing she's his anchor. The only thing that will get him back.

Get them both back.

"Oxygen level, fifty-nine percent."

Beetle closes on Elliott.

"Get ready!" he says.

He twists his body upright, no longer flying like an arrow toward his target. Splays his arms and legs out wide like a spider, ready to wrap himself around Elliott.

Thea looks down in horror. The slack in Beetle's lifeline is almost gone. *And so is my oxygen*, she thinks, but then pushes the thought from her mind.

Seconds later, there's a sharp tug at her waist.

"Beetle, talk to me!" she shrieks as she's ripped off the ground.

"Almost there . . ."

"Please, please," she whispers, watching the ground shrink below her. She twists around and catches a glimpse of Beetle, arms and legs still wide—

"Got him!" he yells.

His mic registers the jostle and struggle to secure his grip on Elliott. Thea's own lifeline reels out behind her, still connected to the harpoon line at the far end, but Beetle's momentum is carrying both him and her farther from the surface.

When her line hits its limit, it could rip Elliott out of Beetle's grasp.

"Hold on to him, Beetle! I'm gonna slow us down."

Thea wraps her gloved hands around her lifeline and gradually tightens her grip as it slips through, not wanting to stop them too abruptly. But her efforts seem to be doing little to slow their momentum at all. She can't determine how much pressure she's exerting due to the thick Kevlar weave on her gloves, and she knows she's running out of line—and time.

She has no choice. She squeezes hard.

Her forearms burn and her hands cramp, but now she can feel herself slowing. She maintains her grip, squeezing as hard as she can, and when she reaches her allotted one hundred fifty meters of lifeline, the tug as she stops is a gentle one.

"Oxygen level, forty-six percent."

"Good work, Captain!"

Rory is in her ear seconds later. "Thea, you need to let go."

She realizes she's still got her lifeline in a death grip. She releases it.

But the autoreel doesn't engage. She twists the locking mechanism back and forth a few times. Nothing happens.

"My autoreel isn't working."

"It may be too taut. Try to get yourself some slack!"

She looks behind her and sees Beetle wrapped around Elliott. Registers the asteroid surface in her peripheral vision rising to meet them. Unlike the *Zephyr*, Beetle and Elliott have no means to match the spin of the asteroid. If she doesn't hurry, they won't reach the harpoon line before they hit the ground.

"Oxygen level, thirty-nine percent."

She grabs the line again and tries to pull herself back down it toward the surface. The extra tension from Beetle's lifeline and the two bodies behind her don't make it easy. Her arms and shoulders pulse and pop under the strain, but she manages to inch herself forward. She pulls again, and it's a bit easier. Eventually she's able to pull herself hand over hand a few feet.

"Try the autoreel again," Beetle says. "Quickly."

She twists the mechanism and tugs at the line. This time it engages. She feels herself being pulled down to her trolley, still attached to the harpoon line. Light refracts off the surface like sunlight off a lake as she draws closer and closer.

Just like calm water, she thinks.

But it's not calm water. Her hip strikes iron, and pain shoots across her pelvis and down her legs.

The autoreel keeps pulling her forward, sending her bouncing across the surface. She skids and thumps across the metallic landscape, closing in on the harpoon line.

She knows when Beetle and Elliott touch down only because she can feel the autoreel at her chest suddenly straining, trying to pull them forward too. But the weight of three people, and the friction of them dragging against the surface, is now too much for it. It's no longer needed anyway. She twists the mechanism to shut it off, then tries to stand.

Her foot slips off the slick surface, and she falls down face-first.

My boots.

"Thea, I need you," Beetle grunts.

Thea reactivates her magnetic soles and turns around. Beetle and Elliott came down at the base of a small swale. Beetle is trying to pull Elliott across the ground but is making little progress.

"Oxygen level, twenty-six percent."

Thea looks back toward the harpoon line. It's at least a football field away, and Beetle's line is maxed out, which means she can't reach him before she hits her own lifeline's limit of one hundred fifty meters. There's no time to go all the way to the trolley to unlatch her carabiner, so she takes her multitool out of its compartment near the small of her back and starts sawing at her lifeline.

"Thea, stop!" Rory says. "What are you doing?"

"Beetle needs my help." The line is starting to fray under the tool's keen edge.

"No. I'll come down."

"There's no time. It has to be me."

"You're oxygen's below twenty percent."

"I'll make it."

She hacks away the last strands of the lifeline and then heads for Beetle and Elliott. As her boots adjust, she bounds across the surface, fueled by adrenaline and the urgency of the oxygen countdown. The ground is relatively flat, which will help as they drag Elliott home.

She reaches them just as her oxygen indicator reads *sixteen percent.*

"How is he?"

Beetle hands over one of Elliott's ankles. "He's still out. And there's no telling what's under that," he says, pointing to Elliott's hand and forearm, still encased in the pink sealant.

Even in the near-zero-g and the slick flat surface, it's hard to haul him across the ground. They struggle to keep their grip, especially as Elliott's suit snags on bits of iron. And all the while, Thea's oxygen ticks down.

The alarm comes back with a vengeance when her level hits ten percent. No silencing it now. Rory and Lola scream through the comms system for them to move their asses. Thea and Beetle strain to pull their friend across the ground, desperate to get back to their ship. As they get closer to the harpoon line, the ground slopes down toward it, and they're able to cover the final distance quickly.

Beetle drops Elliott's leg and grabs his friend's carabiner. "Activate the trolley when I say!"

Thea kneels next to Elliott as Beetle attaches the carabiner to the cable trolley at the back of the harpoon line—originally Thea's trolley—then twists the knob until the number on the side reads *twelve meters per second*, the highest speed.

"Now!"

Thea hits the activate button on her wrist keypad. Elliott's instantly sucked off the ground and into the sky as the trolley flies toward the harpoon bay above.

"Oxygen level, three percent."

Beetle is at her side, lifting her into a standing position. He pulls her arms away from her sides and kicks her feet wide apart.

"Stay like this and hold still," he says, grabbing the remnant of her lifeline attached to her suit and yanking it toward them. As it slithers across the ground from the spot where she cut it, Thea realizes what's already occurred to Beetle.

Her carabiner just went up with Elliott. She can't connect to the trolley.

"Can't we just go up together?"

"I don't know if the trolley can handle it. And we can't risk getting stuck midflight."

He gets hold of the frayed end and starts crisscrossing the line over her body, looping it between her legs and over each shoulder in an alternating pattern. After each pass over her shoulders, he tugs hard to make sure there's no slack in the line.

"I'm sorry. This will not be comfortable."

But the pain in her crotch and across her shoulder blades is an afterthought.

Because her oxygen level reaches zero.

"Small breaths," Beetle says, trying to reassure her, no doubt responding to the terror he sees in her eyes. "You still have whatever oxygen is in your suit."

As he gets close to the end of the slack in the line, he begins weaving it through the attachment point on the trolley he took down to the surface, creating an intricate knot. She sips at the last bits of oxygen, trying to stay focused and not let fear swallow her—or let herself swallow a huge lungful of what little air she has left.

"Stay with me, *ma chère!*"

Thea's knees wobble.

Beetle spins the trolley's speed dial to twelve, and activates it using his wrist keypad.

A second later, she's skybound.

As she zips toward the ship, she notices that the area around her is filled with sparkling bits of rock and metal. Debris blown free during the explosion. She watches it twirl and flash. Beyond the glitter, the starfield twinkles in the distance.

So many stars.

I can touch them, she thinks, reaching out with a gloved hand. But she can't. No matter how many swipes she takes, the pretty stars slip through her fingers.

Her heads-up display begins to wobble and fade.

The stars begin to wink out.

One by one.
And then in big groups.
Going, going . . .

16

Noble Gases

THE AIR TASTES PLASTICKY. Thea sucks in slow and steady, squeezing the sides of the balloon to get as much of it as she can. Holds it for a few seconds, her lungs on the verge of bursting . . . then lets everyone in on the secret.

"Mr. Evans eats farts."

Her friends burst into hysterics, slapping the water and splashing each other. Thea coughs out the last of the helium and joins them. Her neighbor, Joey, drops his foam noodle and frantically swims to the edge. He gets out holding his crotch, red-faced as he races for the pool house bathroom, which makes the kids roar even louder.

"Time for the piñata," Thea's mom calls, waving them over.

Everyone scrambles to the shallow end where parents are waiting with towels. Thea's mom hands her the scratchy pink one. Thea quickly swipes her face and arms, then tosses the towel aside and runs across the hot concrete to where her dad is waiting under the big oak.

A fat, yellow Pikachu swings from a branch.

"Okay sweetness let's see what you can do," he says,

handing her an old broomstick, one end wrapped in electrical tape, before tying one of his faded handkerchiefs over her eyes as a blindfold.

He spins her around and everyone counts.

One, two, three, four, five!

Thea nearly topples over when he lets go.

She digs her toes into the cool grass, steadies herself, and takes a swing.

Nothing but air.

Her guests call out hints. She makes an adjustment, rears back, and swings again.

Another miss.

She pivots, then a wide-arching swipe.

Still nothing!

"Here, gimme that," her dad says, snatching the broomstick from her hands. "You're not doing it right."

She pulls the blindfold down and sees her dad sizing up the piñata. But instead of the jolly Pokémon character, it's now a papier-mâché *Zephyr* hanging from the branch. He rears back and delivers a mighty blow, ripping the brittle paper-and-paste ship off its string and driving it down to the grass.

Then he lifts the broom handle high over his head and drives it into the heart of the ship with a mighty *whack*.

"If you're going to break it, Thea, you gotta do it the right way!"

He strikes it again, and again, and again.

"Stop!" she screams. "You're destroying it!"

"Stop!"

"Daddy!"

She jolts forward, knocking her oxygen mask askew.

"Easy, luv. You're okay," Rory says, gently guiding her shoulders back down before adjusting the mask. His face is flush, the hair in his goatee wild. "You lot scared the shite outta me."

When Thea reaches up and touches his cheek, he claps his rough hand over hers to hold it there a few seconds.

"How's Elliott?" she asks.

"Slightly concussed, and he fucked up his hand pretty good, but he'll be okay. Lola and Beetle took him to sick bay."

Thea takes a deep breath, relief flooding through her. "What happened?"

"A pocket of xenon. There must have been a tiny spark when Ell activated one of his charges. And that's all it took."

"Why didn't it show up on the scan?"

"We're trying to figure that out now."

Thea closes her eyes and listens to the distant hum of the motor in the harpoon bay, still coiling the heavy tungsten line onto the spool.

"How's the ship?"

"Took some damage. But nothing major."

She pulls off the mask and sits up, suddenly on alert. "What kind of damage?"

"Don't worry. Most of the bigger stuff stayed below our orbit. But some of the ejecta caught us."

Thea needs Rory's help to get up. Her lifeline is still coiled around her torso, and her suit weighs a million pounds in the ship's artificial gravity. "Help me out of this. I want to go see Elliott. Then I want to see what happened to my ship."

———

"You saved our bacon," Thea says.

"It's a veggie lasagna. No bacon," Beetle says, setting the platter in the middle of the table.

"I meant down there, smartass."

He gives her a toothy smile and takes the seat across from her. "You too, Captain."

Rory digs out a big spoonful, plops it unceremoniously onto a plate, and slides it toward Thea. "Eat. It'll do you good."

He picks up another plate and looks to Lola, who is lost in her tablet. Her fingers stab and swipe at the screen.

"Oy, girlie. How 'bout you?"

She looks up and wrinkles her nose.

Beetle puts a hand to his chest. "I'm deeply offended, *madame*. I worked for minutes and minutes heating up this delicacy."

"Maybe later," Lola says and goes back to her tablet.

"What are you working on?"

"I'm running a linter on our probes' source code to see if there's a way to boost chromatic depth and avoid the sorts of optical aberrations that made me miss the xenon. I think it's probably dark-spectrum shit or maybe some baseline shift, but that's no excuse. I should have anticipated that the iron exterior was gonna fuck with the data."

She glances up at her silent friends, forks poised near mouths agape, eyes darting back and forth at each other to see if any of them followed what was just said.

"I'm gonna make sure our probes see shit that can blow up."

*Ahhh*s and nods tell her they understand.

"But I still think that when we get back to Darkside, we should invest in newer probes."

Thea drops her fork.

"I know it'll be pricey," Lola says, already on the defensive. "But maybe we could find someone willing to sell us a previous-gen setup. If even half our string were composed of upgraded tech, our range would be tons better."

"What are you talking about?" Thea says. "We're not going back."

Everyone stops and looks at her.

"We're not going back," Thea repeats.

"Thea," says Rory, "we have to regroup. Repairs will be easier at dock. And that'll give Lola a chance to look into the probe situation."

"Absolutely not. It took us almost three weeks to get out here. We head in now, we're talking months before we can bring in any money. And that's *if* we can get on another cluster that hasn't been mined to shit. Besides, I thought you said repairs were minor."

"They are, for the most part."

"Then we can do them out here."

Rory frowns. "We *can*, but—"

Thea pivots to Lola. "Can you do whatever the fuck it is you just said to make sure shit doesn't blow up again?"

"I already am," Lola says, crossing her arms.

Thea looks back at Rory. "There you have it. We're staying."

Beetle chimes in. "What about Ell?"

"What about me?"

Elliott's standing in the doorway to the galley wearing loose-fitting pajamas and a threadbare flannel bathrobe. A big toe pokes through a hole in one of his slippers, and his right hand and forearm are wrapped in a white bandage.

"You should be in bed," Beetle says.

"Lying there was making me crazy." Elliott takes a seat at the table. "What are we talking about?"

Rory's about to explain, but Thea cuts him off.

"They want to go back to the station and *regroup*. But everything we need to do, we can do out here. So we're gonna keep going. Unless you need to go in to see the station medic for anything."

Elliott looks to Rory, Beetle, and Lola for confirmation that nothing is dire and that there's an actual choice on the table. Beetle and Rory nod. Lola shrugs.

"My grandfather was a boxer," he says. "When he was just

twenty years old, he held the title of featherweight champion in all of South Africa. He was one of the best fighters of his generation, and my hero growing up. Man was tough as leather. One day I come home from school, and he's in the kitchen making something I assure you smelled a good bit better than whatever that is there," he says, waving at Beetle's creation.

"Forgive me if it's not coq au vin," Beetle says sourly. "I'm a little tired from saving your ass."

Elliott grabs Beetle's collar, yanks him forward, and plants a kiss on his forehead, then continues his story.

"I walk in the door, and with one look at me, Oupa could tell I'd been fighting again. And losing. My shirt and pants were dirty, and I had a fat lip and a swollen eye. So he called me over, sat me on his lap, and told me about his very last professional fight.

"His opponent, he said, was ten years younger, six inches taller, and weighed three or four stone more than him. And he had a twenty-to-zero record. Undefeated! It was my grandfather's greatest challenge yet.

"No one picked Oupa to win that fight. His own brother, it turns out, had placed a bet against him. *Against* his own brother! Can you imagine? But it didn't matter, my grandfather said. He didn't need anyone to believe in him, because he had faith in the tools God gave him. His hands. His heart. His mind."

"So . . . he *encouraged* you to get into fights at school?" Thea asks. "I mean, apologies, but doesn't sound like you were very good at it."

Elliott chuckles. "I wouldn't say he *encouraged* it. But he did tell me the thing that has stuck with me to this day. He said that as long as you have belief in something, you'll have everything you'll ever need in this world."

He leans forward, resting both his good hand and the damaged one on the table.

"I believe in *us*. I don't know why. It doesn't make much sense. And God knows there's no evidence to support my belief. Not yet anyway."

"Yeah, you nearly blew the fuck up, man," Rory interjects.

"That is true. But I believe, nonetheless. So I say we go on."

Lola frowns. "You're the guy who's been holding back this whole time. Why the change of heart?"

"Because we got the hard part out of the way. We got knocked down," Elliott says, holding up his bandaged hand as a case in point. "Now all we need to do is get back up."

Thea slaps her hand on the table, causing plates, glasses, and cutlery to jump. "It's settled then. We keep going."

They make plans as they finish their meal. Beetle and Rory settle on a strategy to repair the damage to the hull, while Lola and Thea go over deep field scans and try to identify their next target.

After a while, Elliott pushes away from the table and grabs a box of crackers from the cupboard on his way out of the galley. Thea follows, coming up behind him.

"Thanks for the support back there," she says.

"No problem. It's the right call."

"Hey, you didn't really finish your story. Did your grandfather win that big fight?"

"Oh, gosh no. He got knocked out in the first round. Wasn't even close."

And with a wink, Elliott heads back to sick bay.

17

Line of Sight

A PILL-SHAPED CONGLOMERATE SHIPPING CONTAINER, filled with platinums from the outer rim, is shot from the railgun. It sparkles and flashes in the sunlight as it hurtles toward Earth.

Like microdosing a spouse, she thinks. *Slipping the poison into their food bit by bit so they don't realize they're being murdered until it's too late.*

The sounds of the day crew draw her attention back to the reason she's here. They file out of the holding area one by one, weariness radiating from them. She's been watching this crew and knows there's usually a fifteen-minute gap from the time they leave to when the next shift arrives, which should give her plenty of time to slip inside, get what she needs, and get out.

She adjusts her position behind a stack of crates to maintain line of sight on the keypad next to the holding area door. A gangly, tall guy in a grimy yellow jumper is the last one to leave. He enters his code to lock the door behind him.

2-6-6-2-7.

B-O-O-B-S.

Of course.

As he hustles after the others, she moves to the door, enters the ridiculous code, and slips inside.

The shipyard holding area is no different from any other warehouse, except, of course, for its location. A wide conveyor belt runs down the center of the space and passes through an airlock in the south wall, from which it extends all the way out to the landing pads adjacent to the shipyard's main building. Deep shelves filled with boxes and crates line the walls on either side of the belt. The shelves on one side are labeled *Intake*, and on the other side, *Processed*. The latter cargo will be loaded onto the Hyperloop, bound for Darkside Station.

Since she's a resident of Darkside now, it's been easy enough for her handler to slip her encrypted data discs or biometric-coded holosticks containing directives via normal shipments. But his last message said he needed to *talk*, which is tricky. Even with encryption, she can't be certain that someone wouldn't be listening on the lunar satellite network. So calling from Darkside is only something she'd do as a last resort. The shipyard is the best bet since it provides direct line of sight to Earth. But she can't use an ordinary line. She needs something more secure. Something buried somewhere among these shelves.

She moves quickly down the intake aisle, scanning the labels as she goes. Most of the packages are from the International Agribusiness Consortium and are addressed to the Lunar Farming Division of Darkside. Scientists in Iowa made significant progress on a family of root vegetables that can grow in the moon's cultivated regolith. She imagines the cafeteria will be featuring a lot of carrot and parsnip dishes in the coming months.

She looks for her package but can't find it. Doubles back, checks everything again. It isn't here.

She crosses the room and heads to the Processed shelves.

The first thing she notices is that all of the labels have tomorrow's date, which means the night crew will probably load everything onto the Hyperloop this upcoming shift. She has to find the package before that happens. If she misses the call window, she won't be able to reach her handler again for a few weeks, since she's expected back at Darkside soon. And she's already been in here for ten minutes. The night crew is on its way.

She frantically jogs up and down the aisle, head on a swivel. Begins to think that she's going to have to abandon the search in order to get out of the room before she's discovered. But then she sees the package on a shelf above her, tucked up against a roll of fabric. The end of the box is stamped with the intended recipient: Darkside Municipal Court.

She uses a lower shelf to boost herself up and snag it.

The package is locked by a digital seal.

She enters the code sent by her handler, and the box flaps pop open. Inside she finds an accordion folder filled with signed briefs, extradition paperwork, and other official documents. None hold any interest to her, which makes sense, as they aren't for her. Down beneath the paperwork is what she's after: a self-contained satellite burner handheld.

She closes the package, places it back on the shelf, and heads for the exit—

Just as someone starts working the keypad on the other side of the door.

Looking for a place to hide, she dives under the conveyor belt and scrambles to the nearest support column. Perhaps by squeezing up against it she won't be seen from the door.

She checks her watch and sees that she should still have three minutes before the night crew arrives. They're early.

Except it's not them. She hears the voice of the tall dude from earlier. "Hang on. I just gotta get my coat."

She slides a few inches away from his feet as they pass uncomfortably close to her hiding spot. He disappears for only a few seconds, then returns.

This time, his feet stop right next to her. He makes a noise that sounds like a growl.

Fuck, fuck, fuck.

A brown-and-yellow blob of snot splatters on the floor, inches from her hand. It takes every ounce of her control not to flinch away in revulsion.

Then his feet move on, and after a few seconds the door closes behind him.

The next shift will be arriving very soon. Too soon. But she forces herself to wait thirty seconds—avoiding looking at the loogie the whole time—before rushing out of the room, making sure to lock the door behind her.

———

PAIN RIPPLES through her forearm as she reaches for the light switch. When she rubs the spasming muscle, she sees a faint glow beneath her skin. The tracker. The pain lasts only a few seconds, but long enough to tell her that her handler's growing impatient.

A wide beam scans her face as she holds the burner at arm's length. When the green laser winks out, a prompt asks her to repeat the sentence displayed on the screen.

"Rage against the dying of the light."

As soon as she utters the last syllable, the screen flashes red, then green.

He picks up right away. Not a good sign. "You've been lying to me."

"Hello to you too," she says.

"I came across something interesting in a recent report from Darkside's Near Earth Objects Division. It appears a crew discovered a high-potential asteroid that was compromised by pockets of hard-to-detect xenon. Highly explosive. Seems they barely got out of the situation unscathed. So, being good citizens, they filed a notice with the NEOD to include the asteroid cluster on its fleetwide list of hazardous targets."

"What does this have to do with me?"

"The notice was filed by Watts Astromining."

"I know what you're thinking, but listen—"

He cuts her off. "No, you listen to *me*! Leadership wanted to pull you after what happened with the *Victor Hugo*. *I* stopped them. *I* assured them that you were the right operative for this assignment."

"That was an accident. It wasn't supposed to go down like that."

"I don't care. This isn't just on you anymore. It's on me too now. I put my fucking neck on the line for you. And now this?"

"Do they know?"

"No. I buried the report."

She lets out a sigh, then allows the silence to stretch a bit.

"I didn't lie, you know."

"Don't you dare! Not telling me the *Zephyr* was flying again is the same thing, and you know it."

"Why does it matter?" she asks.

"You know damn well why it matters!"

"My relationship with the captain doesn't change anything."

Silence. Thick, sticky silence.

She doesn't know him very well. That's the way it's supposed to be. She doesn't even know his real name. But in this moment, she thinks she may have pushed him too far. So she swallows down her instinct to fight and instead gives him what she thinks he actually wants.

"Okay, look—I'm sorry. I knew how leadership would react, and I didn't want this to affect my mission. I can still do my job. I promise."

He breaks his silence. "Why should I believe you?"

"Because you know how much I believe in what we're doing. You know what I've sacrificed for our cause."

She can't lose this. Not now.

She looks at the elapsed time on the burner's screen. They have only a minute before the embedded encryption code terminates the call.

"Tell me what I can do," she adds, almost pleading—or at least working hard to make it sound that way.

"Go back and wait for instructions," he says, voice flat, emotionless. "And don't ever lie to me again."

"I won't," she says, but the call has already ended.

She stares at the dead screen, replaying the conversation in her mind. It was dumb not to tell him. Of *course* he was going to find out. She'd just hoped it wouldn't be until later, after she'd made more progress.

Made herself indispensable.

She grips the burner in both hands and snaps it in two. Then heads for the Hyperloop back to Darkside.

18

Fun and Games

THE STEAM out to the next cluster takes ten days, which gives
the crew the time they need for repairs. Most of the asteroid's
ejecta impacted the ship's keel, the densest part of the *Zephyr*'s
hull, so damage was minimal. One of the starboard thrusters,
however, took a significant impact. A chunk of iron punched
through the outer door, shattering the control servo. It took
several days to fabricate a new servo and a few more to calibrate it.

While Rory and Beetle focused on repairs, Lola modified
the probes. And Thea tended to Elliott.

Scans of his forearm and hand showed that while he had a
good deal of soft tissue damage and a lot of swelling around
his flexor tendons, there were no ruptures or broken bones.
After a few days of nutrient immersions and rest, the swelling
went down, and he was able to regain limited use of his hand.

The down time also helped him recover from his concus-
sion. He kept insisting that he was fine—that his brain was
used to bouncing back from concussions after years of abuse in
half-pipes, football fields, and some mixed martial arts. But
Thea said that was all the more reason for him to take it slow.

Until the night they were playing cards and she caught him with an ace *literally* up his sleeve. Or in his case, the bandage on his forearm. That was the moment she knew he was going to be okay, and the tension she'd been silently carrying around since the accident finally started to subside.

His days on the mend gave the two of them plenty of time to talk, and they found out they had a lot in common. He'd grown up in Johannesburg, and she in Texas, which meant big skies, oppressive heat, rednecks, and lots of spicy, saucy meats were shared experiences. They'd also both had absent parents. Elliott's father was a diplomat who spent as much time on the road as Thea's dad did, though their "roads" were very different, and neither of them had really known their mothers. Elliott because he was adopted, and Thea because . . . well, because she found out too late that she had never *really* known her mother even back when she thought she did. Or at least not the weak, selfish version who threw away her marriage and daughter when things got too hard.

They argued over which was better, baseball or cricket. Rhythm and blues or punk rock. Indo-Mexican fusion or classic Italian. They agreed on politics and international climate policy. Hated anything related to time travel or the multiverse. *I mean, come up with a new idea already.* And both could spend hours and hours just sitting on the bridge, staring at the stars.

Thea thinks about all of this as she watches him sleep behind the navigation console. She'd shut off parts of herself during the years she took care of her dad, especially the part that let herself be vulnerable and open to possibilities. There was just no time or place for that. But as she studies Elliott's face, listens to his gentle snoring, she can feel something inside her coming alive. Something emerging from its dormancy. She's exhilarated and afraid in a way that seemed impossible not that long ago as she sat by her dad's bedside and read *The*

Old Man and the Sea to him over and over and over again, desperate for any sign of recognition in his glassy eyes. She feels happy in a way that also makes her feel guilty. Because she's still learning it's okay to feel like this.

That she's allowed to be okay.

She nestles into her chair, closes her eyes, and loses herself in the soft hum of her ship, a perfect white-noise nightcap to the day. But just as she's about to drift off, there's a ping from the main display.

She tries to ignore it, but it chimes again. Then a third time.

Reluctantly, she rubs her eyes and checks for the source of the notification.

It's coming from the probes. They found something.

Part of the outer edge of the cluster is circled in red, a dialog box alongside it. She zooms in and sees that the probes have discovered an asteroid with a high probability for cerium. Cerium is abundant back home and fetches a low price at the shipyard.

It's not even worth going after.

But then she sees that the spectroscopy analysis also indicates the presence of lutetium in the same target, and she nearly falls out of her chair.

"Ell, wake up."

Elliott snores.

"Ell!" she tries again.

Behind her, the bridge door hisses open.

"Holy shit!" Lola yells as she charges onto the bridge. Finally Elliott wakes, jerking so fast that he bumps his sore hand.

"How'd you know already?" Thea asks.

Lola aggressively shoos Elliott out of his chair. "Are you crazy? I've always got the feed going in my cabin." She kicks off her slippers and plops down behind the navigation controls.

Her hair is a purple-and-black maelstrom as she types, her knees bouncing out a frenetic rhythm.

"What's happening?" Elliott asks. He sleepily stumbles toward Thea, cradling his hand.

"Payday," Thea says. "That's what happening."

Lola throws the cluster map onto the main display. A trapezoidal prism dominates the screen, slowly rotating and dotted with asteroids of varying sizes and shapes. Like a jar of flies, the asteroids travel as a unit, but each one wobbles and tumbles independently within the interior of the prism, making it impossible to see a way to the singular asteroid near the center of the cluster, lit with a green glow.

"Beetle! Old fucker! We need you both up here now!" Lola calls over the shipwide hailer.

"Rory's gonna love that," Thea says.

"He'll be fine when he sees what we found. Trust me." Lola pulls her knees up and spins around in the chair as they wait.

Thea nudges over to Elliott. "You ready for this?" she whispers, nodding at the display.

"Not sure what *this* is yet," he says. "But I'm with you, of course."

They hear Rory coming, his profanity growing in volume as he storms up the corridor. "Bloody hell! Two fucking hours I've been asleep. Two!"

His diatribe goes to eleven the instant he stomps onto the bridge. Beetle shuffles in behind him, burritoed in a blanket, only the slits of his half-closed eyes visible.

"This better be good, girlie. Or so help me Christ, I'm gonna go crawl into your rack and leave you to deal with Frenchie's all-night nose whistle."

Lola leaps out of the chair and then spins it toward him. "Calm down, Grandpa. Have a look."

Rory pushes the chair aside and moves behind the navigation console. His anger turns to puzzlement as he looks at the readings. Lola moves the chair again, this time positioning it behind him so that he can drop into it. Which he does when he sees what they've discovered.

"Fuck me. This is just what the doctor ordered."

"Yeah, but can we get in there?" Lola asks him.

"I'd crawl up a dog's arse to get at some lutetium."

"What did you just say?" Beetle asks, throwing off his blanket and moving toward the main display. And in the process forgetting that he's dressed only in a banana sack.

"Shit, man," Elliott says, fishing the blanket off the deck and handing it back to Beetle. "No weapons on the bridge."

Beetle takes the blanket but doesn't seem to have heard the jab. "Did we really find the holy of the holies?"

"Doesn't look like much of it," Rory says, "but sure as shit, it's enough for *this* lot."

"Last I heard, lutetium was going for about twenty grand a kilo," Beetle says.

"Can you do it?" Lola asks Rory once again.

He enters a sequence of maneuvers into the plotter and hits enter. A blue line begins to weave through the cluster, heading toward their target. Midway through its journey, the line intersects an asteroid and turns bright red.

A dialog box covers the flight path: *Collision probability 100%.*

Rory tries a new sequence, and this time the line gets closer to the target before it turns red. *Collision probability 100%.*

Third try, he almost gets there.

And on the fourth, he does.

Collision probability 0.02%.

"All right, all right," Thea says. "We're in business!"

"No, it's no good." Rory sits back in the chair so hard he bumps Lola's chin.

"Hey, watch it," she says, slapping the top of his head.

"What do you mean?" Thea asks. "What's wrong?"

"Once we get there, we're gonna have to be in there a while," Rory replies. "You can't just drill down and rip. The miners are going to take some time. It'll be delicate. Every ounce of lutetium we lose is big money. Watch."

He hits a key, and the animation continues. The icon representing the *Zephyr* stays green for a while, then flips to red.

"One hundred percent chance of a collision within the first forty-nine point six hours," he says. "It isn't enough time."

The bridge goes silent. Beetle sits down on the floor and goes back into burrito mode.

"Hold on," Elliott says. He steps closer to the main display and points to an area just below their target. "Zoom in here."

Rory pecks at the keys, and an asteroid appears on the main display. A dialog box appears beside it with additional information.

"Mostly cobalt. Nominal spin," Elliott says. "Speed looks right. Easy anchor and then a straight draw out."

Rory pops forward. "I see what you're after, mate. That might work."

Thea and Lola exchange confused looks. Beetle's nose whistles.

"Gonna come down to the scatter, I think."

"Yeah, and the burn needed to reel her in."

The display changes back to its previous view. But this time, the blue line that appears charts a path to the cobalt-laden asteroid.

"What are you guys talking about?" Lola asks.

"Give us a second," Rory says.

They huddle as Rory works the keyboard. A dotted orange line appears on the screen, originating at the cobalt asteroid and extending to the outer edge of the target cluster.

"Here goes," he says, and punches a key.

As the animation plays, the dotted line slowly turns solid as it extends outward. The lutetium asteroid appears in its path.

When the orange line intersects with their target, Thea expects one of the dialog boxes of death. Instead, the line and the asteroid both turn green.

"You think?" Elliott says.

Rory grins. "Fucking A, I do!"

"Can one of you please tell us what the hell is going on?" Lola says.

"We're not going to go in and get her," Elliott says. "We're gonna bring her out here."

"I think we're gonna need more explanation than that," Thea snaps.

Elliott's grin matches Rory's. "We can get to the lutetium asteroid, but we can't stay in place long enough to extract the goods. So instead we're going to snag this *other* asteroid—made almost completely of cobalt, so it's super sturdy—and once we have it, we'll let out the harpoon line until we're clear of the cluster. *Then* we start drawing that big sucker toward us, timing it so that it'll collide with the lutetium asteroid and knock it off course."

"Like using a cue ball . . ." Lola says, a rarely given look of appreciation on her face.

Elliott nods. "Exactly. We then release the cue ball and get in position. The target's gonna hit some smaller, drifting debris on its way out, but nothing that'll threaten the payload."

"Friggin' brilliant!" Lola shouts. She races over to rouse Beetle, who actually went back to sleep during all this, and Rory follows. Thea takes advantage of the distraction.

"Nice job," she says, giving Elliott a peck on the cheek.

"Hey, isn't that a workplace violation?"

"For sure," she says. "You should complain to human resources."

He grabs her hand with his sore one and gives it a small squeeze.

"No, I don't think I will."

19

Score

"WELCOME to the latest episode of *Interstellar Billiards*! I'm your host, Bastien Bardot, coming to you live from the outer rim of asteroid cluster H72B, where renowned table shark Rory "Pocket Pool" Abernathy is trying to pull off, no pun intended, the Cobalt Cue Ball Caper."

"Where're we at, Lola?" Thea asks.

"Thirty seconds."

"As one of his bunkmates, I can tell you that Mr. Abernathy has been practicing his *stroke* almost incessantly. Trust me, folks, I grew up with four brothers, so I've been around this game a long, long time. And I've never seen someone so dedicated to their craft."

"Beetle," Rory growls, "when we're done here, I'm going to murder you."

"Fifteen seconds," Lola says.

"Ell, keep an eye on the main. I don't want to switch to auxiliary until we're on vapor."

"I ran the numbers three times. We should have enough fuel to adjust the cobalt asteroid's vector without tapping into our reserve."

"Five seconds."

"Here we go!" Thea says, then resumes annihilating her thumbnail with an incisor.

"Firing main thrusters."

The *Zephyr* shudders as the harpoon line draws taut. They're caught in a momentary stalemate as the engines strain to affect the cobalt asteroid's trajectory, with neither the ship nor the asteroid budging.

"We gotta go!" Lola says. "Punch it!"

Rory keys a sequence into the navigation controls. Thea's certain that if there were an actual pedal to put to the metal, his foot would be through the bridge's floor.

An alarm rings out.

"What's that?" Thea asks.

"Harpoon tolerance warning. We're close to the edge. But if this bastard doesn't move soon, we're gonna miss our intercept window and have to cut it loose," Elliott says.

The alarm continues to blare as the ship fights to alter the ancient object's well-worn groove in space for the first time in countless millennia. For a fraught moment, it seems like the cobalt asteroid is going to successfully refuse. But then the alarm stops, and the bridge is silent again.

"There she goes!" Elliott shouts.

"What about the intercept? Still on track?" Rory asks.

Lola's fingers fly over her keyboard.

"Talk to me, girlie!"

The image on the main display changes to a wide view of the asteroid cluster, illustrating the cobalt asteroid's new trajectory. But the latest projection has it missing the lutetium asteroid by approximately ten meters.

"Can we adjust?"

"Hold on!"

Lola continues to work. Moments later, a new projection appears, showing the two asteroids intercepting as planned.

"We just need to maintain our tether for a few seconds longer," she says. "I'll tell you when to disengage the harpoon."

"No, send it to my terminal," Rory says.

"I've got this. Trust me. On my mark."

All eyes are fixed on the projection on the main display as it refreshes. No one breaks the silence until . . .

"Now!" Lola yells.

Rory disengages the harpoon from the asteroid. When he confirms that it's clear and its line is in the process of being reeled back on board, he begins to maneuver them away from the cluster and toward the spot where the lutetium asteroid should emerge from the cluster.

"It's like watching a car accident in slow motion," Thea says.

"Let's hope so," Rory says.

Lola's knees are drawn up to her chest, and she's gently rocking back and forth as the cobalt behemoth draws closer and closer to their potential payday.

"Looks spot on," Thea says, nudging her to break the tension.

"We'll see," she says.

The next few minutes pass slowly, but Thea feels the tension on the bridge ratcheting up as the two asteroids draw closer. Closer . . .

They collide. The cobalt asteroid's mass dwarfs that of the lutetium asteroid, so the collision does little to change its path. But the lutetium asteroid is immediately sent on a new trajectory, one that, according to the updating projection, will take it out of the cluster and right into their waiting hands.

A cheer goes up on the bridge. Thea runs from person to person, hugging them all.

"Nicely done, kid," Rory says, tipping an invisible cap at Lola. "Let's finish the job."

Lola scoots her chair back to the terminal and does a quick

analysis, smiling the entire time. "The target's rotational pattern is a bit wonky, but it should be manageable even for a crusty fuck like you," she says.

Rory lets her have this one. She's earned it.

"She's a wee one, so I can probably stop the spin altogether once I grab it."

"Running close-range spectroscopy," Elliott says.

On the display, splotches of blue and brown decorate the surface of the asteroid.

"The blue is the cerium, and the brown is normal rock," he says. He strikes a key, and a ribbon of green appears near the asteroid's center. "That's the lutetium."

Rory draws a red circle around a section of the display. "If I anchor to the chunky bit here with one of our smaller shots, that'll give the miners the cleanest base to start clearing out the rock."

"That lutetium ribbon is pretty thin," Elliott says. "You're gonna have to leave some fat around it or she'll break off when we reel her aboard."

"Shouldn't be a problem," Rory says, hitting a few keys. The image on the display now shows most of the brown rock gone, leaving just blue and green portions behind. "The cerium pockets are dense, so there'll be plenty of cushion once the miners shear away the rock. But it'll take some time."

Elliott strokes his chin. "Actually, I think we should ignore most of the cerium and concentrate the miners on just giving us a healthy margin around the lutetium. Getting rid of both the rock *and* cerium would be a simpler mining pattern, and a lot faster."

"What would we be giving up if we shaved off most of the cerium?" Thea asks.

"Not much, really," Beetle says. "Cerium is almost as worthless as gold or silver these days."

"What do you say, Cap?" Lola asks.

Thea feels a sudden spark of adrenaline shoot through her. She's utterly amazed by her crew, and optimistic about what they might do together, and the feeling makes her bold, decisive.

She looks around the bridge. "Let's get this done and head back to town."

———

THE ASTEROID IS SMALL—ONLY about two football fields in length—but they need to clear almost ninety percent of the surface away from the ribbon of lutetium at its core. So they deploy a third of their fleet, twelve miners in total.

The miners descend in a single file, gliding down the harpoon line at regular intervals. Upon reaching the asteroid, the miners crawl to their designated quadrants like crabs across an ocean floor. The ones atop rock secure themselves by deploying a central corkscrew from their main body and fixing it into the substrate; the miners atop cerium simply tack-weld their feet to the metallic surface.

Lola then activates the drilling pattern. Laser picks extend from the heads of the miners and rip away the cerium and rock. Within the first few minutes, one of the miners' picks sputters and dies, but Lola is able to adjust the pattern so that two other miners compensate for the malfunction.

When no more glitches are detected, Rory backs the *Zephyr* away from the asteroid, maintaining the harpoon tether, and deploys the catch canopy. The miners are drilling at angles designed to send the debris away from the ship, but it's impossible to predict with one hundred percent accuracy how the breakaway particles will be ejected from the surface. Rory makes sure to gain enough distance from the asteroid so that the canopy will intercept anything that could possibly threaten the ship.

And then there is nothing left for the crew to do—except wait for the machines to do their job.

"Can you believe back in the day they used to do this by hand?" Beetle says. He's watching the main display, which shows what looks like a laser battle taking place down on the asteroid.

"I lost a few friends over the years," Rory says with a sigh. "Punctured suits and exploding picks. Was a shitshow back then. Thank God for these little crabby bastards." He looks to Lola. "How long?"

She spins around in her chair. "Can't be certain, but I'm projecting about thirty-eight hours before they're done."

"That gives us plenty of time to celebrate," Thea offers. "Who's in?"

The crew answers by racing each other off of the bridge. Thea quickly finds herself standing all alone, laughing.

By the time she gets to the galley, Rory is already pouring shots. Elliott hands her one, then proposes a toast.

"To the *Zephyr*. Long may she fly."

Thea throws back the dark liquor, delighting in its burn, then thrusts out her cup for another.

They finish the bottle, then a second one. Beetle makes a delicious stew, then spends the rest of the night strumming his mandolin. Rory and Elliott continue their ongoing digital rugby battle, and Thea and Lola decide to start watching a classic television series about people who've crash-landed on some sort of monster-infested island that Thea argues must be purgatory, but Lola thinks is just Hawaii before the continental plate shift swallowed it.

Elliott is the first to call it quits—probably because he's finally up a game. He heads off to bed, and Rory, as the loser, has to carry a sleeping Beetle to his bunk, the man's nose whistle well lubricated by the rum. Lola's also drifted off, curled up on the couch, so Thea throws a blanket over her.

Alone once again, she heads to the bridge. She drops into her captain's chair and dims the lights so that the only illumination is from the main display and the dancing lights of the miners' lasers. She's on the verge of drifting off herself when she feels a light touch on her leg.

She opens her eyes and finds Elliott standing above her.

"What are you doing up here?" he asks.

"Just wanted to check."

"Yeah, me too," he says, looking at the main display. "Things look good. Right on track. You should go to bed."

"Okay," she says, reaching for him.

She pulls him down and kisses him, gentle at first, then with growing intensity, all the buildup over all the days and weeks finally coming together as the perfect ending to the perfect day . . . their best day.

———

THE REST of the haul goes smoothly. The miners shear away the majority of the asteroid, leaving just a Stonehenge-like rectangle of mostly lutetium attached to the end of their line. Once they've hauled the monolith aboard and repressurized the cargo bay, the crew gathers around it for a photo to commemorate their first catch.

Thea will look at the picture often in the years to come. Lola riding piggyback on Rory; Beetle in front of them, down on his knees and flexing his biceps; Thea resting her head on Elliott's shoulder just as she'd done the night before.

There would never be another moment that she'd wish for more than the one that was captured that day. A moment of innocent happiness and joy.

Before it all went so wrong.

20

Dynamics

"I THINK I'm going to throw up," Thea says, leaning her head against the glass and staring down into the refinery, where their haul is being fed into one of the massive furnaces.

"It'll be fine. You'll see," Elliott says, rubbing her back.

"Explain it to me again."

"They heat the entire thing to around sixteen hundred degrees Celsius."

"Sixteen sixty-three, to be exact," Lola says, jumping in.

"Fine. Sixteen sixty-three. That's the melting point of lutetium."

Lola jumps in again, clearly unhappy with the pace of Elliott's explanation. "They gather the liquified lutetium, run it through a massive, magnetic molecular sieve, form it into a shippable size, and then cool it. That's when we'll get an exact weight and know what kind of moolah we're looking at."

Just then, Rory and Beetle come running up to them.

"It's at eighteen thousand," Beetle says.

Rory says nothing. He's bent over, sucking hard, trying to regain his breath. Finally he manages a few words. "Conglomerate fucks brought in a bunch of lutetium last week. Pushed the price down."

"It's still a great number," Elliott says. "I think we're gonna make it."

They pace back and forth as their catch burns down below. Beetle passes around some jerky he bought from the Norwegians. Elk, but nicely spiced and better than the glorified Slim Jims they'd been eating for the last few months. They chew silently, waiting for the foreman.

Eventually he emerges from the refinery floor. "Watts Astromining?" he says, consulting his clipboard.

"That's us," Thea says.

"After sifting normal rock and other base materials, your load contained two hundred twenty-five kilograms of cerium, which we've rubblized as discussed."

"And the lutetium?"

"It came in at just over one hundred forty kilograms. About three hundred ten pounds."

"Holy shit!"

"We've cubed it for transport to the shipyard. You can pick up your cashier's paperwork at Municipal in about an hour. Congratulations."

The foreman seemingly expects questions, because he stands there and stares at the blank looks on their faces for a few seconds before turning to go. Even after he leaves, no one moves.

"That's over two and a half million dollars," Lola finally says out loud, confirming the calculations they've all been running in their heads.

"You think that'll do it?" Thea asks, knees wobbly.

"Only one way to find out."

They all take off running for the Hub, Rory bringing up the rear and grumbling the whole way.

Thea's old buddy Molly is behind the information counter when they arrive. The teen stiffens and sets down her tablet when she sees Thea and her crew. Thea gives her a sly smile and a wave. The team stands side by side and stares up at the Leaderboard. The timestamp says the last update was ten minutes ago.

"How often does it update?" Thea asks.

"I'm sorry, what?" says Molly.

"The board. How often does it update?"

"Every hour."

"Fucking hell," Rory says. "My lungs are about to explode."

"That's not that long," Elliott says. "We can grab a bite from one of the vendors." He rests a hand on Thea's shoulder. "Come on. We'll know soon enough."

The crew turns to go, but Molly stops them.

"I can do it now if you want," she says.

"What's this now?" Thea asks, rushing back to the glass divider.

"I can refresh the stats for you. If you want."

"Why would you do that?"

The girl leans forward so only Thea can hear.

"No one ever gave me any trouble for that crack I made about Dock D, which I totally didn't mean by the way," she says, then takes out her gum and slaps it under the console between them. "Anyway . . . I assume that's because you never told anyone what I said."

"I didn't," Thea confirms.

"Well . . . that was cool of you. Thanks."

"No worries. This makes us even," Thea says, patting the glass, then stepping back to stare up at the board.

Molly goes to a computer at the rear of the booth and enters a few keystrokes. The Leaderboard clears, and the word

"Updating" appears. As they wait, Thea grabs Lola's and Elliott's hands. When Beetle joins in, Rory has no choice.

The five of them watch as the board flashes white, then black, then white again.

And the new rare earths leaders appear.

The Conglomerate remains at the top, followed by crews from China, Japan, Russia, Ukraine, Brazil, Norway, Germany, and North Korea, in that order.

And at the very bottom, in tenth place . . .

Watts Astromining.

Rory lifts Lola into the air and swings her around.

Beetle shimmies his head and shoulders through the opening in the glass divider and plants a kiss on Molly's cheek.

Thea grabs Elliott's face and kisses him long and hard. They tried to keep their relationship discreet on the journey back to the station, so this bit of PDA serves as their hard launch to their crew, who all claim later to have known all along.

Thea and her team—a civilian operation—have announced their presence in the biggest way possible.

And people take notice. Some notice due to the jubilant, raucous scene in the Hub and then later that night at the station's pub, where Rory drinks everyone under the table before passing out on top of it. More take notice when stories about the *Dark Horse at Darkside* begin to spread. The prodigal daughter and her crew of misfits.

But eventually everyone *has* to take notice, because the ascendancy of Watts Astromining does something no one expects. It marks a change in the power dynamic that has been in place for years. The playing field suddenly feels level. It gives other civilian operations hope that they, too, can compete with the big boys, and it energizes the rank-and-file refinery, ship-yard, and station workers, making them feel that people *just like them* can make a difference. The crew of the *Zephyr* become folk heroes of a sort. Famous among the lunar inhabitants.

People take notice.

Lots of people.

And not everyone likes it.

PART III

Distress Calls

21

In Crowd

"OUR RECENT EFFORTS have been concentrated on 12658 Eros, a midsized asteroid cluster coming into range in thirty days. As you can see on this slide, its astral orbit is extensive, which means it hasn't been in our neighborhood in decades."

Click.

"The leading edge of the cluster has a few hot spots, but it's mostly made up of unremarkable smaller objects and base materials. However, long-range spectral analyses indicate the presence of a large quantity of rare earth elements concentrated near the interior of the cluster."

Click.

"Unfortunately, a few of the most promising targets have serious gnat issues, so we don't recommend expending the time and resources going after them. But we think a focused effort on the lower-risk objects can still be lucrative. If you turn your attention to your tablets—"

"Explain to me why we wouldn't go after those targets."

Darcey is clearly flummoxed by the interruption. "I'm sorry, Admiral?"

"You said it yourself. There are rare earths there. Why aren't we getting them?"

Darcey clicks to a different slide. "As you can see, sir, these targets have a significant swarm of silicate and other debris encircling them, which puts them outside of normal Conglomerate harvesting protocols. I can show you a close-up if you'd like." She raises her clicker again.

"For fuck's sake! Stop clicking that damn thing and answer my question!"

Darcey sets the clicker on the conference room table and looks at the silent faces all around her. No one seems ready to jump in and offer help.

"What was your question again, Admiral?"

Brian Allgood, Admiral of the Conglomerate Astromining Fleet, gets up from his chair so abruptly that it rolls back and crashes against the conference room wall. He stomps to the front of the room and pokes at the screen. The image on Darcey's slide winks out with each finger strike.

"I'm willing to overlook the fact that you dismissed the leading edge, despite the fact there's some money to be made there, if not a lot. But these interior asteroids are lit up like Christmas trees. I'm seeing neodymium, lanthanum, terbium, and gadolinium. And you're telling me we're going to let them fly right on by because they have a few gnats floating around?"

"Sir," someone tries to interject.

"You shut the fuck up. I asked her, not you."

"Yes, sir," Darcy says. "We are."

The admiral's face reddens. His jaw is quivering as though he's only barely holding back a tsunami. But before he can explode, Darcey runs him over.

"We aren't going after the scrap out front because we're the *Conglomerate*, not the cleaning crew, sir. Let the Germans and the Chinese and the pissant civilian operations pick up the crumbs while we go after the real meat. If we spend time screwing around with the gnatty shit, you can bet that everyone else in the fleet is going to swarm the other rare-earth-rich targets. We need to be first to the trough, eat our fill, and crowd out the rest. That's how we win."

The room is silent. Stunned.

"With all due respect, sir," Darcey adds, wiping a bead of sweat off her forehead and taking a step back.

Her boss silently stares her up and down. Then a broad smile breaks out across his face.

"Everyone out!" he says, never breaking eye contact with Darcey.

The room empties quickly. The last one out is Allgood's assistant, who whispers something in his ear before leaving the room.

"What's your name again?" the admiral asks, now surprisingly calm.

"Darcey Grey. I'm a payload specialist on the *Sierra*."

"Lot of eating metaphors just now, Payload Specialist Grey. What gives?"

"Skipped breakfast, sir."

"Me too," he says. He nods at the untouched plate of pastries in the center of the conference room table, and directs her to take a seat. They both grab slices of blueberry coffee cake. "Why'd you do it?" he asks.

She swallows her bite before it's fully chewed. "Do what, sir?"

"I asked you a straight question and you actually gave me a straight answer. Not many people do that."

"I've noticed, sir. I just think . . . well, speaking frankly, sir. All of us came all the way out here to do a job. Maybe the most important job in history. And I take mine seriously. I'm a serious person. Which means I don't waste time with . . . niceties. There's just too much to do."

"You mean to say you don't like kissing ass."

"No, sir. Admiral, sir. I don't, sir," she says.

He drops his cake onto the table with a chuckle.

"Your strategy is sound. God knows I love leaving scraps to the countries that said no to joining the Conglomerate. I've made it my personal mission to fuck those nations who decided to go it alone every chance I get. But there's been a surge in civilian operations. Three are currently in operation out of Dock D, and my contacts in ship building tell me that two more are said to be starting up by the end of the year. Getting a bit crowded, don't you think?"

"It's just a fad, sir. Like boot-cut jeans. They look good on one person, then all of a sudden you can't walk down the street without seeing every dad bod and soccer mom rocking them."

"True, but the person wearing them well right now—this Watts Astromining—is climbing up the Leaderboard. I hear you know the captain."

So that's what this is about, Darcey thinks.

"Yes, sir. Thea Watts and I were in grad school together for a little while. Until she dropped out to take care of her dad."

"I knew Billy. He was as smart as they come. If his daughter is anything like him, she's going to be a force to be reckoned with."

"She is, sir. No doubt."

He slaps the table and stands.

"Here's what I want you to do," he says, waving her back into her seat as she starts to get up. "I want you to talk to her about joining us."

Darcey coughs out a few crumbs, then swallows hard. "I don't think she'd give up the *Zephyr*, sir. Her dad's legacy and all."

"No, of course she won't. We'll buy their operation. Merge it into the Conglomerate fleet. She keeps her ship and crew and flies under our flag."

Darcey sets down her pastry and wipes her sticky hands

together as she considers his proposition. "Very interesting idea, for sure. But like you said, Watts Astromining is doing well. Seventh on the Leaderboard right now. It'd have to be one hell of an offer."

"You leave that to me."

"I appreciate the vote of confidence, sir. But the *Sierra* leaves tomorrow morning for 12658 Eros. I won't be here when the *Zephyr* arrives."

"Yes, you will, Payload Specialist Grey," he says, heading for the door. "You're on my ship now. Welcome to the *Bellwether*."

22

Beacon

THEA JOLTS awake to the sound of light knocking. The clock says it's the middle of the night. She looks at Elliott to see if he heard it too, but he pulls the blanket over his head and nuzzles deeper into his pillow. She hopes the noise was just part of a dream, but the knocking comes again.

She has to crawl over Elliott to get out of the bed, then quickly fishes her robe off the ground and pulls it around her to ward off rising gooseflesh. When she cracks open her cabin door, Rory's there, fending off a jaw-splitting yawn.

"What's going on?"

"Lola wants us on the bridge."

"All of us?"

Rory glances past her as Elliott lets out a deep snore.

"Nah, leave Sleeping Beauty here. We'll call him if we need him."

Thea pulls on her boots and follows Rory. When they arrive on the bridge, Lola's bent over the communications console, fingers working the panels like a concert pianist. The image on the main display shows a miner crawling past their harpoon's anchor point.

"Everything okay down there?" Thea asks.

"The drill site's fine," she says, waving them over. "But I'm picking up a weird signal."

"From where?"

"I'm trying to figure that out now."

Lola hits a button that switches the main display from a live shot of the yttrium-laden asteroid they captured two days ago to a view of the surrounding cluster as mapped by their probes. The avatar representing the *Zephyr* is on the left side of the screen. A red glow pushes toward it from the opposite side of the display, but it gets dimmer and fragmented as it gets closer, and is nearly gone by the time it reaches the ship's avatar.

"I know the signal's being sent from somewhere on the other side of this cluster, I just can't lock it down. It's tough to even pick it up because of all the interference from the base metals in these rocks." Lola looks at them for the first time since they came onto the bridge. "I'm not one hundred percent sure, but . . . I think it's a distress call."

"Fucking hell," Rory says, moving over to get a closer look at the main display.

"Can we reel out some more line?" Thea asks. "Maybe backing off will help with reception."

"I thought of that, but we won't be able to get far enough away that it'll matter. We're still mostly surrounded by the cluster."

"Zoom in on the top edge there," Rory says, pointing to a section of the cluster displayed above their avatar.

Seconds later, the display changes to depict swirling rock and debris surrounding a large asteroid shaped like the letter C. The asteroid is slowly rotating like a wheel with a blowout on one side.

"We have a spectral analysis of this zone?" Rory asks.

"Yep, hang on."

Lola swipes and pecks at the control panel. The objects on

screen take on different hues, like cosmic Skittles tumbling through the void, but the big asteroid stays mostly dark, with only a few dots of green and yellow speckled across the surface.

"It's mostly rock, with bits of iron and cobalt," Lola says. "Where are you going with this?"

"You said the signal is getting scattered by all the garbage in the cluster, right? But it doesn't look like there's a lot in this area that'll interfere with it. What if we positioned a probe just past this C-shaped fucker?"

"Use it to bounce the signal toward us," Thea says, following Rory's line of thought. "I like it. Can you run a simulation?"

Lola gets to work, typing and swiping, and eventually nodding. The display changes to show an animation of a blinking green object fixed in the zone they just studied. It's relaying a beam of red toward the *Zephyr*'s avatar.

"It could work," she says.

"How long do you need for the modifications?" Thea asks.

"Give me twenty minutes." She rises from her seat and slaps hands with Rory on her way to the cargo bay and her fleet of probes.

"Guess we'll have to wake Sleeping Beauty after all," Rory says to Thea. "We may need to move fast."

———

THE MODIFIED probe rockets from the ship, following the flight path designed by Lola. It zips and zooms around the cluster before taking up its position on the outer edge.

At first, it doesn't pick up the signal any better than the *Zephyr* did, but that's resolved with a minor vector adjustment. Soon the mystery signal is being relayed loud and clear.

"Confirmed," Lola says. "It's a signal from a distress beacon."

"You sure it's a beacon?" Elliott asks.

"I'm positive. It's an automated mayday."

"That's not good," Beetle says, letting out a whistle and dropping into the seat next to Lola.

"Who else is out here?" Elliott asks.

Lola glances at her screen again to confirm. "Based on the latest report from Darkside, we're supposedly the only ship in this sector."

"Maybe whoever it is just lost comms?" Thea says, turning to Elliott.

He shakes his head. "Those beacons are only launched in extreme cases."

"Can we tell which ship it belongs to?"

Lola hits a key, and the distress beacon's message is displayed on the main screen. "There's no ship identifier in the message. All we're getting are coordinates."

"It doesn't matter," Rory says. "There's a code out here: Anyone in need, we go." He takes up his pilot seat and swings himself in front of the helm.

"How long will it take to get our miners on board?" Thea asks.

"A few are pretty dug in," Lola says, studying the screen in front of her. "Maybe an hour or so?"

"That's too long," says Rory. "I say we bring in the harpoon and leave the little buggers going. Best case, this whole thing is a mistake, and we can come right back."

"Agree," Beetle says, his hand in the air as if he's voting in favor of Rory's motion. Which apparently he is, because Elliott and Lola join Beetle by putting their hands in the air too. They all look to Thea, who puts her hand up as well.

"Let's do it," she says.

She can see the worry on Elliott's face and imagines he might be reliving what happened aboard his old ship before it went down.

"You okay?"

He touches her cheek, which sends an electric shock through her body. She puts her hand atop his and lets herself revel in their connection. Her worry for him, and his immediate recognition and gratitude, cements something she's been feeling build for weeks now. Something real. Something she can't deny any longer.

"Beetle and I will go get the cargo bay ready," he says. "There's no telling what we're getting ourselves into."

Got that right, she thinks, letting his hand go.

Elliott nods to Beetle, who follows him off the bridge. Thea watches them go, then sits in the captain's chair, her head and heart racing.

"All right, girlie," Rory says. "Let's get the harpoon up here and get going."

Lola brings up a view of the surface and activates the sequence that retracts the teeth on the harpoon bolt. Soon the bolt yanks free from its anchor point, and the *Zephyr* is untethered from the asteroid.

As the line is being reeled in, Rory slowly backs them away from the cluster. He maneuvers through a sparse debris field toward their relay probe and the area with the C-shaped asteroid. Then, as the field finally clears, he punches the main thrusters, and they head off toward the source of the distress call.

———

TIME IS critical when you're responding to an emergency beacon at sea. The longer it takes you to get to the beacon, the farther ocean currents will carry it away from the ship in distress. This problem of drift is magnified in the frictionless void of space. Without an anchoring mechanism, an emergency beacon's launch momentum will simply persist, sending it farther and farther away and complicating any rescue scenario. To compensate, the International Astromining Alliance engineers designed emergency beacons that can stay at a fixed distance from their mothership. Every beacon carries enough fuel to maintain its relative position for up to two weeks, which is the length of time that most life support systems can sustain a crew after a ship becomes disabled. If you find the beacon in that timeframe, you'll find the ship and her crew.

If you don't . . .

So when the *Zephyr* loses the mystery beacon's signal two hours into their rescue operation, they fear the worst. Six hours later, when they arrive at the location of the last transmission, those fears are confirmed.

Twisted aluminum and steel twirl and tumble amid a debris field that spans nearly three kilometers. Flash-frozen beads of liquid reflect the *Zephyr*'s searchlights like marbles of tempered glass scattered across a highway. There are mangled plates, beams, and trusses. Dented canisters, crates, bins, and boxes. Shredded wires, plastic piping, and insulation. All of it mixed with the stuff of everyday life: clothes, boots, packets of food, a coffeemaker, canvas bags, a toilet.

And at the heart of the destruction, two halves of a ship, ripped at the middle and spilling its guts into space.

"*Mon dieu*," Beetle says, making the sign of the cross.

"Who is it?" Thea asks.

"Can't tell yet from this angle," Rory says. "I'm going to try and get closer."

He engages the starboard thrusters. Intermittent arcs of light and bright flashes emanate from inside the ship as the *Zephyr* swings around the carcass.

"Lola, scan for radiation," Elliott says. "That looks like the reactor to me."

"Yeah, numbers are off the chart," she says, her voice

cracking. "But we should be okay so long as we don't get too close."

They skirt almost one hundred eighty degrees around the devastation before they can make out a hull insignia and the image of a Norwegian flag.

"It's the *Lillehammer*," Rory says.

Thea's heart breaks as she takes in the destruction. The Norwegians were so kind to her. She'll never forget how they rallied around her and took care of her on their journey to the moon, which feels like a lifetime ago.

But before the crew's shock can fully register, a person in an EVA suit drifts through their searchlights.

And they're moving.

23

Survivor

No one says a word. No one breathes.

They stare at the main display, waiting for the drifting figure to move again. To confirm that what they saw wasn't some sort of shared illusion or a bit of groupwide wishful thinking that amid so much destruction they'd find a beacon of hope.

The person's leg kicks. Arm twitches.

And they all start talking at once.

"Oh my God!"

"You see that? You all saw that, right? It wasn't just me?"

"What do we do?"

"Oy, calm down."

"We have to get them."

"Can we get closer?"

"I can run a multi-object velocity estimate to try and plot a way through the debris field. If we position our hull in such a way that it absorbs the brunt of the——"

"Everyone, shut the fuck up!" Rory yells.

As they all catch their breath, Rory points to the display.

"Boys, if I fire the harpoon into the stern, right about

there, do you think one of you could trolley down and grab them?"

"That's probably our best bet, yes?" Beetle says. "But it has to be now. We don't know how long they've been out there."

"What if you hit something vital in that part of the ship?" Thea asks. "Or some*one*?"

"The fuel tanks are the only thing back there in this class of ship," Lola says. "And considering all the frozen liquid around here, my guess is the tanks are empty."

"All right then," Thea says. "Do it."

"We should trail a second trolley down the line too," Elliott puts in, "and run it from the bay so we can get them onboard as fast as possible."

"Agreed," says Beetle, already on his feet. "I'll go down and hook them, you run them back up the line. Let's go."

"Hold on," Elliott says, holding out his fist. "You know the drill."

Beetle stands in front of him, fist out, then starts the count to three. "*Un, deux*—"

"Wait," Thea interrupts. "No rock-paper-scissors. Beetle, you go out. Ell, you handle things in the bay. I need you to stay on board in case we need to come up with a plan B."

"But this is how we've always done it," Elliott says, fist still held out.

"Not anymore."

Beetle looks back and forth between them, then races off the bridge. Elliott turns to Thea, clearly annoyed. She can tell he wants to say more, but there's no time.

His *Aye, Captain* is terse, laced with contempt.

Rory and Lola exchange glances as Elliott hustles after Beetle, then they turn their attention to the *Lillehammer*'s hull.

"Gimme a grid," Rory says.

A red grid appears on the display across the *Lillehammer*'s hull, with alphanumeric notations along the x and y axes.

Rory studies it for a few seconds, considering his options. "I'm thinking C-three?"

Lola's fingers fly over her console. "That should work," she says.

Rory enters a few commands, then activates the shipwide hailer.

"I'm sending the harpoon now. Stand by, boys."

Beetle's voice comes through the control panel. "Roger."

Rory hits a button, and seconds later the harpoon rips into the *Lillehammer*'s stern, striking the grid at C-3, dead center. The slack in the harpoon line ripples behind the entry point but is quickly drawn taut. Rory sits back and strokes his beard, which is something Thea's only ever seen him do when he's thinking really hard or he's nervous, like when he's bluffing in poker. She's nervous too, watching the floating figure meters away from their harpoon line. Given the extent of the destruction here, saving even one person would be a miracle.

Come on, damn it. Give us a sign. Anything.

The figure just drifts, no longer moving.

Then Beetle appears on the display, descending along the harpoon line with a second cable trolley in tow.

"Come on, baby," Rory says, tugging strands of his beard loose.

Lola paces next to him like a tiger in a cage. Then she pounces, reaching past Rory to key the comms system on his control panel.

"Beetle, do you read me? You're going too fast."

It's Elliott who responds. "I'm running both trolleys from the bay," he says. "Don't worry. We have a plan."

Now it's Thea's turn to lean over and hit a button on Rory's controls. A small window pops onto the main display, showing the interior of the harpoon bay. Next to the cannon, Elliott is in an EVA suit and bent over the control kiosk that manages the trolley system. He senses the camera on him and gives it a thumbs-up before resuming his work.

Beetle begins to let out his lifeline. A lot of it.

"That's too much," Lola says, reaching for the comms again.

But Rory grabs her wrist. "Leave them be. The boys know what they're doing."

Beetle's cable trolley slows to a stop a few meters from the adrift Norwegian crewman. The momentum from his rapid descent carries his body upward like the ball at the end of a pendulum. Once he's parallel to the crewman, the cable trolley starts drawing back toward the *Zephyr*. At the same time, Beetle lets out more of his line, which counteracts the snapback that he'd have experienced from the trolley suddenly pulling him in the opposite direction. As a result of Beetle and Elliott's coordinated effort, Beetle begins to slowly drift toward the Norwegian.

The distance between them closes . . .

Beetle reaches out . . .

. . . and grabs the drifting figure.

He activates his lifeline reel. As it takes up the slack, he grabs the carabiner from the trailing trolley and connects it to the Norwegian's EVA suit. Moments later, the Norwegian is being pulled back toward the *Zephyr*.

"Yeah, buddy!" Lola screams, drumming the back of Rory's chair then whacking the top of his head like a cymbal.

"That boy is a fucking madman!" Rory says.

Thea lets out a huge sigh. She waits for her wobbly knees to settle, then races off the bridge. Rory and Lola aren't far behind. By the time they reach the cargo bay, Elliott and Beetle are already hauling the Norwegian crewman into the airlock separating it from the harpoon bay. Elliott initiates the pressurization and decontamination process, in case of any residual radiation from the *Lillehammer*'s reactor.

It feels like forever, but the airlock indicator finally turns from red to green and the door hisses open.

Thea immediately drops next to the Norwegian. A splatter of red covers the inside of the helmet, preventing her from making out a face. She finds the latches on either side and takes a deep breath before twisting the helmet and lifting it off.

The young man inside has blood everywhere, even dripping from his white-blond hair. More blood burbles from his mouth as he takes a shallow, ragged breath.

His crystal-blue eyes flutter.

"Oh God, Jakob," Thea says, then squeezes his gloved hand the way he did hers on the shuttle to the moon all those months ago.

24

Stakes

JAKOB LETS out a feral howl when they try to move him. His head thrashes back and forth, his eyes wild with pain.

"I'll get a med kit," Lola says, then races away.

"Jakob, look at me," Thea says, her face so close to his that she has to blink away droplets of blood spraying from between his clenched teeth. "It's me, Thea. Do you remember? From the shuttle."

His eyes lock on hers. She smiles down at him, nodding her head, trying to reassure him as he struggles to make sense of what's happening.

"Thea?" he says, tears pooling in the corners of his eyes.

"Yes, it's me. I'm here."

"How?"

"You're going to be okay. We've got you."

He suddenly becomes aware of the people standing around him and where he is—and more importantly, where he no longer is, which seems to offer him a brief moment of respite.

Rory kneels on Jakob's opposite side. "Can you tell us what happened, son?"

Jakob winces, teeth clenched, blood dribbling over his chin. Then finds the strength.

"We were refueling. Our sipper door jammed when we pulled in the line. Ice buildup—"

A wave of pain washes over him.

"Leak around the intake valve," he continues after the pain subsides. "I was doing an EVA to fix it when I felt—"

He clutches his midsection. Muscles, tendons, and veins striate his neck as his entire body seizes. He shudders, twists—

Then stops.

His arms flop onto the deck and his head lolls to the side.

Thea rests a hand on his cheek and gently turns his face toward her. His eyes roll up into his head as he teeters on the verge of consciousness.

"Come on, Jakob. Stay with me."

But Rory leans in close and presses the question. "What did you feel?"

Jakob manages to focus his eyes on Thea, but it's obviously a struggle. "Vibra . . ."

"Vibrate," Rory says. "The ship vibrated?"

Jakob sucks in a deep breath. His chest rises off the deck. Fingers curl into claws. Eyes dart side to side as he mouths something silently, again and again and again.

He begins to convulse.

Lola tears around the corner, medical bag in hand, but pauses when she sees Rory and Thea struggling to hold Jakob's flailing arms and legs still. Elliott helps, his hands gripping Jakob's blood-slicked head in an effort to keep him from smacking his skull against the deck.

"Give me the bag!" Beetle says, clapping his hands together.

Lola hands it over and he digs through the contents, tossing aside rolls of tape and bandages as he searches. But before he can find what he's after, Jakob goes still.

Rory places his hand on Jakob's chest and an ear near his mouth.

"What's happening?" Thea says.

She's waved off by Rory as he tries to listen. And then he's suddenly straddling Jakob's body and administering chest compressions.

Beetle digs an autoinjector from the medical bag and jabs it into Jakob's neck. Then he pinches Jakob's nose and waits for Rory's count.

Thea backs away to give the two men room. Elliott moves next to her and takes her hand, then waves Lola over to join them.

Sweat drips from Rory's face as he administers a steady stream of compressions, pausing only long enough for Beetle to breathe bursts of oxygen into Jakob's bloody mouth.

They work hard, but to no avail.

After fifteen minutes, Thea puts an end to it.

"That's enough. Let him rest."

Rory punches the floor as Beetle wipes his mouth, leaving a red smear on the back of his hand.

"Thank you for trying," Thea says.

"I'm sorry for your friend, *ma chère*."

"Did you find out anything before . . . you know," Lola says, trailing off apologetically.

"Not much," Rory says. "He was outside when it happened, poor bastard." He leans over and closes Jakob's eyelids.

"What about the rest of the crew?" Lola asks.

"We're still attached," Elliott says. "Beetle and I could go over and look for other survivors."

"No way," says Thea.

"There could be survivors, Thea. Maybe they sealed off part of the ship. Or managed to get into suits before shit went bad. We don't know."

"You're right—we *don't* know!" Thea snaps back. "We have no idea what happened over there. Which is why you're not going."

"She's right, Ell," Rory puts in. "That kind of damage can only have come from the reactor. We're talking major radiation."

Elliott looks like he wants to argue the point, then concedes. "We should at least do a thorough sweep. Look for any signs of atmosphere over there. Just to be one hundred percent sure."

After a few seconds of silence, Thea wrenches her eyes from Jakob's face and nods to Lola. She signals to Rory, and the two of them head for the bridge.

"Are you okay?" Elliott says to Thea.

"I'm fine." She tries to make it sound true. Rising to her feet, she heads for the door, then stops. "Can you guys . . .?"

"We'll take care of him," Beetle says softly.

Without looking back and with only a small *thanks*, Thea hurries out of the bay.

———

As Rory predicted, radiation saturates the shredded portions of the ship. There's no longer any doubt. The *Lillehammer*'s main reactor experienced some sort of catastrophic failure.

Thea and her crew circle the wreckage for hours, desperate to find any signs of life, no matter how improbable. They transmit on every fleet frequency, scan for temperature fluctuations, power consumption, and pressure variations. They even send out a fan of flares near the *Lillehammer*'s bridge, hoping the signal might rouse someone. Let them know they aren't alone. That there's reason to hope.

But all their efforts are met with silence.

Finally, as the last flare sputters and dies, leaving the *Lillehammer* in darkness, Thea calls off the search.

"Lola, drop a marker beacon. We'll broadcast the location back to Darkside for a recovery crew. Rory, let's get back to that cluster and finish the job."

She swivels around in her chair and begins making her way off the bridge.

"Hold on," Elliott says. "You want to go back to mining?"

Thea turns and stares at him, confused. "Why wouldn't we?"

"Come on, Thea. Really?"

Exhaustion hits her like a body blow. Her limbs feel like sacks of sand, and the blood pulsing at her temples seems ready to escape all over the bridge. She needs to lie down more than she's ever needed anything, ever.

"Where is he?" she asks.

"You mean Jakob?"

"Yeah. What did you do with his body?"

Beetle jumps in, clearly trying to diffuse whatever's going on. "We put him . . . I mean, the body bag, in the harpoon bay. For the, umm, cold. That way . . ."

"Good. So we can go then?"

"Thea, listen," Elliott says. "Protocol for when something like this happens is for the surviving crew to get back to Darkside as quickly as possible."

"But there *is* no surviving crew." Thea rubs a ravine into her forehead.

"You know what I mean."

"Darkside is over two weeks away, Ell. Meanwhile, our miners are less than a day from here crawling around on my next set of docking fees, overdue supply bills, and your next paycheck. Jakob ain't gonna get any deader, so we go get what we came for and then we'll take him home."

"I agree," Rory adds. "We should be able to get our haul

on board pretty quick. Plus think of all the fuel and time we'll save. I know it feels shitty, but it makes sense."

"Great. Settled then," Thea says, and quickly stalks off the bridge.

Elliott catches up to her in the corridor. He grabs her arm and spins her around.

"What's going on with you?" he says.

"Not now, Ell. I need to close my eyes for a while."

"Look, Thea, I get it. Especially seeing as you got to know the *Lillehammer* crew a bit. But you realize this kind of thing hits us all, right? When a ship goes down like that, it reminds everyone what's at stake."

"You don't need to tell me how this works. I may not have been doing this as long as you, but I understand. Trust me. I spent my whole life listening to the horror stories of ships going down and wondering when something like that was going to happen to my dad."

"I'm sure you have. But there's a big difference when it's *your* ship."

Thea shoves him against the wall, suddenly infuriated.

"Don't you think I *know* that? Jesus, Ell! I worry about how my decisions affect you guys every waking moment of every single day. I know that if I make the wrong call, *you* guys are the ones who pay the price!"

"Is that why you sent Beetle out there instead of me?"

She takes a step back, caught off-guard.

"What?"

"Is it?" he asks again.

"I sent Beetle because he was the right person for the job!"

"I don't believe you," Elliott says. "I think you did it because of what's happening between us."

"That's not true."

"I think you sent Beetle out there instead of me because you were afraid."

"Of course I was afraid! I didn't want to send *either* of you. But we had to do something."

"So you made the call?"

"Goddamn right I did!"

"Just like the call right now to go back to the cluster instead of returning to Darkside?"

"That's the job, Ell! Mine and mine alone."

"But it's not," he says, stepping in front of her so she can't disengage. "You're the captain, Thea. No one denies that. The *Zephyr* is yours. But it's *ours*, too. We're a team. More than that, we're a family. You're not alone anymore. That's the difference I'm talking about. You don't have to do this by yourself."

She feels her eyes welling with tears. From his words, certainly. But also from the pressures of the day taking their toll and the sadness crashing in on her while her defenses are at their lowest.

"We're out here doing this bizarre, batshit-crazy job," he continues, "but at least we're doing it together. So long as you don't shut us out. Don't shut me out, Thea."

Suddenly exhausted, she leans into him and rests her head on his chest. "When I saw him floating out there, all alone . . . all I wanted to do was get him. No matter what it took. But then I imagined it was you, and my insides turned to ice."

She pushes back and meets his gaze.

"You're right, Ell. I'm afraid of losing *this*," she says, resting a hand on his heart. "And I know that could be a liability. But I can't help it."

"You don't have to. I feel it too."

"Then what are we going to do?"

"We're gonna make Beetle do all the dangerous shit, obviously," he says, then quickly ducks the smack aimed at his head. He chuckles. "It's gonna be okay. I promise."

"But you can't. You can't *promise* me that."

He takes her hands in his and looks into her teary eyes.

Kisses her forehead. The tension coursing through her slowly dissipates.

"You're right, I can't," he says. "But what I have here—not just you and me, but everyone, and this ship, and even the job itself—makes me happier than I've ever been in my life. So no, I can't promise that everything's always going to be okay. But I *can* promise you that I'm going to fight like hell. For all of us."

She takes his hand and turns to pull him after her down the corridor, but he hesitates.

"I should go check on them," he says, thumbing toward the bridge. "They might need me."

"Right now, I need you more," she says. "Captain's orders."

25

Thief in the Night

THEA WATCHES the dark liquid stream into her mug. Inhales the rich, earthy aroma and delights in the instant endorphin rush it provides. The espresso is critical, especially after a night that brought very little sleep, thanks to the unshakable image of Jakob's blood-splattered face playing over and over in her mind. But today, feeling each and every one of the hundreds of thousands of miles she is from home, the subtle scents of dirt and nuts and charcoal rising from the thick head of foam are even more important to her than the caffeine kick.

"Thea, we need you on deck," Rory says over the hailer.

She loads another pod into the machine, definitely feeling a double shot is in order, and then keys the comms panel.

"On my way."

When she reaches the bridge, she finds Rory, Beetle, and Elliott standing in front of a live view of the cluster they'd been mining before responding to the *Lillehammer*'s distress beacon. Lola is head down, working at her station.

"I've triple-checked," she says, fingers a blur on her keyboard. "These are the right coordinates."

"What's going on?"

172

"It's gone."

"What are you talking about?" Thea says, joining them.

Elliott points to the main screen. "The asteroid we were mining. We can't find it."

"Ping the miners across all frequencies," Rory says, then heads back to the navigation controls.

"I know that. Don't you think I know that?" Lola snaps.

"Could the radiation from the *Lillehammer* have affected our sensors?" Thea asks before Rory and Lola's bickering can take flight.

"Nah, it'd be all or nothing," Rory says. "They'd either work or——"

Lola cuts him off. "Got something," she says.

The image on the main screen zooms in on one of their miners. It's floating in space, lifeless, and anchored to a jagged shard of rock. A cloud of debris encircles the machine, bits of rock and metal bouncing off its body.

"Bloody hell," Rory says, pounding on the arms of his chair.

"Someone picked our pockets," Beetle grumbles, then issues what Thea can only imagine is a string of profanity in French.

"Maybe a rogue object came through and knocked her off course," Thea says. "A comet or something."

"I scanned the field and compared it to our previous map," Lola says. "All the objects in this cluster are in their same relative positions. And the odds of something ripping through here and striking only *our* asteroid are astronomically small. No pun intended."

"Plus, there'd be a bigger and more widespread debris field from that sort of collision," Rory adds.

"So you're telling me that someone came by and just . . . scooped up the whole damn thing. How many ships can do that?"

"A few, actually," Elliott says. "That rock was too big for *us* to handle in one gulp, but its child's play for some of the big boys out here."

Elliott turns to Rory. "The miner's onboard sensors may have captured enough to tell us what happened. Can you get us close?"

"Roger," Rory says. "But she's probably not gonna let go of that piece of rock she's holding on to. It looks too big to come in through the harpoon bay hatch. You should go out the cargo bay instead."

Not again, Thea thinks, but she doesn't let her anxiety show. She faces Elliott.

"Walk me through it."

He nods. "Beetle mans the controls while I go out and get a tow line on the miner. If I can get it to power up, I'll have it release the bit of rock it's connected to. If it won't, Beetle reels me in and together we bring in the miner."

Though neither mentions it, it's undeniable they're both thinking about their recent argument . . . and maybe the reconciliation afterwards, which is another reason for this morning's double shot.

"So?" Elliott says. "What do you think?"

Thea downs the rest of her cup. "I think you've got work to do," she says, "and I need another espresso."

———

ONCE DEPLOYED ON A JOB, miners work as a unit and are able to compensate for changing conditions or malfunctions. But when a miner is disconnected from its group, it goes into protective mode, shutting down most of its systems to preserve power, which is what happened to the miner drifting just outside the *Zephyr*'s cargo bay.

Rory maneuvers the ship to within fifty meters of the

miner, matching the machine's trajectory and spin, and Elliott floats out to meet it.

"You got me, Beet?" Elliott says, fogging the inside of his helmet. The last time he did an EVA, he kind of blew up, so he's a bit on edge, though he won't admit it, especially not to Thea. Climate control kicks in, sucking away the fog so he can see clearly.

"Roger. What's your status?"

The miner is still anchored to an iron-rimmed section of the missing asteroid's crust, and from this close, Elliott can see the tack welds at the base of the miner's feet. "She's on there pretty good. No chance of disconnecting it unless I can get it to power up. Stand by."

He secures the tow line to the miner's body, then swings around to the opposite side to access the primary control panel. A few screws later, he's inside.

He tries several times to bring the miner back online, but it's unresponsive.

"I can't get it to power up," he says. "We'll have to bring the whole thing in."

"Roger," Beetle says. "You ready to come back?"

Elliott double-checks the heavy carabiner connected to the miner. "Ready."

The tug against his lifeline is gentle. Beetle's a pro, so Elliott's ride back to the *Zephyr* is a breeze. Once inside, he disconnects his lifeline and gets ready to help guide in the miner and fragment of asteroid it's clutching. Beetle engages the motor and begins to reel in the miner's tow line.

"Stand by," Beetle says, and gets a quick *Roger* from Rory, who's monitoring their progress from the bridge along with Thea and Lola.

Everything is going smoothly until one of the welds on the miner's feet breaks, sending the miner and asteroid fragment onto a new trajectory. Beetle kills the motor and watches as the end of the tow line disappears out of sight.

"What was that?" Rory asks.

"Weld snapped. She's vectoring starboard," Beetle replies.

"I see it. Hang on."

Rory uses the port thrusters, and the end of the tow line slowly comes back into view. After a bit of maneuvering, the miner is once again centered on the cargo bay doors. Beetle reengages the motor and reels the miner to the precipice of the opening, then Elliott attaches it to the crane hoist. Minutes later, the miner is on board.

As soon as the cargo bay repressurizes and artificial gravity is re-established, Lola races to the fallen miner as if to an emergency room patient. But Thea moves directly to Elliott.

"You good?" she asks as soon as his helmet comes off and she sees his sweaty hair.

"Piece of pie," he says.

"Don't worry, Captain. I'm fine too," Beetle says with a sarcastic smile.

Rory has come down as well, and hovers over Lola, who's fiddling with something inside the miner's primary control panel. "How's it looking, girlie?"

"Power coupling's fried." She yanks out a black rectangle of metal with a ribbon of multicolored wires dangling from one end. "Hopefully the data on the drive is intact."

As she takes the drive to one of the cargo bay terminals to run it through diagnostic and recovery programs, the crew examines the remains of the asteroid.

"Take a look at this," Elliott says, pointing to a melted edge of the asteroid fragment.

"Could that have been from the other miners?" Thea asks.

"No," Rory says, "angle's all wrong. Plus look at the beading. I'd bet that's from a harpoon plasma cone."

"A what?"

"Some of the big trawlers have plasma cutters attached to their harpoon lines. The cutter spins around a fixed point on the line and blasts out a cone of plasma that shears off everything beyond where the harpoon is lodged into an object. It ain't precise, and you can lose a lot of material in the process, but it's fast."

"So it's a perfect solution when you don't want to get caught with your hand in someone's cookie jar," Thea says, slapping the melted edge.

Lola waves them over to the terminal. "Guys, I've got something."

When they've all gathered around, she plays a video captured by the recovered miner's camera. At first it just shows the surface of the asteroid, with another miner visible and crawling along a ridge in the distance, but she's queued it up to start just slightly before the moment of truth. Suddenly the entire image shakes and a cloud of debris rises from the surface.

"Go back to before the image goes wonky," Rory says. "And slow it down. I thought I saw something."

Lola goes back to before the camera begins to shake, and following Rory's instructions, she zooms in past the crawler on the ridge. This time they all see it: a quick streak against the blackness of space, something from off screen racing through the image and hitting the asteroid.

"That's the bastard's harpoon, right there!"

Now Lola fast-forwards. The debris in front of the lens thickens, then begins to disperse. Just before it completely clears, a blast of white light fills the screen.

"And *there's* the plasma cutter," Elliott says.

Lola sets the video to play at normal speed again. Minutes later, the light is gone, and dust and debris once again dominate the view. But the dust is now also interspersed with occasional clear shots of space. Dust, then space, then dust again as the now free-floating miner tumbles.

They watch it for what seems like an eternity, their anger growing in the face of the damning evidence.

Thea breaks the silence. "Go back!"

Lola stops the video and slowly rewinds, not sure what she's looking for until Thea taps the screen.

"There," she says.

Lola freezes the frame and zooms in. Through a scattering of debris, they can just make out the dull gray hull of a ship.

And what might be letters.

"Can you clean up the image?" Thea asks.

Lola opens a Pandora's box of windows on the screen. It's hard to follow what she's doing, but after a minute of crunching and cleaning, the fuzzy image grows less fuzzy.

The name of the ship is now clear as day.

The *Bellwether*.

26

Shock and Awe

THE CONGLOMERATE DOCKS are always busy, but the intensity increases whenever their flagship is in town. As Thea pushes through the crowd, she gazes up through Dock A's transparent roof at the massive ship docked above. *My entire ship could probably fit inside that bastard's cargo bay*, she thinks, watching the ship's bay doors begin to close.

She stops two young crewmen as they step off the lift.

"Where's the captain?" she asks.

"You mean the *admiral*."

"Yeah, fine. Where is he?"

"Who are you?"

Thea points at the *Zephyr* insignia on her jacket sleeve.

The two men exchange glances. "I don't know where he is," one says, and they both turn to go.

She maneuvers in front of them. "Bullshit." She makes a show of reading the names stitched above their breast pockets. "Is he up there?"

"The admiral's a busy man. You're gonna have to make an appointment just like everyone else."

Thea makes an effort to turn down the heat a notch.

"Look, fellas, I'm sorry. I really need to talk to him right away. Can one of you please just radio up top and let someone know that Captain Thea Watts is here to see him?"

Their nods make her think that maybe the catching-flies-with-honey thing has some merit.

"Please. It's important," she adds in a final attempt to motivate them.

The two men look at each other, then break out into grins. "What's the matter, Captain?" one of them says. "*Lose* something?"

So much for honey.

Thea smiles and nods along as if she's in on the joke.

Her chest tightens.

Ears start to burn as the blood rushes to her head.

The tension builds, looking for release . . . and finds it when her haymaker connects with the man's chin.

His partner drops his shoulder pack, ready to intervene, but he's too late to protect his crotch from Thea's knee.

As he drops to the floor, the first guy bear-hugs Thea from behind, pinning her arms to her sides. He lifts her off the ground, swinging her away from his fallen colleague as she kicks and twists and tries to break his grip.

"Put her down!" a voice shouts.

They all turn toward a woman standing with her hands on her hips. She's dressed in Conglomerate command blue.

Darcey.

"Lieutenant, this woman—"

"Do it, now!"

The man drops Thea, then quickly raises his arms in defense as she wheels around on him.

"Thea, knock it off!" Darcey orders. Then to the two men: "You two, get lost."

The man who'd hoisted Thea off the ground picks up his friend, who's clearly still feeling the aftereffects of Thea's knee.

They give quiet *Sorry ma'am*s to Darcey, then shove their way through a smattering of onlookers.

"What the fuck do you think you're doing?" Darcey says, grabbing Thea by the elbow and steering her away from the crowd.

"Lieutenant?" Thea asks.

"We can't all be instant *captains*. Some of us have to work our way up the ladder."

"When did you join the *Bellwether*?"

"A few weeks ago."

"So then, *you* stole from me too."

"I don't know what you're talking about."

"Come on, Lieutenant Grey, sure you do," Thea says. She eyes her old friend up and down. "You've come a long way from our college days. Back then you wouldn't be caught dead working for the Conglomerate, let alone be one of their brass."

"I grew up," Darcey says, meeting Thea's glare. "And it's time you do the same."

It's been a long time, but the look on Darcey's face is a familiar one. When she's focused, she goes still. All business. Deadly serious and calm.

"What are you talking about?" Thea asks.

"Come with me," Darcey says.

———

THEA WANTS to hold on to her indignation, focus on the injustice of it all. She and her crew answered a call for help, put their ship and their lives in harm's way, and were rewarded with treachery. She wants to demand immediate retribution and secure what she feels is a much-deserved apology. She wants to regain what was lost—no, what was *taken*. But the second she steps off the lift into the *Bellwether*'s enormity, all she wants to do is catch her breath.

Her bitterness and anger are temporarily swept aside in favor of a much different emotion: awe.

The smooth, curved walls of the ship's cargo bay radiate a soft glow, filling the space with a warm, inviting light. Hoists, cranes, and slings are suspended from elegant parabolic arches that curve throughout the cavernous space, complementing a twistingly complex system of conveyor belts and chutes. The clangs, bangs, and revs of the machinery blend together into what feels like a syncopated rhythm, creating a mesmerizing space jazz worthy of Marsalis or Davis, or at least the Mos Eisley Cantina band.

Darcey leads her down what appears to be the *Bellwether's* main thoroughfare. Rounded portals to Jefferies tubes are spaced along the passageway at regular intervals, and steady streams of people flow into and out of corridors that branch off like arteries. Everyone is in crisp uniforms, walking with great purpose. Even so, many can't help but give Thea a side-long glance as she and Darcey pass.

They turn a corner and nearly collide with a woman who steps out of a door marked *Engineering.* Her head's down and her eyes are focused on the tablet in her hand, so she barely registers Thea and Darcey's presence before sidestepping around them. But it gives Thea an opportunity to gaze through the open door into the beating heart of the *Bellwether*.

A spiral catwalk wraps around a tall, cylindrical reactor, bespeckled with lighted panels and rainbow wire clusters. A thick blue tube emblazoned with *H2O* extends from the reactor to the wall. Several feet below and on the opposite side, a larger red tube elbows out and runs parallel to the reactor, disappearing somewhere below the catwalk.

Thea can't help but marvel at the engine that powers the Conglomerate's astromining dominance. She senses the reactor's power, can actually *feel* it on her skin and in her lungs, the very air charged with an electric current. She takes a tentative step forward, but the door slides closed, shutting her out.

She notices Darcey is watching her, sporting an intense look of satisfaction.

"I know, right?" Darcey says, then waves Thea forward.

Soon they're sitting at a small round table in one of the officers' conference rooms. Thea pretends to admire the table's rich oak surface.

"How've you been?" Darcey asks.

Thea gives her an *Are you serious* look. "We really gonna do small talk? Or are you going to give me back what's rightfully mine?"

"We'll get to that," Darcey says, tapping something into a flat inset panel on the table.

"No, we'll get to it now, because that's the only reason I'm here."

Darcey sighs. "You know the rules, Thea. Any unmanned target remains open to acquisition by other mining operations unless the target in question has been registered with Municipal."

"That's bullshit, and you know it. Our miners were crawling all over that rock. If you had pinged any one of them, our call sign would have come up. And this wasn't some spray-and-pray strategy—we didn't scatter miners everywhere as a way of laying claim to the whole cluster. That rock you stole was the only target we were mining."

"Doesn't change the fact that you weren't there, Thea."

"We weren't *there* because we were answering a *distress call*. In fact, we were the only ship who did."

"I know. I read the report you filed," Darcey says, reaching across the table and taking Thea's hand before Thea realizes what's happening. "What a tragic accident."

Thea snatches her hand away. "Why are we here, Darcey?"

Darcey sits back and folds her arms. "Jeez, Thea. I'm just trying to be nice. I didn't mean to *offend* you."

"Don't worry, I've gotten used to it."

Now Darcey's anger rises to match Thea's. "What did I ever *do* to you, anyway?"

"Nothing," Thea says, waving dismissively. "Nothing at all."

"You *left*, Thea!"

"To answer a distress call!"

"I'm not talking about that. I'm talking about Cambridge."

Caught off-guard, Thea pauses, but not for long.

"How dare you. I didn't have a choice," she says. "My dad had no one else."

"I know that. But it feels like you're *blaming* me because I got to finish and you didn't."

"Don't flatter yourself."

"It was hard on me too, you know. We used to be a team," Darcey says, a hitch in her voice. "We *used* to be friends."

"Oh, I'm sure it was *awful* for you, sucking up all the recognition with me out of the way. International Astromining Alliance grant winner and Cambridge royalty. Must have been terrible."

"I'm not going to apologize for my success."

"I'm not asking you to."

"Then what do you want?"

"I want what you *stole* from me!" Thea snaps, slapping her hand on the table.

"Which time?" Darcey says, leveling her gaze at Thea. "Then, or now?"

Thea feels the blow deep in her marrow, not only because of the implicit insult, but because of the truth hidden inside it.

"We were never friends," she says. "You know that, right? You were just convenient to me, so I kept you around. But we were *always* rivals. You were my adversary then, and you're my adversary now."

As Thea's words land, the door opens, and Brian Allgood glides into the conference room, all smiles and saccharine.

"Hold that thought," Darcey says, then stands at attention.

"You must be the intrepid Thea Watts," Allgood says, taking Thea's hand in his and holding on a few seconds too long. "We've all been watching your rise up the Leaderboard. Good work, I must say. Big fan."

Thea manages to get her hand back, but only because Allgood decides to pull up a chair across from Thea, positioning it so that their knees are almost touching. Despite the closeness, he still leans forward to the point that Thea has to sit all the way back in her chair to maintain a modicum of personal space.

"Catching up with your old buddy here?" he asks, thumbing toward Darcey but never breaking eye contact with Thea.

"You could say that."

"Were you excited when she told you the news?"

"We didn't quite get there, Admiral," Darcey says.

"Goodie, then I get to do it." Allgood flashes his blindingly white teeth like a cannibal on a nudist beach.

"Do what?" Thea asks, pushing her chair back a few inches.

"You know, before all this . . ." he says, twirling a hand above his head, "I was a warden."

He pauses for dramatic effect, slowly nodding his head and grimacing as if he too can't believe his own humble beginnings.

"Yep, I looked after the residents of Angola Penitentiary in the great state of Louisiana for almost eleven years. Ten years, four months, and twenty-seven days to be exact. Do you know how it is that I know it was exactly ten years, four months, and twenty-seven days? Because that's what I'm all about, Ms. Watts. Precision."

"Really now? Do tell me more."

Allgood is undeterred by Thea's sarcasm. "Precision is how you maintain order," he says. "It's what keeps the trains running on time. Precision is how you keep a prison full of animals, guarded by goons and bullies, from tearing itself to pieces. You establish a system that allows for zero variability, and then you make sure that everyone follows that system. The same holds true up here. Believe me. The Conglomerate isn't the best because we're the best-funded operation, though we are by a long shot, or because we have the best technology, which we most certainly do. We're the top dog up here because of *precision*. Full. Stop."

"And what if people don't?" Thea asks, taking advantage of the break in his monologue.

"Don't what?"

"Follow your system?"

For the first time since he entered the room, Brian Allgood's smile fades. It's brief, and he quickly catches himself. He puffs out his cheeks and lets loose with a fake chuckle. But in that momentary lapse of his practiced good humor, Thea's certain she's dealing with a man accustomed to getting his way.

Thea doesn't wait to hear his response. She doesn't care. "Thanks for the philosophy lesson," she says. "But honestly, Admiral, the only thing I want right now is my haul."

"*Our* haul," he says.

"My *old pal* already tried to feed me that protocol bullshit," Thea says, thrusting her finger at Darcey. "We were all over that rock, and you guys know it."

"That's not what I mean."

"Excuse me?"

"It's okay. Take your time." That grin again. It's infuriating.

Thea turns to Darcy. "What the *fuck* is he going on about?"

"Don't you see?" Allgood says. "Your ship has come in, so to speak. I'm making you an offer to join the Conglomerate. To be part of my team."

After a few seconds of looking back and forth between Allgood and Darcey, waiting for a punchline that doesn't come, Thea lets out a sharp cackle.

"Hear him out, Thea," Darcey says.

"Sure. Okay, go ahead," Thea manages.

Allgood steeples his fingers and gnaws on his thumbs while he stares Thea down. When he finally starts again, she sees the deep dents in the pads of his thumbs.

"You keep your ship and your crew," he says. "We'll move you over to Dock B and pick up all docking fees, repairs, supplies, et cetera. All the necessities for you and your team to keep doing exactly what you've been doing."

"How magnanimous. Oh—but what about your precious *system*?"

"Don't worry. I'm sure you'll love it."

"I'm afraid we operate a little differently, Admiral," Thea says, checking Darcey's face to see if there's some sort of joke taking place here that Thea's not yet getting.

"I'm willing to give you some latitude . . . so long as you meet expectations."

"Which are?" Thea asks, leaning in, now actually enjoying the repartee.

"The Conglomerate will give you a quota we expect you to hit each cycle. You'll be given specific rare earth elements to search out, so you'll be able to focus your efforts instead of taking whatever fate gives you out there, and we'll agree in advance to purchase your quota at a predetermined rate. This means you and your people will be shielded from any fluctuations in price and will have a guaranteed paycheck . . . so long as you deliver, of course."

He sits back with an air of satisfaction, like someone pushing back from the dinner table after eating a big steak. All that's missing is him drumming his fingers on his belly.

"That it?" Thea says.

Now it's Allgood's turn to laugh. He even hams it up for Darcey, shrugging his shoulders as if to say, *Can you believe her?*

Thea brings the show to an abrupt stop.

"Thank you, but fuck no."

"Wait," Darcey says. "Thea, let's talk about this. I don't think you're considering all of the possibilities here. I mean, not that long ago you came up here to sell your dad's ship."

"It's *my* ship. And you guys sent that weaselly fuck to shit all over the *Zephyr* and then lowball me. Said at best it could be a tender vessel."

"And you proved everyone wrong. Good for you. So take your prize. This is a great offer."

"Maybe, but the answer is the same," Thea says, turning her attention back to Allgood. "All I want is the haul you *stole* from us. That's it, nothing more."

Allgood shoots up from his chair. "I value my time, Ms. Watts. And this has turned out to be a colossal waste of it."

He sneers at Darcey, then heads for the door.

"What about my haul?" Thea says.

Allgood turns, his trademark smile once again plastered on his condescending face.

"If I recall correctly, I think that particular catch turned out to be pretty disappointing. Mostly rags and just a tiny bit of some random platinums. Low-value stuff. Aren't I right, Lieutenant?"

"I believe so, sir. I'll confirm with the payload team."

"You're really gonna do this?" Thea says, looking back and forth between them.

"Be sure to transmit any credits we might owe to Ms. Watts," Allgood says. "Less any reimbursable amount due to the *Bellwether* for processing and fuel, of course." He levels his gaze at Thea. "After all, fair is fair."

Thea leaps to her feet. "I'll go to Municipal. Tell them and everyone else at the station what you did."

"I expect you will," he says with a wink. "See you out there . . . *Captain*."

Then he's gone.

Darcey slaps the table hard enough to hurt her hand. "You're an idiot, you know that?" she says, rubbing her palm.

"And you're a fucking thief. You're gonna go down *with* him once I report this."

"Grow up! This is the Conglomerate we're talking about. No one's gonna take your side in this, least of all Municipal."

Thea comes around the table and gets in Darcey's face. "You're a disgrace. You should be ashamed."

Darcey shrugs off the insult. "About six months ago, I heard the admiral made a similar offer to the Norwegians. Gave them a chance to join us and make up for deciding to go it alone in the first place, which would have made the *Lillehammer* one of ours."

Thea feels as though she just got punched in the mouth. She stares at Darcey in disbelief.

"What are you saying?"

"I'm saying, this is a dangerous business, Thea. Maybe if they had listened, taken the deal and had been in our care . . . the last member of their crew wouldn't be at Darkside's morgue right now, getting ready to be sent home in a box." Darcey's gaze is not just cold, it's icy. "I hope you didn't just make the same mistake."

Darcey pushes her chair back into place at the table, setting it right again, following protocol. "Wait right here. I'll have someone escort you out," she says, her voice flat, not looking at Thea as she heads for the door.

It takes effort, but Thea regains enough of her composure to ask. "Darcey, did you just threaten me?"

Turning back with a smirk that could rival Allgood's, Darcey says, "That's crazy. We're friends, remember?"

PART IV

Voids

27

New Threat

THE CONGLOMERATE FLEET, which flies on behalf of the Conglomerate's eighteen member nations, consists of eight ships. Its flagship, the *Bellwether*, is the largest mining vessel ever constructed. It's able to haul three times more cargo than any other ship at Darkside Station. Its sister trawlers, *Segundo* and *Tertius*—also known as the Twins—are smaller, more nimble vessels designed for mining dense asteroid clusters. Their contingent is rounded out by two scout ships, *Sierra* and *Pencari* —which set probes, analyze data, and direct the trawlers—and three tender ships, referred to simply as T-A, T-B, and T-C. The tenders' main functions are to shuttle supplies from Darkside and refuel the other vessels so they can focus on the business of identifying platinum-rich objects and mining them.

This group of eight ships, the only multivessel astromining operation in existence, is responsible for more than half of all rare earth elements harvested from near-Earth asteroids. And in the six months since Brian Allgood's offer to the *Zephyr* to become their ninth member, Thea and her crew have encountered every one of those ships—and never in a good way.

On one occasion, Lola set a string of probes in the path of an approaching asteroid cluster only to discover that they'd been "upstreamed" by the Conglomerate. That's what it's called when a crew knowingly sets their probes ahead of another crew's string, highjacking their position. By the time the targeted cluster passed through the *Zephyr*'s probes, the Twins were already in the process of mining its most promising targets.

Another time, the *Zephyr* went to a slow-moving comet to refuel, only to arrive and find all three Conglomerate tenders attached in such a way that the *Zephyr* had to wait for one of them to withdraw before they could get at the icy surface. It wasn't unusual to encounter the Conglomerate's tenders at refuel points, but it was decidedly suspicious to find all three in one spot, especially with no other Conglomerate ships in the sector. And when all three tenders proceeded to suffer sipper malfunctions at the same time, delaying their departure . . . there was no longer any doubt that the move was deliberate.

But the most frustrating incident involved asteroid cluster Zeta Twenty-Two. Zeta Twenty-Two was a known platinum-dense cluster with an orbital path that brought it into range every forty-four months, making this only its sixth-ever appearance since the inception of astromining. The *Sierra* and *Pencari* were dispatched weeks in advance to set a comprehensive string of probes that would map the entire cluster. They had done something similar before with other clusters, and everyone knew the drill—basically, wait until the Conglomerate trawlers settled on their targets, then build your own maps and go after whatever targets were left. But with Zeta Twenty-Two, the Conglomerate decided to *share* their intel. They transmitted their scouts' findings to all of the ships in the area.

Every ship except the *Zephyr*.

The cluster was swarmed.

Rory figured out what happened and asked a friend of his on the Beijing crew to send him the Conglomerate cluster map. He didn't get it. His friend told him that Admiral Allgood threatened that any ship sharing the map with Watts Astromining would be *on his list*. And as the *Zephyr* discovered during those six long months, "his list" was not a place anyone wanted to be.

So Zeta Twenty-Two came and went, and the only ship that didn't benefit was the *Zephyr*.

Thea tried lodging complaints with Municipal, just as she had lodged the promised complaint after the *Bellwether* stole their haul when they were responding to the *Lillehammer*'s distress call. But the complaints were all dismissed summarily, proving that bureaucracy and politics truly know no Earthly bounds.

Luckily, however, Municipal provided temporary relief from the Conglomerate's torment when they summoned *all* captains back to the station for an unexpected mandatory briefing.

––––––

"WHAT'S YOUR PLAN, KILLER?" Elliott asks, setting his spanner on the floor. Thea is dancing back and forth like a boxer in her corner as they wait for the lift.

"I'm thinking of going straight for the jugular."

"Right out of the gate?"

"Why not? He's been doing it to us for months."

"Sure, sure. But what about appealing to Municipal again? It'll be harder for them to ignore you while you're standing right in front of them."

"They made their position clear. They're in Allgood's pocket."

The lift clangs to a stop and the doors hiss open. Thea is

about to board the lift until Elliott stops her, gently grabbing her arm and turning her to face him.

"Look, I trust you. We all do. But let me just say . . . this guy has made our job, which is already hard, even harder. And all just to prove a point."

"I'm not giving in, Ell. He's not getting his hands on this ship."

"I'm not suggesting that at all. None of us want to work for the Conglomerate. All I'm saying is that maybe you can find a way of neutralizing him. Appeal to his ego. Play up some story of family legacy and just wanting to take our small little piece of the pie. Just wet our beaks. Something along those lines. Maybe if you do that, he'll lose interest and find some other crew to harass."

Thea shakes her head. "I hear what you're saying, I really do. But I'm sorry. I just can't do it. He's a bully, and I refuse to kiss his ass. It's not how I'm wired."

Elliott smiles and draws her into a hug. It takes a few seconds, but she can feel the tension inside her release as she sinks into his warmth, breathes in his scent. Earl Grey mixed with engine oil and sweat. She could stay here all day. Forever. But first, she has business to take care of.

"How long will you be?" Elliott asks.

"The meeting is only scheduled for twenty minutes, so we should aim to get out of town by noon."

"All right, I'll radio Rory. He and Beetle went to pick up those parts we need for the reactor."

"Make sure they get back right away. You heard the fleetwide chatter. There's gonna be a mad rush to get out of here."

"Anyone have any idea what this is all about?"

"No. Municipal is being super tight-lipped."

"Speaking of lips . . ." He cups her chin and gives her a

long, deep kiss. When he finally decides to disengage, Thea won't let him. She grabs the back of his head and pulls him toward her, adding an ass grab at the end for good measure. He reaches for her, but she pushes him away and wags a finger in front of his face.

"I gotta go do this thing. Don't worry. I'll deal with you later," she says, stepping into the lift.

"Go get 'em, Captain."

———

THE CONFERENCE ROOM is at the apex of Darkside Station. Starlight streams in through a mostly glass ceiling, its panels arranged in the same configuration as the original International Space Station cupola: a circular window surrounded by six trapezoids. The design is intended to evoke the type of global collaboration that existed among nations and private organizations during the ISS's decades of service to mankind.

Gasira Achebe, the head of Municipal, glides around the room, greeting each of the captains as they take their assigned seats. Her diamond earrings and nose ring twinkle against her rich, dark skin and all-black business suit. When she takes Thea's hand in a firm grip and stares straight into her eyes, Thea feels like she's being drawn into twin black holes.

"It's nice to finally meet you, Captain Watts. I was a great admirer of your father."

"You knew my dad?"

"I was only a clerk at the time. But on the few occasions I had dealings with him, he was always pleasant. He handled his business very well, if I remember correctly. Helped maintain the order of things, which, as you undoubtedly know by now, is critical up here."

With a final penetrating gaze, Achebe moves on.

Thea takes her seat, realizing that the discussion she'd intended to have with Achebe about her grievances with the Conglomerate had just taken place. Achebe had shut it down before Thea could even begin.

She looks around the table at the other captains as they exchange curious glances and shrugs. It's clear no one knows why they're here, but everyone's surprised that Achebe herself is going to be doing the briefing instead of one of her magistrates.

Brian Allgood is the last one to enter.

"Hello, everyone," he says, arms out wide as if Caesar had just stepped into the arena and expects the applause of his subjects. Saito, captain of the Japanese fleet, is the only person other than Thea who doesn't give Allgood their attention. In fact, when Thea rolls her eyes and makes a subtle jerk-off motion, Saito rewards her with a smile and small nod.

Fostering international relations, she thinks.

Allgood finally takes his seat, and the room settles.

"Thank you all for coming," Achebe begins, drawing all eyes to her, the timbre of her voice like a cello, deep and rich and resonant. "I know this isn't ideal. I assure you, the decision to summon you all back to the station wasn't taken lightly, but what I have to share is very sensitive. It's not the sort of information I want to communicate over open channels, and certainly not the sort of information I'm willing to leave open to interpretation. I wanted you all to hear it directly from me, and at the same time.

"With that said . . . after a lengthy investigation, we've concluded that the destruction of the *Lillehammer* was an act of sabotage."

Achebe pauses, letting the stunned silence lengthen until Saito breaks it.

"How do you know this?"

Achebe nods as if she anticipated the question. "The destruction emanated from the engineering section of the ship, located at the point where the vessel was severed in half. Given the structural damage in that area, including certain fused alloys and residual radionuclides, there's no question that the *Lillehammer*'s reactor suffered a meltdown. But that wasn't the only malfunction.

"When the investigative team did a full sweep of the wreckage, they confirmed that not a single section of the ship was sealed off, either by the crew or the ship's emergency systems, and no escape pods were deployed. Every section of the ship decompressed when the reactor went critical and the hull breached. This is obviously very unusual, and indicated there had to have been a simultaneous computer malfunction. Sure enough, our forensics team discovered a Trojan horse buried deep in their mainframe's code."

"So it was someone on their crew?" Allgood says.

"Why would you assume that?" Thea asks, acknowledging his presence for the first time.

"Who else would have access to their computers?" he says dismissively, then turns to Achebe. "Are there records of a system architect visit or other tech support?"

"Not in nearly three years," Achebe says. "But we're fairly certain it wasn't anyone on the crew."

"How could you possibly know that?" Allgood says, looking around at the other captains for support.

"Maybe because they're all dead," Saito says.

"One of them could have cracked up. It's happened before."

"Captains, if you'll let me finish," Achebe says.

They settle down, and after a beat, she continues.

"You all receive encrypted systems updates from your nation's space agencies or private organizations," Achebe says matter-of-factly, and receives nods of confirmation from around the room. "Usually these are transmitted to the ship-yard relay station rather than the lunar satellite network for security purposes and then sent to you as a physical copy via the Hyperloop."

"We know this," Allgood says irritably.

"Yes, of course. But what you probably didn't know, Admiral Allgood, is that we keep a copy of the transmission as well." Achebe steeples her fingers in a gesture that could be interpreted as either sinister or meditative. Thea decides that it's most likely a *Serenity now* pose brought on by Allgood's inter-ruptions.

"The last known system update for the *Lillehammer* was just over a year ago," Achebe continues. "So we asked the Norwe-gian government to resend the last update to us along with the encryption key. We compared what they sent against what the shipyard originally received, *and* against what was recovered from the *Lillehammer*'s operating system. The code sent by the Norwegians was clean. But the one in the shipyard archive contained the Trojan horse, as did the one recovered from the *Lillehammer* wreckage. Which means that the alteration to their update took place up here."

"So, basically, what you're telling us is the saboteur's on the moon," says another captain, barely containing her frustration. "Which means it could be anyone at the shipyard, Hyperloop control, or here at the station."

"That's right," Achebe says. "Which led us to look more closely into the *Victor Hugo* incident."

A cold sweat breaks out across Thea's back. Achebe must sense this, or more likely she simply knows that Beetle and Elliott landed on the *Zephyr* after the *Victor Hugo* went down. Either way, she looks at Thea as she continues.

"Our investigators took a fresh look at the ship's wreckage and the damage at their dock. And while we can't definitively ascertain what led to the tethering and launch malfunctions, we can't rule out tampering."

"Well, shit," Thea says, already imagining the conversation to come with Elliott and Beetle.

Another captain speaks up, his voice a challenge. "This is concerning news, certainly, but what I want to know is, what are you going to *do* about it?"

"Our investigation continues apace," Achebe says calmly, not rising to the bait. "And when the perpetrator or perpetrators are identified, believe me, we will act, swiftly and severely. But I've called this meeting not to tell you what *I'm* doing, but what *you* can do. What you *must* do.

"First, I recommend you scrub your systems immediately and thoroughly. Just because you haven't had anything happen yet, doesn't mean it won't. The Trojan horse that took down the *Lillehammer* lay dormant in their systems for months before it triggered.

"Second, be vigilant. Until we catch whoever's responsible, the entire astromining community is at risk. Only share information with one another and with us. Now is not the time to deepen entrenchments. I know you all compete out there for product, but now is the time to measure those short-term profits against the longer-term objective of securing this operation—and with it, your livelihoods.

"Finally, I ask you to share this information with no more people than is absolutely necessary. Limit your communications to essential crew only. My team's investigation will be made significantly harder if this news goes wide."

Achebe makes sure to meet the gaze of everyone around the table, not moving on to the next person until she receives some form of acknowledgment. When she's completed her circuit of the table, she adjourns the meeting without fanfare and briskly leaves the room.

The chatter begins the very moment the door closes behind

her. People break off into groups to share their impressions, rumors, speculation, and hearsay. Of course Allgood has the largest cluster of captains around him. Thea talks to Saito for a few minutes, then decides it's time to leave. But before she can, Allgood walks over to her.

"Captain Watts," he says loud enough for all to hear, ensuring that everyone's attention is on him. "I look forward to collaborating with you out there. And back here, too, of course. I think we'll make a good team."

Thea takes his outstretched hand before having a chance to think better of it. Which is what enables him to lean in and talk in a lower voice that only she can hear.

"This is temporary. Once we catch this motherfucker, it's back to the doghouse for you and your whelps."

Thea rips her hand from his and storms out of the room.

As she weaves through the crowd in the Hub, a tumult of emotions in tow, she notices that the Leaderboard is just about to post an update. She stops, waits for the latest tally . . .

And sees that Watts Astromining is no longer listed on the board, having fallen outside the top ten.

Fucking Allgood, she mutters, and punches her thigh.

"Hey there, Captain," a voice calls.

Thea sees Molly waving from inside the booth below the Leaderboard. The girl gives her a sympathetic smile as she points up to the bad news on the Leaderboard and mouths *sorry*.

Thea nods and is about to leave, but then she looks once more at the girl, screwing in an earbud and blowing a green bubble, and she's overcome by a sudden urge to protect her. She has to warn her that things aren't safe, that everything has changed.

She catches Molly's attention and waves her over.

"What's up?" the girl asks.

"Listen, I can't tell you why, and I don't want you repeating this to anyone, but I need you to stay on alert. Okay? Be extra safe around here. No kidding."

"What's going on?"

"It's complicated," Thea says, glancing around to be sure they aren't overheard. "But if you hear anything that sounds weird, anything that strikes you as odd at all, I want you to come find me or radio me."

"Like what?"

"I don't know. You know this place better than most. Trust your gut."

"You're freaking me out a little bit."

"I have that effect on people," Thea says. "The passcode for dispatch is *Mister Softee*. If we're out in the field, that's how you get me. Understood?"

"Mister Softee, huh? Old boyfriend?"

Thea laughs for the first time all day. "Sure. Something like that."

"Can I ask you something?" Molly says.

"Sure."

The girl hesitates, looking a little sheepish, an expression that's out of place on the face of the ardent punk rock space girl. Then she meets Thea's eyes. "Why are you telling me this?"

Thea holds up a fist for her to bump. "Just watching out for my people, that's all."

———

THEA GETS BACK JUST as Rory and Elliott are loading the last of the supplies on the lift.

"You're gonna love this, boss lady," Rory says, setting down a heavy red case with steel straps, the words *Printer Polymer* etched in the side. "My boy Bobby Bean hooked me up with a great deal on this shit."

Thea has no idea who Bobby Bean is. "Sounds great," she says.

"How'd it go?" Elliott asks.

"We have a truce with the Conglomerate."

"How'd you manage that?" Rory asks, eyebrows raised.

"Because we all have a much bigger problem."

28

New Assignment

ALLGOOD ROUNDS THE CORNER BRISKLY, an entourage in tow and tripping over themselves to bear witness to whatever he's saying. Everyone in Dock A makes way as the group heads for the *Bellwether*'s lift, where Darcey is waiting for him. She recognizes a few captains from rival operations amid the small cluster of people shouldering each other aside like autograph-seekers hoping to get a scribble before the star athlete hits the locker room.

She also notes that Thea isn't among them.

His followers must sense their time with him is nearly up, because they tighten the circle around him as he reaches the lift. He shoots Darcey a silent plea, but she's already in motion.

"Apologies, everyone. Admiral Allgood is needed immediately on some urgent Conglomerate business," she shouts.

"Thank you, Lieutenant Grey," he says, hands up as if surrendering to the call of duty. "As I said at the meeting, this issue will face the total weight of the Conglomerate, as well as receive my full *personal* attention. If we all do our parts, things will be just fine."

He waves off a last-ditch effort by the Russian captain, and he and Darcey board the lift. As soon as the doors hiss shut, he falls back against the wall and lets out a deep sigh.

"Thanks for that. They're all a bunch of fucking lemmings. No wonder we're kicking their asses."

"How'd any of them end up in the captain's chair?"

"What they lack in conviction or intelligence, they make up for in brown-nosing."

"How'd it go?" she asks, trying to sound as nonchalant as possible.

"They've determined that the *Lillehammer* was sabotaged. Maybe the *Victor Hugo*, too. Of course, I got a heads-up from one of my people on the inside, so I knew all that going in."

Darcey keeps her eyes pinned to the floor and nods in a way that she hopes displays deep contemplation—and does nothing to betray the accelerated thudding in her chest.

"Do they have any leads?" she asks.

"Not yet." He straightens up and smooths his hair back. "And if this saboteur has half a brain, which it seems they do, then it won't be hard to stay ahead of the goons and morons that Achebe has working for her. They're going to need us to help figure it out. And that's where you come in."

Darcey meets his gaze as the lift reaches their ship. He studies her as the doors open. Quiet. Waiting for a reaction.

She snaps to attention. "What do you need me to do?"

"Good," he says, looking satisfied, his finger on the button to hold the door open. "I want you to coordinate with our security teams across the fleet and here on the ground. Devise a plan. Send out a net. Use whatever resources are necessary to uncover the saboteur's identity. But priority one is making sure *our* ass is covered. Once we're secure, *then* we help everyone else. Got it?"

"Yes, sir."

He steps out of the lift, then reaches back inside and hits the down button.

"Can you handle this, Lieutenant?"

"Don't worry," Darcey says. "You picked the right person for this assignment."

He gives her a tight nod, then turns to go.

Darcey has the discipline to hold back her smile until the doors close and the lift begins to drop.

29

Safety Measures

LOLA'S KNEES bounce up and down, her fists clench and unclench. She folds her legs under her for a few seconds, then stretches them out again. Shoves her hands into her armpits and chews her lower lip bloody. Does everything she can to keep herself from attacking her keyboard as Thea tells them about the saboteur.

When Thea finishes, Rory waits barely a half beat before releasing a stream of profanity so acerbic and withering that the saltiest of sea dogs would clutch their pearls, real or imaginary, make signs of the cross, and mutter apologies to any and all other deities out there just to be on the safe side.

Beetle joins in with what sounds like the French version, the two of them creating a blasphemous bilingual symphony that fills the bridge.

But it's Elliott's reaction that worries Thea the most.

The news seems to hit him like a sledgehammer. He sits silently, staring at the floor. Flinches when Thea touches his shoulder, so lost in his own thoughts that he doesn't hear her say his name or notice when she kneels next to him.

"Talk to me, Ell."

He rests his hand on hers. "Sorry. It's just a lot, you know."

"I know."

"My crewmates on the *Hugo* . . . they were murdered."

"Yes."

"And your friend, Jakob. And his people too."

Thea just nods, not knowing what more to say.

"We won't let that happen to us," he says to her. Then louder, to the rest of them: "Let's make sure it doesn't happen to us, all right?"

"Fucking right," Rory says, slapping his armrest.

"Where do we start?" Thea asks.

Beetle answers first. "I say we tear apart engineering. That's where the bastards hit the *Lillehammer*, so we should start by . . ." He trails off as his eyes are drawn to Lola, who appears to be on the verge of going critical.

"Lola?" Thea says.

Lola snaps out of whatever fever state she's locked in. She looks over at Thea, her fingers splayed like a wizard about to shoot bolts of lightning from the tips.

"It's okay, Lola," Thea says. "Go!"

Unleashed, Lola attacks her keyboard, her fingers moving so quickly that the sound is a sort of white noise, like a rainstorm or waves crashing on the shore. Beetle starts toward her, a question poised on his lips, before Rory grabs his collar and pulls him back.

"Better not," he says. "Bother her now and you might lose a limb. Let's leave girlie to it up here. We'll head to the cargo bay and come up with a plan."

"*Oui*, sounds good," Beetle says.

Thea takes Elliott's hand. When she looks into his eyes, she sees herself reflected there. She loves that she's both there and here, despite the circumstances.

"Let's get to work," she says.

———

THE TREACHERY that destroyed the *Lillehammer* sat dormant inside her systems for a long time. That freaks Lola the fuck out. So she digs into every one of the *Zephyr*'s systems, sometimes scanning code for anomalies line by line. Where possible, she backtracks and reinstalls things from known clean states. Every one of the *Zephyr*'s operating systems is subject to an intense series of forensic analyses and debugging. Even upgrades Lola installed herself don't escape her scrutiny.

By the second day it becomes clear there's no getting her off the bridge. Except for the occasional bathroom break, which she runs to and from, she stays at her station. The crew takes turns keeping her fueled with meals and a steady supply of energy drinks and sugary treats. Rory eventually drags her mattress onto the bridge and sets it next to her workstation.

While Lola digs, the others comb every inch of the *Zephyr*.

They pore over old service records. Written documentation of calls from Darkside engineering is confirmed using the ship's video logs and Dock D security footage. They identify everybody who's been on board since Thea took command. When they double-check the work performed, all of it meets specifications.

They examine all cargo brought on board. Unpack and repack every box and crate, interrogating the contents.

They check each probe and every miner for anything suspicious, fixing every bit of wear and tear with new, freshly printed parts using their onboard printer even though it would be cheaper and faster to just run over to any one of the vendors at the Hub for a replacement.

They even check all their packaged and frozen food, which turns out to be a good thing, because some of it expired and needs to be replaced. Thea even finds an ancient pack of Lorna Doones her dad had stashed on a high shelf in the mess.

By the time they finish, and Lola is *finally* tucked away in her cabin to make up for a lot of lost sleep, they've spent an entire week at dock. The *Zephyr* is the last ship to leave, which will put them at a significant disadvantage when they finally get out to the grounds. But they all agree that peace of mind is worth the tradeoff. Because they feel in control again. At ease. Certain that they've done everything, checked everything, left no stone unturned.

They feel safe.

Ready for whatever comes next.

They're wrong.

30

Broken Promises

PRINTER POLYMER.

  Printe- Polymer.

  Printe- -olymer.

  Print-- --lymer.

A white tendril of smoke rises from the darkening spot.

The ringlet thickens and turns caustic green as the spot grows, consuming the words etched into the side of the heavy red carrying case.

As the malignancy spreads, the case begins to crater and crack. The chemical reaction reaches the case's steel straps. Sparks flicker and jump off the steel as if from a newly lit sparkler, showering the floor with glowing shards of metal.

Thick billows rise from the carcass of the red case, mixing with the conflagration erupting from the straps and creating a lightning-infested storm cloud quickly filling the *Zephyr*'s cargo bay.

The shipwide alarm sounds as the floor begins to melt.

THEA STARTLES and rolls out of bed. She tries to process what's happening as Lola's shriek comes over the hailer.

"Cargo bay, now!"

Fear ices up Thea's spine as Elliott hauls her to her feet.

"Ell, what's going on?"

"I don't know."

They rush to the door and are nearly bowled over by Rory and Beetle as they race past.

"What's happening?" Elliott calls after them.

"Fire!" Beetle screams. He and Rory disappear around the corner, bare feet slapping on the metal decking.

Elliott and Thea exchange a quick, fearful glance, then chase after them.

Lola's frantic voice comes over the speakers. "Should I open the cargo bay doors? Someone talk to me! What do I do? Roreeee!"

Up ahead, Rory finally answers her, shouting loud enough for Lola to hear him on the bridge. "Not yet!"

Rory's peering through the window in the sealed doors that lead into the cargo bay when Thea and Elliott reach them. Beetle is waving them in like a third-base coach waving a runner home.

"Where is it?" Elliott asks.

"I can't see anything!" Rory says, punching the wall.

Thea pushes past him and looks through the window at the cloud of blackness obscuring everything inside the cargo bay.

"Is it secure?" Rory says to Beetle, who shakes his head.

Rory keys the intercom. "Girlie, listen to me. I want you to open the harpoon bay doors. Got that? The *harpoon* bay doors only."

"Hold on!" Elliott yells before Rory can click off the intercom. He gets Lola's fear-riddled *Fuck, fuck, fuck* in response.

"Just have her open the cargo bay doors," Elliott says to Rory. "It'll suck out the oxygen and kill the fire."

"Our haul isn't secure," Rory counters. "We'll lose it, plus a ton of our equipment. But if she opens the harpoon bay doors, then opens the airlock between the two bays, she can pull the smoke out that way and we can see what we're dealing with."

They both look to Thea to settle the argument.

She decides quickly. "It took three weeks to bring that haul in. It'd be great if we don't have to lose it." She gives Rory a hard look. "But if it looks bad, we pull the plug and have her throw open the cargo bay doors. Agreed?"

Rory nods, then keys the intercom once more. "Lola, the harpoon bay doors. Do it now!"

A warning indicator begins to flash above the airlock leading from the cargo bay to the harpoon bay, sending blood-red bursts of light through the thick smoke and confirming that the harpoon bay is now exposed to vacuum.

"Okay, now open both sides of the airlock, but not all the way. Use the manual override."

"How far?" Lola shrieks.

"About halfway. Go!"

Seconds later, the cloud on the other side of the window begins to dissipate as it's sucked through the open airlock and out into space through the harpoon bay doors.

Thea presses her forehead to the glass and scans the cargo bay. She's finally able to see the source of the fire.

"There!" she shouts. The red case, or what's left of it, is jutting from a hole in the cargo bay floor, emitting a steady stream of thick, black-and-green smoke that now streams directly toward the partially open airlock.

"Looks like there's some damage to the inner hull on the starboard side," Elliott says, clearing the way for Rory and Beetle to see. "If we don't do something about that, it could rupture."

Rory pushes in and mutters as he looks through the

window. Then he straightens and turns his gaze to Thea and Elliott. Realization dawning.

The source of the fire is the case containing the 3D printer material he purchased from his buddy Bobby at Darkside. The amazing deal he bragged about just weeks earlier is the thing now melting a hole in their ship.

"*Baise moi*," Beetle says. "It's sinking into the floor!"

"What do we do?" Thea says.

Rory doesn't answer. He stumbles back from the door and runs a hand through his greasy hair.

Elliott turns to face them all. "We have to move. Beetle and I will suit up and go in."

Beetle doesn't wait. He hightails it to the lockers to grab EVA suits for the two of them.

Thea looks once more at the burning hole in her cargo bay floor and the damage to the hull just behind it. "Fuck it," she says. "Let's just open the cargo bay doors. I don't care about the haul."

"No, you guys are right," Elliott says. "We can put out the fire and then seal up any damage with foam. Easy-peasy."

As Beetle rushes back with their suits, Elliott grabs Thea by the shoulders. "It'll be okay. I promise."

"Don't. We've had this conversation before."

"I know." He gives Thea his best, most reassuring smile. "But it's all I've got."

"I'll go," says Rory. He's recovered from his initial shock, as evidenced by the excess of blood that's returned to his now-flush face. "It should be me."

"We can't leave Lola up on the bridge alone. If a breach occurs, you're the only one who'll be able to handle the ship."

Rory is about to object, but Elliott stops him short.

"We got this, man."

Rory touches his friend's arm in a silent thanks, then runs up the corridor toward the bridge.

Elliott and Beetle begin pulling on their EVA suits.

"Let's be on the safe side and go seventy percent on the boots," Beetle suggests. "It'll be a bitch, though."

"Roger."

Elliott adjusts his boots' magnetic strength, then looks at Thea. "Wait until I signal you. When we've got it contained, tell Lola to close everything up and repressurize."

"Ell—"

"I know, love," he says, grabbing the back of her head and pulling her toward him. He kisses her, nibbles her lower lip, then presses his cheek against her forehead.

Pulling back, he snaps his helmet in place and turns to Beetle, who blows a playful kiss to Thea. After a quick visual inspection of each other's suits, they trade thumbs-ups.

"We'll be back soon," Elliott says.

"Be safe," she says to them both, then puts her back to the wall and reaches for the panel that will open the door into the cargo bay.

Beetle and Ell both nod, and she slaps the panel.

As the door slides open, Thea can feel the tug of escaping air trying to pull her inside. She flattens herself further against the wall as Elliott and Beetle step through into the cargo bay, then she slaps the panel again. The door closes behind them, and the tug vanishes.

She watches through the window as they move across the cargo bay to the smoking case. It looks like they're walking through mud as they yank their magnetized boots off the deck with each deliberate step. When they make it to the cratering floor, they stand opposite the evacuating smoke, staring down at what's left of the case.

Elliott drops to one knee and looks inside the hole. He points to something, then points at the damaged starboard hull of the ship directly behind the case.

Beetle thumbs toward the tool locker. Elliott nods, points to himself, and then in the opposite direction.

Thea wishes she could hear them. She sends Elliott vibes, willing him to look at her and help her understand the conversation they just had. But he doesn't. He walks across the bay toward the tool locker. Only when he arrives at it and picks up the foam cannon does he look in her direction. He makes a spraying motion.

Thea gives him a thumbs-up and an enthusiastic nod. At the same time she pounds her thigh with her other fist, the one he can't see. The one expressing her actual frayed and fractured nerves.

By the time Elliott makes it back to the smoldering case with the foam cannon, Beetle is prodding it with a heavy steel pole that they normally use to break rock away from captured chunks of asteroid. He manages to snare it, then bends at the knees as he tries to lift it. It takes a bit of maneuvering, but he manages to fish the smoldering case free, leaving it dangling from the end of the pole like a snared trout.

Elliott then sprays the pink foam, filling the cavity in the floor and coating the damaged inner hull in a sweeping motion.

Beetle walks toward the airlock, pole thrust out before him. Steady. Careful.

He's just about reached the airlock when the case tumbles from the end of the pole.

Sparks fly as it strikes the metal deck.

Thea's heart nearly stops.

Beetle tries to scoop it up again with the pole, but can't snag it. After a few attempts, he resorts to pushing it across the floor like he's playing shuffleboard.

The opening in the airlock door is just wide enough to accommodate the husk of the case. He pushes it through, then peers after it and shakes his head.

It must not have been pulled out, Thea thinks.

Beetle signals to Elliott and shimmies through the opening, still carrying the steel pole.

As he disappears from view, Thea turns her attention back to Elliott. He's still spraying pink foam, which has now piled up all around the hole in the floor and thoroughly coats the damaged portion of the starboard hull.

He pauses. Examines the stiffening foam. Then activates the cannon again, pouring more foam atop the pink peaks.

Beetle re-emerges, squeezing his way through the half-open door, stabs the pole into the deck like a spear, and gives Elliott a thumbs-up.

Elliott stops spraying and returns the gesture. He inspects his handiwork, then looks at Thea and points in the direction of the bridge. That's her signal that it's time to call Lola.

Thea keys the intercom and tells Lola to close the harpoon bay doors. Lola and Rory cheer in response.

Thea looks back into the cargo bay at the man she loves. Lets out a deep, emotion-filled sigh.

Then watches as he's sucked through the giant hole that suddenly appears behind him in the starboard hull of the *Zephyr.*

31

Drifting Away

THEA STARES in disbelief as Elliott disappears through the rupture, followed by almost every other untethered object in the cargo bay.

An array of hand tools, a jackhammer, the heavy grinder, sawhorses, their new arc welder.

Elliott.

Coils of harpoon cable, straps, anchors, a ring of carabiners, a spare EVA suit.

Elliott.

Every ounce of terbium and lanthanum from their last haul. Scrap iron, cobalt, and quartz. A disassembled miner from Lola's workbench and her purple laptop. Their spare 3D printer and its mobile cart. All of it mixed in a haze of ice erupting from a burst coolant line.

Elliott!

Empty ration tins, plates, utensils, and their storage unit. A half-empty bottle of whiskey, a deck of cards, and Beetle's red, white, and blue Tour de France jacket.

Beetle!

She looks over to see Beetle clinging to the steel pole he

used to push the smoldering case out through the harpoon bay, the end of which is stabbed into the metal grating on the floor. He's straining against the suck of space coming from the gaping hole in the hull, but he manages to pull himself forward and wrap one leg around the pole, then twist his body so that he's got one foot underneath him, his magnetized boot against the pole.

He stabs at his wrist control pad to cut the magnets . . .

. . . then leaps forward like a frog from a lily pad and grabs the edge of the partially opened airlock.

The maneuver takes only seconds, which is all he has. He hauls himself into the airlock just before the emergency system seals the door shut.

The evacuation of the cargo bay slows and eventually stops as the atmosphere inside disappears.

Thea can't move, can't think.

She stares at a bright ribbon of stars through the jagged hole in her ship and the debris field of their lives. Litter on a galactic highway.

The hailer sounds. She hears someone calling her name. Over and over again. But she can't process what's being said. It's impossible. Because he's suddenly there. Through the hole in their ship, she sees him.

Elliott!

Tumbling, tumbling away.

The sight of him shocks her into action. She takes off for the bridge, screaming as she runs.

Seconds feel like years as she races along the main corridor, bouncing off the walls, processing neither the blaring ship-wide alarm nor Rory's bellows. All she can think about is the image of Ell's triumphant smile after containing the fire—and his look of complete surprise a split second later.

And her need to get him back.

Right now.

She bursts onto the bridge. Rory is at the helm, yelling something to Lola, who is bent over her screen.

"Do you have him?" Thea says.

"What the fuck happened down there?" Rory says.

"Do you *have* him!" Thea screams, her vocal cords on the verge of snapping.

Rory finally turns to her. "Who?"

"Ell got sucked out when the wall blew."

"What?" Lola says, her head swiveling back and forth between Rory and Thea, desperate for someone to make sense of what she's hearing. Then a flash of clarity hits, and her fingers fly over the keyboard.

"What about Beetle?" Rory says.

"He made it inside the airlock to the harpoon bay."

On cue, Beetle's voice comes over the bridge comms. Crazed. Desperate. Pleading for them to get their friend.

"Hold on . . ." Lola says.

An image appears on the main screen. The aft camera, showing a cloud of debris billowing from the underside of the *Zephyr*. The view swings and zooms, swings and zooms, moving so fast that it's almost impossible to register what it's seeing before it moves again, the camera searching for its next target, faster than a human brain can process.

At least a normal brain.

Then suddenly . . .

"There he is!" Lola shouts.

Elliott floats in the center of the screen, surrounded by glittering rocks. His arms and legs are splayed out and his face shield is clouded, impossible to see through.

"What do we do?" Thea asks, pleading.

"Umm, okay. Okay . . ."

"Quick!"

"Open the cargo bay doors," Rory says. "I'll swing around so that he'll float right near us, and we can grab him."

"Rory . . ." Lola says in an uncertain whisper.

"I'll suit up and attach myself with a tether. It'll be fine. It should have been me anyway."

"Rory—"

"I'll get him, Thea. I'll—"

"*Rory!*"

Lola's scream finally shuts him up. He looks over at her and sees her pointing at the screen, her face sheet-white and her lips trembling.

Thea sees it too. Elliott has drifted around to face away from the camera.

Revealing a long tear up the back of his EVA suit.

Rory stares at Elliott's corpse, shaking, the last vestiges of his plan to save his friend still on his lips.

Then gone for good when Thea collapses to the floor.

32

Cold

WHEN HER DAD wasn't home for Christmas, which was the case most years, Thea and her mom would spend the holidays with her grandparents on Lake Winnipeg. Those trips had all the idyllic trappings of a Hallmark holiday movie. Ice skating and sledding. Roasted marshmallows, hot chocolate, and maple cookies. Jimmy Stewart, Bing Crosby, Boris Karloff. You name it, and Pops and Nana had it and then some. But it wasn't the sugarplums and mistletoe that made Thea love those days at the frozen lake beneath the towering Canadian pines. It was the cold.

Texas was a blast furnace of heat and misery and about as unmerry a place as you could get in December. So when Thea and her mom took those vacations, Thea would spend as much time as she could outdoors. But the days weren't enough. After everyone went to bed, she'd sneak out, lay on the dock, stare up at the stars, and imagine she could see the *Zephyr* skating across the night sky.

The best times were when it would snow. She'd stay as still as possible, watching the flakes drift down in the moonlight until her cheeks and nose were numb.

Most of the time she'd get away with it, too. But one time, her mother caught her and came charging down the hill, screaming.

God damn it, Thea, it's freezing.

You'll catch your death out here.

Out here.

Out here.

Thea wipes a slushy tear from her cheek and lets out a long, slow breath in the deep freeze of the harpoon bay. She watches it cloud before her face then slowly climb toward the ceiling as the memory fades.

You were right, Mom.

She turns onto her side, pulls the thermal blanket to her chin, and looks at him. Or rather, looks at his body bag.

She's spent time here every night, lying beside him in the cold until she starts to go numb. And when the numbness of her body finally matches what's in her head and in her heart, she stays a little longer, happy to not feel anything at all.

Free of the pain of feeling, if only for a moment.

Like now.

She's drifting off to sleep as she hears the door slide open. The light leaking into the harpoon bay momentarily obscures the person walking toward her, but she can tell who it is by his heavy sigh.

"What do you want, Rory?"

"We'll be at dock within the hour."

"Okay, thanks."

He doesn't say anything, but he doesn't leave, either. She tries to ignore him, let herself slip back toward sleep, but she can't. The thought of him standing there, looking at her curled up next to the corpse of her boyfriend, is too much to bear.

She throws off the covers. "Is there something else?"

"I wanted to let you know that when we get back, I'm

gonna take some time away. Maybe go home to Scotland for a bit."

She stands up too fast and has to lean over and massage the tightness in her left knee. Once she can flex it again, she hobbles toward him.

"You're leaving?"

"Look, Thea . . . I know you're mad at me. For what happened with the case and everything." He doesn't meet her gaze, and her heart breaks at the sight of his tears. "I'm so sorry, luv. I truly am."

She hugs him, realizing it's the first time she's done so since Elliott died. She holds him, and they cry together for a while before she gently pushes him away. This time, she forces him to look at her.

"I'm so sad," she says, swallowing hard and having to pause for a second. "I loved him, and he loved me. And that hasn't ever happened to me, and it probably never will again."

He tries to interject, but she stops him, needing to continue lest she break entirely.

"I'm also furious. So much that I think it might consume me. But Rory, I'm not mad at *you*. This isn't your fault. I know you want to blame yourself, but it's *not* your fault. And I'm not going to let whoever did this to us end it."

She feels a warmth growing inside her that's been absent since Elliott died. A warmth ignited by rage.

"I loved that man," she says. "But I love you too. All of you. You're my family.

"You're all I've got."

The hulk of a man before her fights to collect himself, his fists and jaw clenching until he's able to find a modicum of composure.

"What do we do?" he says finally.

"We start with the guy who sold you the case." With a final

glance at Elliott's body bag, she steers Rory toward the door. "We start with Bobby Bean."

33

Tones of Home

MOST OF THE fleet is in town, so the Hub is packed. A cacophony of languages echoes off the curved walls, creating a mesmerizing multilingual din. The normally stale air is humid from so many bodies packed together.

Thea imagines this must be what it's like in an Olympic village. People comingling, representing their homeland with colorful hats, jackets, and shirts emblazoned with their country's flag. Everyone momentarily united by a shared goal and passion to compete. Allies today on this neutral ground, breaking bread or sharing a pint, but tomorrow's adversaries. The analogy is punctuated by the glowing Leaderboard, listing the top nations in the race to collect rare earth elements.

A steady stream of people enters and exits the general store carrying crates, boxes, and bags of supplies. Thea and Rory have to make way for store clerks pushing loaded-down hand trucks through the crowd. As they trundle past, she can't help but think of the giant list of supplies they'll need if they're going to replenish everything that was lost in the accident.

Not an accident, she catches herself, swallowing down her rising emotions and fighting to stay focused.

What happened was no accident.

After patching the hole in their ship, they examined the decking and found what they believe were traces of hydrofluoric acid along the edges of the melted steel. They'd scrutinized everything on board the *Zephyr*, including the contents of the red case, after Municipal ruled that the *Lillehammer* was sabotaged, so they're certain it contained only 3D printer polymers. That left only the case itself as the culprit. Some acid delivery device must have been embedded in its structure. Unfortunately, they weren't able to find the remnants of it amid the massive debris field to validate their hypothesis.

"His table's over there," Rory says, pointing toward the vendor stalls.

"Remember the plan."

"I'll keep it together. Like I said, I don't think Bobby did this. He ain't the sharpest knife in the drawer. But if I get a whiff that this fucker is hiding something, anything at all . . ."

"I know," she says. "I'm with you. But we need this guy to play ball."

"Don't worry," Rory says, stroking his beard. "He'll play."

Rory's like a snowplow, the scowl on his face and width of his shoulders responsible for parting the crowd. But when they reach their destination on the opposite side of the Hub, they find only an empty table.

"Oy, where's Bobby?"

A woman at an adjacent table rests her soldering iron in its holder and flips up the eyepiece connected to a leather headband around her sweaty brow. She looks Rory up and down before responding.

"Who are you?"

"A friend of his."

"I imagine any friend of his wouldn't need to ask."

"I've been out of town. Do you know where he is?"

The woman glances at Thea, eyes focused on the *Zephyr* logo on her jacket.

"I know that ship," she says, waggling a bony finger at Thea's chest. "You Scottie's kid?"

"Thea," she says, stepping in front of Rory.

The woman's hand is like sandpaper when she gives Thea a quick shake.

"Saw you on the Leaderboard. Glad you got her up there again, even if just for a little while. *Zephyr*'s a good ship. Some of my handiwork on there still, I reckon."

Thea glances down at the green motherboards stacked on the table and nods, feigning recognition, which draws a crooked smile from the woman.

"We really need to talk to Bobby," Thea says. "Can you help us?"

"Haven't seen him in a few days."

"Do you have any idea where he might be?"

The woman glares at Rory and starts to shake her head, but Thea is quick to read the situation and grabs one of the motherboards from the nearest pile.

"How much?"

The woman's demeanor instantly changes. She takes the motherboard from Thea's hand.

"This one here's one of my best." She turns the faded green board over in her hands. "I can't let it go for anything less than four hundred."

Thea fishes a five-hundred-credit note from her pocket and holds it out. "How's this for the board and info on where I can find Bobby?"

The woman snatches the bill and slaps the motherboard against Thea's open palm, sealing the deal.

"He lives in Seven. Building four."

Thea says a quick thanks and turns to go, pulling Rory

behind her. As soon as they're out of sight of the woman's table, Thea throws the motherboard in the nearest bin.

"Nice work," Rory says.

"I've never been down to the Neighborhood."

"Oh, you're gonna love it. Picket fences, green grass. Burgers and pie on picnic tables. It's a dream."

———

THE NEIGHBORHOOD IS BUILT into the foundation of Darkside Station. It comprises eight cul-de-sacs branching off a circular common area, like the petals of a flower. Each cul-de-sac has seven low-rise tenement buildings, all of which look the same —squat gray cinderblock structures made from the blasted lunar rock cleared during Darkside's construction.

This is where all six hundred twenty-five permanent residents of Darkside Station live.

In an attempt to provide some sense of normalcy to the residents who've come to work at the station, the Darkside architects painted the ceiling sky blue. The lighting is also set to match the day cycle on Earth, complete with regular sunrises and sunsets.

No stars, though. People get their fill of those up above.

The sun is setting on the Neighborhood when Thea and Rory arrive, an orange-yellow glow illuminating everything. "Charming," Thea says as the streetlights flicker to life. "So, is this like every other place? You know, a good side of town and then a fun side?"

"One and Two," Rory says, pointing to the corresponding cul-de-sacs, "are reserved for Darkside Administration, visiting dignitaries from back home, and Hyperloop and Municipal staff. Definitely not the *fun* part. Or the *good* part either, for that matter. Three is for security staff. The rest are for everybody

else. Refinery workers, fabrication, transportation, maintenance, Hub vendors, you get the drift."

"Why just numbers instead of names?" she asks as they
walk, Rory leading the way.

"Official story is because the people working up here serve all
of humanity, so they went with 'the only true universal language.'
But I dated this girl from Municipal for a little bit, and she told
me the founders went with numbers to try and avoid workers
segregating themselves based on some of the age-old shit from
back home. You know, like your fellow Texans, for instance,
refusing to live on Joseph Stalin Court. Dumb shit like that."

"You really think that would happen?"

"I don't think people up here are any more enlightened
than they are back home," Rory says. They weave around a
twosome sitting on the curb, covered in grease from head to
toe, sucking on e-cigarettes. "If you ask me, people are just
people, no matter where they are."

Thea used to wonder why anyone would come all this way
to work these sorts of jobs. The Neighborhood certainly
doesn't help answer the question; it only deepens it. But in the
time that she's spent up here at Darkside, she's come to understand there is a gravitational pull to the place. If you're going
to break your back for a living, you might as well do it on the
friggin' moon.

"How'd you meet this guy?" she asks.

"You mean Bobby?"

"Yeah. Sounded like you've known him for a while."

"He was an indie operator for a bunch of the civilian operations back in the day. We crossed paths here and there. He got
squeezed out same as the rest of us once the Conglomerate
and the other national outfits took control. He stayed around
Darkside, and I went to the shipyard. We'd lost touch until just
. . . well, you know."

She can tell how much it still bothers him. No matter how many times she tells him it wasn't his fault, she suspects it'll haunt him for the rest of his days.

"I've known bad guys," he says after a long pause. "Bobby's got his rough edges, that's for sure. But he's solid."

"I believe you," Thea says. "But he's wrapped up in this somehow, and we need to know why."

The ceiling over the Neighborhood is lit a dusky red as they enter Bobby's building. They're instantly met with an aroma of spice strong enough to tickle Thea's nose hairs. Low-fi beats filter through the nearest apartment door and mix with the intoxicating scent to create a comfortable, welcoming atmosphere—a stark contrast to the dull gray uniformity outside.

Rory knocks on the door, and someone calls out in response over the music, which drops a few seconds later. The door swings open to reveal a youngish woman in a fuzzy pink bathrobe. Her skin is snowy white, and her white-blond hair is wet. She's holding a martini glass that she tips back as she eyes Thea and Rory.

"Help you?" she says, sliding the empty glass into one of the robe's voluminous pockets.

"We're friends of Bobby Bean. You know which one's his?"

"You work with him up top," she says, eyes pinned to Thea's flight jacket in anticipation of her answer.

"Bobby and I go back to his pilot days," Rory says.

"Wow, good for you. Still at it, huh?" the woman says. "Which ship?"

"The *Zephyr*," Thea says.

The woman nods, a quizzical look replacing the skepticism on her face when she first opened the door.

"Seen you on the board. I hope you keep giving those Conglomerate fucks a run for their money." She cinches the robe around her as if a cold breeze just blew into her apartment.

"We just got back to town after being in the field for a long while," Rory says. "Thought I'd drop by and give the old boy a visit. Introduce him to my captain too." He nods to Thea. "Can you point us in the right direction?"

The woman steps into the corridor and points down the hallway.

"Go all the way to the end, hang a right. He's the last one on the left."

"Thanks," Thea says.

The woman gives a quick wave then ducks back inside and throws the lock on the door. Moments later, the music returns to its previous volume.

Rory and Thea head down the hallway. They step to the side as an old man emerges from the corner apartment, a trash bag slung over his shoulder. A curry-laced cloud of delight wafts out behind him.

"Smells lovely," Rory offers, and gets a wave of thanks in return.

"This doesn't seem so bad," Thea says as they turn the corner.

But when they reach the end of the hallway and Bobby Bean's apartment, her tune changes. She and Rory exchange glances, both of their noses wrinkled against an entirely different smell. Sour. Sticky.

Bad.

Rory gives the door a quick knock.

"Oy, Bobby. It's Rory. You in there?"

Nothing.

Rory pounds harder and calls out again.

Thea examines the door handle and finds what looks like a dent near the hinge, the metal frame buckled. And before she can say anything, Rory takes a few steps back and throws his weight against the door, easily crashing through into the apartment.

The room is dark, and the odor is overwhelming. Rory finds and flicks on the light switch, and they discover the source of the smell immediately.

Bobby Bean sits in his lounger, an empty rocks glass clutched in a literal death grip. Dark, dried blood from a crevice in his forehead covers his face and chest and pools in his lap.

"Fucking hell," Rory says.

"Damn," says Thea. "C'mon. Let's get out of here."

Thea grabs his hand and manages to pry him away from the sight of his dead friend—

Just as security arrives.

A team in black bursts through the doorway and surrounds Thea and Rory, Tasers in hand.

"We just got here," Thea says, thrusting her arms into the air. "Found him like this. I swear."

Two of the officers flank Thea and Rory, while more canvass the apartment. After a minute, someone from the back of the apartment shouts *Clear*, and the man guarding Rory echoes it toward the hallway.

Where Gasira Achebe, the head of Municipal, is waiting.

34

Secrets

WHILE HER TEAM sweeps the space, bagging and tagging items, including Bobby Bean himself, Achebe sits on the dead man's couch, cross-legged, hands steepled together and elbows on knees, captivated by Rory and Thea's story about what happened aboard the *Zephyr*. They sit across from her like kids in the principal's office, except unlike those kids, they're flanked by security officers. Achebe interrupts only a few times for points of clarification, but otherwise she simply takes it all in, concentration and intensity knitted on her brow as if she's trying to absorb every syllable straight into her brain.

But when Thea mentions the acid, Achebe cuts her off and waves the officers away. She waits until they're alone, then leans forward.

"Are you sure?" she asks, her voice low. Some of her team members are still tagging evidence in the apartment, and Achebe clearly doesn't want to be overheard.

"We don't have the type of equipment that you've got, but we have something better," Rory says. "Our girl Lola's sharper than anyone I've seen, and she thinks hydrofluoric acid melted the decking and weakened the hull. If she says it, it's true."

"Why do you ask?" Thea says.

"Six weeks ago, at the shipyard, we found a small metal container buried in a pile of silver rubble scheduled to be melted into a bolide. It was dumb luck that a worker spotted it and halted the belt feeding the oven. The container had traces of fluorspar inside."

"What's that?"

"Calcium fluoride," Achebe says. "One of the main components in hydrofluoric acid."

Thea has to grab Rory's arm to keep him from bounding out of his seat.

"Where'd it come from?" he asks a bit too loudly, then repeats himself in a calmer voice.

"We don't know."

"Is that why you're here? For him?" Thea asks, nodding over to the body bag.

"No, the woman you met when you came in the building called us. I told her to let me know if any unusual people came around. This . . ." Achebe says, waving at the scene unfolding over her shoulder, "is unexpected."

"Did you check manifests for the container? Or load-on scans from launch sites back home?" Rory says, getting more animated as he thinks through the scenarios.

"We're on it, Mr. Abernathy."

"I'm just saying, I was at the shipyard for a while. I know the process. There's things you can do."

"I assure you, we've got a team of people looking into this. There's a lot of information to pore through. We don't know when the container was sent up, in which shipment it arrived, or who received it. And the container is just a simple tin. Could be easily mistaken for anything from food to machine parts. So that leaves us a lot of avenues to explore."

She calls to a woman who's tagging evidence, and the woman comes over.

"This is Carla," Achebe says, introducing the woman to Rory, who takes her outstretched hand. "I'd like you to take her to your ship so she can confirm your findings." To Carla she adds, "You'll need a chem forensics kit."

Rory looks to Thea, who nods her agreement.

Achebe then turns to Thea. "Captain Watts, can you accompany me back to my office?" Her tone suggests she's offering only the appearance of a choice, not an actual one. "I'd like to continue this conversation someplace more secure."

"Hold on," Rory says, and he pulls Thea out into the hallway where they can be somewhat alone. A few of the neighbors have poked their heads out of their apartments, but Rory's steely gaze chases them back inside.

"You okay with this?"

"Yeah," Thea says. "I'll be fine."

"What do you think of her?"

"I'm not sure why yet, but I think we can trust her. This can't be a good look for Achebe with the powers that be back home. Couple of ships wrecked, and now yet another death."

"Just be careful, okay?" Rory says. "Get done with her and get back."

He pulls her into a bearlike hug, then lets her go and sets off down the hallway, leaving Carla to catch up.

———

ACHEBE'S OFFICE is adjacent to the conference room where she held the captains' meeting weeks earlier, so it shares the same bird's-eye view of Darkside Station. Thea stares down at a line of ships, their glowing umbilicuses connecting them to their docks like arteries.

Which of you is next? she thinks, then has to turn away from the window, disgusted by the thought.

"Have a seat," Achebe says, directing Thea to a small

seating area. She takes a bottle of whiskey and two glasses from a cabinet, then takes the seat across from Thea.

"What ya got there?" Thea asks.

"Johnnie Walker Purple. That hundred-year shit." Achebe pours Thea a few fingers of the amber whiskey. "Brian Allgood's way of keeping the peace."

"I guess *my* bottle got lost in the mail."

"I heard he made you an offer to become part of his team," Achebe says before raising her glass to Thea then draining it in one go. "Smart move turning him down, if you ask me. But be careful with that one. As you've already experienced, he doesn't like hearing the word *no*."

She pours a second splash into her glass and offers the same to Thea. Thea waves it off, and Achebe sets the bottle down and sits forward like she's settling in behind home plate.

"What do you know about how all this got started?" she says, hand circling in a fashion that indicates she's referring to it all, the totality of what's around them.

"Same as everyone, I guess," Thea says with a shrug. "Cellular and battery advances pushed us to the brink. Medical, automotive, and environmental tech pushed us over. And when the availability of rare earth elements couldn't meet global demand, we came up here."

"You got it. That's the story in the history books. Artificial intelligence was transforming everything, and the damage done to the environment by mining the elements negated the environmental benefits we got from the green tech sector. It became a zero-sum game, and meanwhile the world was boiling to death. We had to pivot to astromining to meet the pace of progress. So here we are." After a pause she adds, "But there's something else. The *real* catalyst."

Thea puzzles it out for a few seconds. "You mean the freighter accident?" She remembers the animated debates among her dad and his buddies at barbecues.

"The *Hudong Star*, yes. Very good," Achebe says with a look of admiration on her face. "What do you know about it?"

"I know it was carrying a small amount of rare earths. Very small, but we couldn't afford to lose any back then. But it was mostly hauling cars and offshore turbines, or something like that, right?"

Achebe decides that Thea needs another finger or two before they continue. She tips out some more lubricant into Thea's empty glass and pushes it toward her.

"The *Hudong Star* was the largest container ship in the world. It was the pride of the China State Shipbuilding Corporation. And the day that it sank in the South China Sea, it was carrying nearly *two hundred thousand* metric tons of rare earth metals—the largest remaining reserve on the planet."

"Holy shit," Thea says, utterly stunned.

"With rationing and strategic allocations, that shipment might have kept the global economy afloat for almost a decade. Without it, we were screwed. Everything accelerated after that."

"Why was this kept secret?"

Achebe throws back the rest of her whiskey and settles into her chair. "Have you ever heard of a group called the New Muses?"

When Thea shakes her head, Achebe continues.

"The New Muses believe that technological progress has led to the death of the human spirit, and they are determined, and I quote, to force us 'back to a time when invention and inspiration was the purview of humanity alone.'"

"So they're humanists. Nothing new there," Thea says. "People have been spouting off about this since ChatGPT back in the twenties."

"The rhetoric isn't new, for sure. But the Muses took it way past just waving signs and holding demonstrations. They knew that going after AI, cellular tech, pharma, and the rest of it was impossible. The genie was way out of the bottle already. So they decided to target the single thing they all have in common instead."

"Rare earths."

Achebe crosses her arms and considers Thea for a few seconds, then comes to a decision. "What I'm about to tell you is confidential. I'll ask that you keep this between us."

Thea nods her assent, which seems to satisfy Achebe.

"The *Hudong Star* was sabotaged."

Thea feels the blood rise to her face, and not because of the whiskey. "And this group, the Muses . . ."

"They claimed responsibility, yes. And for a while now I've suspected that the New Muses are behind the recent attacks up here as well. The malfunction that grounded the *Victor Hugo*. The *Lillehammer* disaster. A couple of other incidents that we've managed to keep under wraps. But after today, I no longer just suspect. I'm fully *convinced* that they're behind all this."

"What convinced you?" Thea asks, though she already knows the answer.

"The acid," Achebe says. "The sailor responsible for the *Hudong Star* died when she sank, so no one could question him. But when investigators searched the man's home, they discovered large quantities of fluorspar and sulfuric acid, the key ingredients in hydrofluoric acid."

"So these fuckers are back to their old tricks," Thea says.

"It would appear so."

Thea goes over to the window, her head spinning. Down below, a trawler is hovering above Dock C. A quick spike of fear ices up her spine.

This is what they want, she thinks. *They want us afraid.*

She turns back to Achebe. "Why me? You didn't have to tell me any of this. You could have simply taken the info about my ship and gone about your business."

Achebe stands and approaches.

"I hear a lot of things as head of Municipal, Thea. And I know that the crewmate you lost was much more to you than just a crewmate."

Thea chokes back a sob, caught off-guard by how quickly it rises in her at the mention of Elliott, embarrassed by the speed and intensity of the emotion.

"I wanted you to know as a show of good faith," Achebe continues. "To help you understand that we are doing everything we can to catch these people. We've been after them a long, long time. But also, I told you because I could use your help. We don't know each other well, but I can tell you're not the kind of person who sits back and lets others take care of things for her. So let's work together. Share information. You're unique up here in that you don't have to answer to superiors back home—superiors whose agendas could be a hindrance. You enjoy a freedom of movement that I think could benefit us all in this investigation."

Thea glances out the window once more and sees that the trawler is safe, its docking lights off, ground lighting illuminated.

Safe, for now.

"Thank you for telling me," she says. "And trusting me. And yes, I'm in. I'll help. In any way I can."

Achebe holds out her hand, and Thea shakes it. Achebe holds on to Thea's hand for an extra second and says, "I'm very sorry for your loss, Captain Watts."

Thea turns to go, but Achebe adds one last thing.

"And Thea, please don't share what we talked about here. We need to be very careful. The saboteur could be anybody."

35

Beginnings

The four of them hold hands as the container with their friend's coffin races down the railgun's glowing length. A sob escapes Lola as the container is shot toward Earth, big and blue and beautiful in the lunar sky. As it tumbles through space, bearing Elliott home, their grips tighten. And even after the container disappears from their view, lost in the white swirl of the atmosphere above Africa, no one lets go until Rory pulls the others into a hug and they let the tears come.

It's late by the time they pull out of the shipyard. They have the entire Hyperloop to themselves, but they don't spread out. Instead they cluster together in the middle of the train as if driven by some instinctual need, some biological impulse to close ranks after losing one of their tribe. They stare out the train's windows as it races across the pocked and vacant landscape, cutting across a vast sea of gray and silence.

Then Beetle decides to break the ice.

"Did I ever tell you how Ell and I met?" he begins, his voice snapping them out of their collective trance.

"My troupe was in Johannesburg. It was at the end of a six-month tour, and everyone was very much done with performing. We all just wanted to go home. Especially me. The circus had been my life since I was very young, but I had started to wonder about what I'd missed all those years traveling around the world, going from arena to arena, city to city. It all started to look the same.

"Anyway, on the last night, one of our aerialists got food poisoning. I'd never seen someone shit himself so much. It was amazing. The noise and the stink."

Sign of the cross, then he continues.

"The boss tells me I have to cover his part of the silks routine, which would normally be no problem. I did the silks for years and knew the routine by heart. But there was a big problem *that* day, and Elliott got to see it firsthand."

Beetle pauses for a long dramatic beat, and Lola bites. "What was it?" she asks.

"It was the woman who would be working as my partner in the routine." Beetle slaps his hand on his head for effect. "We had, let's just say, a bit of a past together. She was a woman of great . . . passions. Qualities I share, of course, as you know. But it did not end well with us. So I was very nervous to perform with her.

"That night, I step into the center ring, and there she is. Happy and bubbling, like my old Sophie. Sexy in her red-and-gold sequined suit, wrapping herself in the silk and smiling at me as the music starts and we're lifted into the air. She was exquisite.

"So I'm thinking, this is going to be okay. There are no hard feelings here. And then as the routine starts and we begin to dance through the air, our arms and legs and hands touching, I start to think, you know, maybe . . . maybe there's still something here. Maybe there could be some love still between us. I begin to wonder, you know . . ."

He shrugs. "And then she lets me fall."

The three of them are incredulous, but Beetle holds up his hand attesting to the honest truth like a witness on the stand.

"Are you sure she did it on purpose?" Lola asks.

"Oh yes, no doubt. She reached for me as I was unwinding down the silk, and then at the last second, she pulled back."

"Did you get hurt?"

"No, there was a net. She was cruel, but not *that* cruel."

"Still, you can't be one hundred percent sure, right? What if it was just a mistake?"

"I am one hundred percent sure that Sophie did this intentionally. Because as I was on my back in the net, staring up in shock at what had just happened, there she was, dangling upside-down above me, giving me two middle fingers."

The others erupt in laughter.

"So what does this have to do with Elliott?" Thea asks.

"Ah, that's the best part," he says, a gleeful look of remembrance on his face. "When I left my dressing room that night after the show, she was waiting for me at the side entrance. We started to fight. It was epic. She screamed and yelled and pushed me. At one point she even spit at me. It was very bad, and it went on for a very long time. And then, there he was.

"I'll never forget it. He was wearing a bright green cricket uniform and filthy orange shoes. He looked like a skinny leprechaun, except for the tall bushy hair that I'm pretty sure had some grass and dirt in it. He had a pint of something in one hand and a cigarette in the other."

Thea's eyes well with tears, but she's smiling, too. "What did he do?"

"He gets between us and looks Sophie up and down, which infuriates her. She keeps trying to get around him, but he won't let her. Then when she tells him to *fuck off*, he flicks away his cigarette, dumps the rest of his beer at her feet, hands her the empty pint glass, and gives me a kiss right on the mouth."

"Fuck you. No way he did that," Rory says.

"He did. I swear it. Right on the lips," Beetle says, pointing at them as if there's still a trace of the kiss all these years later.

"What did she say?"

"Nothing! I think she was in shock. Probably still is to this very day. When he was done, he gave her a wicked smile—you guys know the one—and then he took my arm in his like we were going to a dance and led me away."

"What a baller!" Lola says, prayer hands to the sky.

"When we got around the corner, he let go and finally introduced himself, and told me I owed him a pint. It was the first of many we had together."

They laugh until their sides hurt. And when Beetle jumps at Rory and plants a kiss on him to recreate the famous event, they laugh some more.

They spend the rest of the ride sharing stories and tears and laughter. By the time they reach Darkside, all of them are spent, exhausted by the emotion of the day, yet somehow fuller.

Beginning to heal.

36

Breaches

"CAPTAIN WATTS!"

Thea is so tired she can barely muster the energy to turn around. And she regrets it the second she does, because Brian Allgood is waving at her from across the Hub.

"Shit," she says, eyes nearly rolling out of her head.

"Fuck him. Let's go," Rory says, Lola and Beetle close behind him and on course for Dock D. Thea follows suit, ignoring Allgood and thinking of her bed, until he calls out again.

When she looks back, he's jogging toward them.

"You guys go ahead. I'll be right behind you," she says, handing her bag to Rory and waving off his protest before he can lodge it. "Get some rest. We've got a lot to discuss later."

She watches Lola, Beetle, and Rory go, each of them giving a glance back before disappearing among the morning crowd starting to fill the Hub.

"Captain Watts—Thea," Allgood says, reaching out and resting a hand on her upper arm. "I just wanted to express my sympathies for your loss. What a tragedy."

His gesture has an unexpected air of truth about it, which immediately puts Thea on guard.

"Thanks," she says, taking a deliberate step back so that she's once again out of reach.

"How's the rest of your crew?"

"Shaken. Angry," she says, watching the crowd flow around them, all eyes on their exchange.

"I think that goes for all of us," he says, shooting a stern glance at someone who's drifted too close. The young man course-corrects instantly.

"We can't go on like this," Thea says. "No one's safe."

"I'm on my way to the shipyard now to meet with an investigative team from the States. Some people I knew back in my federal days."

"I thought Municipal was handling the investigation?"

Allgood sneers. "Gasira's team has been *handling* things too conservatively, in my estimation. So I decided to augment their efforts with some of my own."

"You mean the Conglomerate's."

"Sure, of course. The leadership is very concerned. We need to protect our interests, first and foremost. Which is why they defer to me in these sorts of matters."

"Acts of terrorism?"

"Any sort of disruption up here, really. Anything that cuts against the status quo I've established."

Like me, Thea thinks, but she doesn't have the energy to go down that road again. Not today.

"Well, good luck," she says in a way that she hopes will end the discussion.

"How's your ship?" he says before she can escape.

"She'll be fine."

"Hull breaches can be tricky. You contact engineering?"

"We're working on it," she says, suddenly on alert.

"Yeah . . . make sure you get on their schedule soon," he

says, rubbing his chin far beyond the length of time needed to satisfy an itch. "From what I understand, they're pretty locked down for a stretch."

"With whom, I wonder," she says, sensing he's working some sort of angle.

"Look, I don't ordinarily do this," he begins, "but given your situation . . . down a man and with the kind of damage that could leave you stranded here at dock for gosh knows how long . . . I'll extend my offer to you one last time. Same deal as before. Join us, and I'll see to it that your ship is put at the front of the queue with engineering."

Thea shakes her head as she tries to process his crassness, but comes up short. Never has she encountered someone so like a snake in her entire life.

"And another thing," he adds, suddenly inspired, or pretending to be, "I'll even let you interview some of our folks to replace your man. People we've already vetted and trained. So you can be sure they all have the necessary skills to do things the right way. But I'll let you decide who fits best with your team, of course."

Un-fucking-real.

"You'd do that? Really? For me?" Thea says, her rage barely contained.

"Sure thing. No problem."

"Fuck you, Allgood," she says through clenched teeth. "I'd sooner fly my ship into the sun than work with you."

He leans forward, flashing his ultra-white smile. "Can't blame a guy for trying. But I was kind of hoping you'd say that. It's better like this. More fun."

She shoves him hard and heads the opposite way.

"All righty then," he calls after her, making sure everyone around hears. "Feel better, Captain."

She glances back and sees him waving at her, a satisfied grin plastered on his face. Like always.

As she heads up the main concourse and turns into Dock D, people give her the kind of wide berth you give a muttering crazy person on the street. Sometimes it's best to just steer clear, and everyone can tell this is one of those times.

She reaches the *Zephyr*'s lift and enters her code into the panel, seething in silence as she waits for it to arrive. The doors barely open before she squirts through to escape the stares.

Seconds later though, as the doors glide shut and she starts to ascend, all thought of Allgood is erased when the lift shudders, its lights flicker . . .

. . . and the refinery explodes.

37

Eye of the Storm

THEA LOOKS down through the glass wall of the lift as a dust cloud billows out from the side of the refinery below. The bloom thickens, and she instinctively moves away from the glass as it approaches. Braces herself for impact. Seconds later, the cloud swallows the lift. She cringes at the *pick pock* of regolith bouncing off the glass, but luckily nothing substantial strikes. The glass holds.

As the impacts slow, she steadies herself and tries the control panel.

The lift jerks upward, then stops. The control panel flashes red. She tries again, but the lift doesn't respond.

She isn't going anywhere. Not without help.

She keys the comms panel to contact the *Zephyr*.

"Guys, I'm in the lift. Are you there?"

Static.

They just got back to the ship, so the bridge is probably empty. But the silence from above is still unsettling.

The dust cloud thins enough so that she's able to see the gaping, jagged hole in the refinery wall. Detritus from inside streams out into the vacuum of space. Hunks of mottled and glittering rock, tools and machinery, a blizzard of crystallized liquid. A hard hat flips end over end, beginning its journey into the unknown.

Then everything goes dark. The power must have cut out station-wide, and the dark side of the moon had returned to its natural state.

Thea can't help but be captivated by the brightness of the distant stars and the vastness of the universe, its grip impossible to resist even at a critical moment like this.

And then a light snaps on from above. She looks up toward her ship, where emergency hull lights have flickered to life.

Lights on the surface appear next, and she can see the refinery once more. The hole in the refinery wall is starting to shrink, pink foam flooding out onto the lunar surface. It gathers in pools as it works to seal the breach. The wall of foam grows, then fills the hole entirely.

Thea lets out a held breath into the rapidly chilling air inside the lift, but then sucks it in again in horror. A worker is caught in the pink death grip, his legs encased in the now rock-hard foam. He futilely pounds at the sealant that has become his cotton-candy-colored death sentence. His mouth goes wide in a silent scream, his arms outstretched and fingers splayed, grasping toward the nothingness of space.

Luckily, the man doesn't suffer long. Not out here.

"Thea, come in!" Rory's voice.

Relief floods through her as she keys the comms panel. The lift remains dark and motionless, but at least the comms are still active. "Talk to me. What's going on?"

"It looks like they hit one of the helium-3 processors."

"What about the reactors?"

"I don't know. Comms are flooded with traffic from all over the station."

The bitter taste of adrenaline hits the back of Thea's throat. "Okay, listen up. I'm dark down here. I need you to reverse some juice down from the *Zephyr* into the lift. I gotta get down there."

"The fuck you are! I'm bringing you up. We're getting outta here."

"Listen to me—"

"Let the rest of the fleet find this fucker. We paid our price!"

"That's exactly why I gotta do this," Thea says, looking down at the stiffening corpse of the worker embedded in the side of the refinery.

"Then I'm coming down too."

"No, *you* need to get the ship ready to take off at a moment's notice in case shit goes sideways," Thea says, trying to project calm. "Rory, please. There's no time."

The comms goes silent. Blood pulses at her temples as she waits, struggling to be patient, holding back a tidal wave of sadness and anger at the unknown person who has thrown her life and the lives of those she loves into chaos. But she knows pushing Rory right now would be the wrong thing. His instinct is to dig in and fight; she has to let him get there on his own.

Her patience is rewarded when the lights in the lift come on and his voice returns. "You go find out what's happening and get back to us," he says. "Promise me."

"I promise."

The lift descends in fits and starts, its movement much like everything in her life. Yes, she's very familiar with this sort of momentum.

Shouts drift up from below. The lift eventually clangs to a stop and the doors slide open. As Thea step outs, she has to jump back to avoid a woman shouldering one of the heavy, lead-lined sacks used to carry unprocessed platinum-rich rubble.

"Hurry up! Cap wants us topside *now*!" the woman yells over her shoulder to someone trailing behind her.

"What's happening?" Thea asks.

The woman's face and bright green jumper are soot-stained. Thea doesn't recognize the logo emblazoned on the woman's chest, which tells her that she must be from one of the newer civilian mining operations in Dock D.

"Saboteur hit processor two. Everyone's bugging out," the woman says, looking past Thea to a young man jogging up. "They sealed the containment doors to the refinery."

"Is there a radiation leak?"

"Who knows." The woman's companion pushes past, struggling against a similar sack. "But we ain't staying here to find out."

As they hurry away, Thea keys her lock code into the control pad to seal the lift doors, then heads to the main concourse, weaving through a panicked crowd of people carrying tools, equipment, and other items. Along the way, she hears the unmistakable sound of ships untethering from the docks above. As she passes the entrance to Dock B, she glances up and sees two of the Conglomerate ships taking flight. Allgood's gang is retreating from the fight.

The crowd intensifies as she approaches the junction to the Hub, people shoving and shouting. A security team is blocking the way, directing everyone back down the main concourse to their docks.

"Let us through!"

"You need to return to your ships, now!" one of the officers shouts, shoving a man at the front of the line.

It looks like the man's about to obey, but then suddenly he spins around and throws a right hook. A few officers tackle the man to the ground. Other people join the fray in an apparent effort to rescue the man, and one of the officers pulls out her stun stick.

The buzz and crackle of electricity stuns everyone—for a moment. But then, rather than serving as a deterrent, the appearance of the weapon only ignites the fighting, sending the frustrated and terrified crowd into a frenzy. The security team is overwhelmed.

They're saved by a sudden burst of intense light from outside that draws everyone's attention. The fighting slackens as all eyes turn toward the large window looking out toward the Hyperloop.

Thea strains like everyone else to make out what's going on. It's hard, because her eyes are still dealing with the lingering effects of the flash. Which is why she doesn't immediately see the boxcar tumbling through space and heading straight toward them.

At the last second, someone pulls her away from the window.

No one else has time to react.

The boxcar smashes into the concourse wall head on, shattering the window and sending thick shards of glass knifing into the crowd. Sealant foam immediately explodes from safety cannons in the ceiling, coating the nose of the boxcar—which is now protruding into the main concourse—the shattered window, buckled wall, and everyone in the impact zone who wasn't instantly sucked through the breach. If it weren't for the foam and the boxcar partially stoppering the hole, they'd all be dead already. But even the sealant isn't fast enough for a hole of this size, and while the pull of the void is diminished, it's still powerful, still a threat.

People dive for safety, screaming in terror. A lucky few make it to one of the decompression closets. Thea scrambles along the floor toward the junction to the Hub as sealant foam continues to rain down behind her. She inches forward, trying to stay as low to the ground as possible. At first it's like crawling through molasses. But it gets easier with each passing second as the foam fills more of the breach in the concourse wall, and the pull at her back lessens.

The suck eventually disappears. The sealant foam cannons sputter, spit, and then stop. An eerie quiet fills the concourse.

She pauses to catch her breath. Thinks for a fleeting moment that they're going to be okay. That the worst of it is over.

That's when a new sound begins. A low hiss. It's slow at first, but picks up speed.

In seconds it becomes a roar.

Everyone scrabbles to grab on to something as the air around them begins to get sucked out into space once more, with a pull that somehow feels even more powerful than before.

The safety door leading back to the docks, which hadn't triggered before, irises closed now, and the door leading to the Hub attempts to do the same. But it's only halfway closed before a metal bench from the Hub area is sucked into the steel blades and jams itself there, stopping them from sealing.

Thea scrambles toward the stuck door and what has now become the single source of rushing air, driving herself straight into the force that's pushing everyone back. She throws herself forward, but her foot slips as she leaps, sending her face-first into the ground. Blood wells from a gash below her left eye.

Just ahead of her she sees a tear in the thin carpet. She kicks forward, grabs the rip, and twists it in her fist. The tear grows as she's pulled backward, but it holds.

She risks a quick glance over her shoulder. A droplet of blood from her lacerated cheek flies off toward where the boxcar is starting to be wrenched back out into space. People are stuck to the breaches in the concourse wall and the crumpled, foam-encrusted face of the boxcar like flies to a fly strip.

Thea locks eyes with the security officer who brandished her stun stick earlier. The woman's mouth gapes in a silent scream as she fights against the pull of space at her back. A man tumbles through the air toward the officer, strikes her body with his own, and sends them both out into vacuum through one of the larger gaps that's appeared in the hardening foam.

Thea reaches with her free hand toward one of the lower door blades. But as she raises her hand into the stream of rushing air, the force of the wind is so strong that it snaps her arm backward, wrenching her shoulder.

She screams in pain and fights to maintain her grip on the carpet. Stars swim before her eyes, not only from the pain but from depleting oxygen. She struggles to take a breath to keep from passing out, and only manages a shallow sip.

She hears the crash of something heavy hitting the door in front of her. A man from the Hub has been pulled into the opening, getting himself wedged between the blades of the door and the bench. Blood streams from his head and shoulders as he writhes to get free.

His struggles cause both his body and the bench to slide forward, closer to Thea. Then the man slips free and flies over Thea's head, followed by two other flailing figures.

Thea can tell by the sound of the air above that the change in the bench's position must have affected the airflow. She tightens her grip on the carpet tear and once again reaches up with her free hand to test this theory. When the stream of air hits her, this time she's able to fight against it and grab one of the lower blades of the door. Her injured shoulder burns under the effort as she pulls herself forward so that most of her body is at the base of the door.

She lets go of the carpet and grabs the opposite side of the blade, then swings her legs around and through the gaps between two of the blades to the other side of the door, making sure not to dislodge the bench above her.

She then pushes herself to one side of the door. The force of the air racing across the Hub shoves her tight against the wall, which is fine by her. She lets herself stay there as she works to catch her breath.

She hears another crash, and looks to her side. More bodies have been sucked into the half-closed door, shifting the bench's position again and bowing it outward. It's not going to hold.

The bench continues to warp, and slip, and then it's gone, sucked through the opening.

Unobstructed, the door irises closed, and the roar of air vanishes.

Thea falls to her hands and knees and sucks in air. She takes her time, allowing her head to clear and her nerves to settle, desperately trying to process all that just happened.

She looks up only when a dark, lithe woman emerges from the stairs leading down to the Hyperloop corridor. She's dressed in a tight, all-black body suit that comes up to her chin, the kind worn underneath a spacesuit. A matching black backpack is slung over one shoulder. Light ringlets of hair sneak around the edges of her tight skullcap, and goggles shield her eyes, leaving very little of her face exposed.

She sees Thea, and the two women stare at each other, neither one of them moving.

This must be her, Thea thinks. The saboteur.

The person who did this.

The person who killed Elliott.

Thea is frozen in place, stupefied by the moment, overwhelmed by the implication.

Until . . .

"Hi, Thea."

That voice.

"I'm glad you're okay."

Then the woman drops the backpack and runs.

Thea finally shakes off her stupor. Her legs are unsteady after nearly getting sucked out into space, but she scrambles to her feet and chases after.

The common area of the Hub is a minefield. One woman

lies unconscious under an overturned vendor booth. A man is kneeling in a puddle of his own blood, which continues to sheet down his face from a gash across his forehead.

The saboteur leaps over a pile of crates, shoulders a general store worker out of the way, knocking her to the ground, and disappears into one of stairwells. Thea races in pursuit, dodging obstacles. At the entrance to the stairwell, she looks up the steps.

No, not up there. Municipal's there.

Her guess is confirmed when she hears a bang from below.

Thea races down the steps, sucking in air, still not fully recovered from the oxygen deprivation. But she's running on something more potent as she takes the steps two at a time.

Hatred.

She reaches the bottom of the switchback stairs and runs headlong into a crowd of people.

"What's happening up there?"

"Did the door seal?"

"What about the reactors?

"Where the hell's Municipal?"

Thea ignores everyone and scans the crowd. "Where did she go?"

When no one answers, she practically screams the words.

"*Where did she go?*"

"Who?" someone says.

"The person in black! Right ahead of me!"

"I didn't see anyone."

Thea uses a man's shoulders to boost herself up. She scans the crowd, but the saboteur isn't there. She ignores another flurry of questions as she heads back up the stairs. Halfway up, she sees it.

A round grate in the wall is slightly ajar, opening into a dark maintenance conduit.

Thea grabs the grate and hoists her legs up into the

conduit. But before she can climb all the way inside, hands grab her. It's the man whose shoulders she borrowed down below. He and several others followed her.

"Who are you?" he demands.

"I'm a captain," she says. "Let go of me!"

Someone must recognize Thea, because another voice cries, "Let go, it's true."

The man releases her.

"I'm chasing after the person who did this," Thea says. "Where does this conduit go?"

"Atmospherics. Electrical. Sanitation," he says, shrugging. "Everywhere."

Of course it does.

Thea scrambles down the conduit, leaving the dumb-founded crowd behind. But before she's out of earshot, she yells back toward them. "Get help!"

A fluorescent strip of yellow light illuminates the conduit. Her hands and knees ache as she scurries forward, and blood drips from the gash below her left eye. She ignores it all, desperate to make up lost time. But then she reaches a junction and is forced to pause.

Which way?

She fights to steady her breathing, but the blood pounding in her head is so loud it muffles all sound. She closes her eyes and listens, summoning Ell's smile. As the image resolves in her mind, she can feel her heart rate slow, clarity returning. She focuses on the way Ell's smile made her feel. Safe and loved and whole.

A clang rings out from the left conduit.

Thea savors the image of Ell a split second longer, then turns left, once again on the hunt.

This part of the conduit is a straight shot, so she is able to concentrate on speed. Her knees go numb from the incessant pounding as she crawls but she presses on.

Just ahead, a shadow in the fluorescent lighting. It's there for a moment, then it disappears around a corner.

Thea inches forward, on alert, knowing she's close. It's so quiet—too quiet.

As she reaches the junction, the saboteur appears! Just out of reach.

Thea lunges for her. The woman kicks her legs and scrambles backward, crab-crawling away, but Thea manages to grab the woman's ankle, yanks her back, and leaps onto her—getting a thumb in her bloody eye in the process.

Thea slaps the saboteur's hand aside and drops an elbow, smashing the woman's goggles into her face.

The woman reaches for the sides of the goggles as if trying to keep them in place. But Thea is already tearing at them, ripping them upward so she can stare into the eyes of Ell's murderer.

She scoots forward enough that she can get a knee on one of the saboteur's flailing arms, pressing down hard with all of her weight. Finally she succeeds in flipping the goggles off.

And Thea looks down . . .

. . . into the eyes of her mother.

The End
Book 1

Acknowledgments

It feels premature to be writing this part, especially with two more books to come. But not thanking some important folks would feel wrong too, so here I go.

When I saw the rocket illustrations David Lindroth did for Andy Weir's *Project Hail Mary* I knew he would be the perfect person to help me bring Darkside Station to life. Thankfully, when I asked, he said yes.

As to the other David behind this and my two previous novels—my editor, David Gatewood—I couldn't imagine not having you in my corner. Or my bedroom closet. Or under the bed. Because you scare me, my friend. Actually, the thought of sending you something <gulp> bad or even worse, boring, scares me to death. So, thank you for being my boogey man.

And to my family, friends, colleagues, students, readers, and anyone else who encouraged or supported me along this journey, it's because of you I can't speak Italian. I've always wanted to find the time to learn it. I think it would be cool. Instead, here I sit, behind a keyboard, making stuff up. It's your fault. *Accidenti a tutti voi!*

About the Author

Lou Iovino was born in Philadelphia, Pennsylvania. He splits his time between working in advertising, writing, and teaching. He lives in New Jersey with his wife and two sons.

For more information, visit www.louiovino.com. You can also find him on the following social channels:

INHERITANCE

A NOVEL

LOU IOVINO

RARE
EARTH
TRILOGY
VOLUME
ONE

Printed in Great Britain
by Amazon